E.L. Kennedy was born in 1927. Her mother was Welsh and her father from Co. Antrim, where she grew up. She began writing in her early teens and in the following years had poems published in various magazines, as well as articles in the *Belfast Telegraph*. She started work as a teacher in 1947. As a young woman she travelled in Europe and kept a record of her experiences. Throughout her adult life she continued writing, both fact and fiction, and she was also a keen oil painter. Poor health forced her to retire from work in 1981 and she died in 1985. *Twelve in Arcady* is her only published novel.

Twelve in Arcady

E. L. Kennedy

THE
BLACKSTAFF
PRESS

BELFAST AND DOVER, NEW HAMPSHIRE

First published in 1986
by The Blackstaff Press Limited
3 Galway Park, Dundonald, Belfast BT16 0AN, Northern Ireland
and
51 Washington Street, Dover, New Hampshire 03820 USA
with the assistance of
The Arts Council of Northern Ireland

Printed in Northern Ireland
by Belfast Litho Printers Ltd

British Library Cataloguing in Publication Data
Kennedy, E.L.
Twelve in Arcady.
I. Title
823'.914[F]   PR6061.E59/

Library of Congress Cataloging-in-Publication Data
Kennedy, E.L., 1927–1985.
Twelve in Arcady.
I. Title.
PR6061.E5957T8   1986   823'.914   86–1038

ISBN 0 85640 351 2 (hardback)
ISBN 0 85640 338 5 (paperback)

*To Rachel D.
and John Kilfeather*

JANUARY

'Where do you live?' asked the school inspector.

'In Arcady,' said I.

Mrs Conlan frowned at me behind his back, and I remembered to make it into a sentence the way she is always telling me.

'I live in Arcady,' I said to him.

'Where is that?' he asked me.

'Arcady is an old factory down by the river,' I said to him, 'but it is in flats now. We live in the first flat at the head of the stairs.'

'And who are we?' he asked me.

'Daddy and Mammy and Agnes and Bertie and Mria and Alec and Doreen and Mervyn and Hector and George and wee James,' I said to him.

'Could you describe Arcady,' he asked me, 'so that I would know it if I saw it?'

'Well,' I said to him, 'it is three storeys high and you go round the side if you want to get into the lower flats. They have two rooms, one behind the other. But ours is up the outside steps. You go up the steps to a balcony and four front doors are on it, ours, and Lyle's, and an empty flat, and Pettigrew's. The upper flats have four rooms, two up and two down. The steps are cement and the balcony is cement, with an iron railing. On wet days the balcony is covered with shallow puddles.'

'Very good,' he said, and asked Vera Gorman where she lives.

She told him her daddy works in Belfast and her mammy has a shop and a post office, and her aunt is a staff nurse, and they live in a white house on the Belfast Road. Vera is an only child. It is a pity of her.

The inspector talked a while to Mrs Conlan, and then asked us to write a short description of our families.

Well, how are you Burke! There are twelve in our house, I

1

thought to myself, so I would not be a quarter finished in the time. He was watching Alice Todd. She has it easy, nothing at home but her mother and brother Don and a canary and her daddy.

I thought I'd better get cracking. That is what Daddy says, get cracking.

My daddy is a tall man with dark hair and eyes and a small moustache. He is thin and brown and was in the western desert in the war. His best friend is Shamus McCann who keeps pigeons and fishes in the river if the police are not watching him. Daddy wears a blue shirt and navy jeans and a big leather belt with rijimentle badges on it, and black tough shoes or wellingtons. He still has his battledress jacket from the war and he wears it when it is cold. He is the best darts player in Guinan's and the best Daddy in Arcady. He is buying a lorry to go into the road-haulage business.

My mammy is very pretty and she has her hair bleached and she says she weights twelve stone but I don't believe it. She is not very tall and has a good figure and can cook very well. She gives me threepence on Saturdays for scrubbing the kitchen floor and I get three toffee chews and give her one. She always chooses the liquorice one.

I am the eldest. I am twelve. Agnes is eleven and wears glasses and is a tell-tale. She is not in the same class as me and I am glad. It would be torture. Bertie is ten and not a lot of use. He is supposed to get sticks from Harper's Planting for our fire, and he forgets, and my mammy is waiting maybe an hour for the sticks before I have to go and get some to keep the fire in. Mria is nine and there is a joke about her and Bertie being Irish twins. She is at home, sick. She has a bad throat this three weeks, and Mammy does not know what is wrong with her. Doreen and Alec are really twins. They are eight. My daddy says it is a pity there are two of them, because he could lick either one single-handed, but he is outnubmered. I mean outnumbered. This is only a joke. He never hits any of us, even on Saturday nights when

2

he has been in Guinan's. Mervyn is seven and George is nearly five. We thought Mervyn would never learn to read but the nurse came to school and found out he could not see, so now he has glasses and can see the very best. He is very fond of reading. George cannot read yet. Hector is between Mervyn and George but he does not go to school because he is not well. He is six, but George has more sense than him. Daddy says we will all have to take great care of Hector because he does not know down from up, or hot from cold, and likely never will. My mammy says she has two babies, Hector and wee James. But wee James is thriving like a gosling and nearly two years old, and is so quick on his feet you can't watch him. He has blue eyes and a pink face and a fluff of white hair, and Mammy is always scared in case he gets out and falls in the river. Once Hector . . .

'Time up,' said the inspector.

I was not near finished. And it was three o'clock. That was the shortest afternoon I ever mind.

I hoped Daddy had got the lorry by now. He says there is lots of work about for an intelligent man with a lorry, doing flits for people and carting stuff for the farmers that are too busy to do it themselves, and he could cart peat from the Far Moss and sell it round the town. My daddy is working at the labour exchange. He only goes three times a week but he gets paid the full week just the same. He says there is little to do but stand, and Mammy laughs at that. He always says if he could get a job for the other three days he would be on the pig's back, but Mammy says, 'Six or nothing, you know you got into a quare row the last time. You nearly got jail, and left me a grass-widow.'

A grass-widow is what you are when your husband runs away. Mrs Conlan's husband did not run away, she put him out. He would not work or give her any money for the house. She is my teacher. He was a commercial traveller and I did not like him. He said something to Mammy one day she was coming into Arcady past the bungalow, so she set down wee James on the ditch and

3

went and warmed both his ears, then came back and picked up wee James and walked on. I was with her.

I wished I was home. Mammy was sick in the morning but she would not let me stay at home. I could have kept Hector and wee James out of her road for a while, and redd up the kitchen, and got sticks, and emptied the bucket. And I could have taken a look at the new people in the cottage. They only came the night before, late, and I had not laid eyes on them yet. I wanted to go over and tell them that their well is condemned, and to get their water from the pump at the steps, the same as we do.

The last one to live in the cottage was old Barney Hake. His name was not Hake, but that was what we called him. I never heard him called anything else. Mammy would not let us go near him, for she said he should be in the asylum. That is where he is now. He ran out one night in his shirt, all the way over the Stock Bridge in his bare feet, and it raining, to the Belfast Road. He said he would walk to Belfast to see Rangers play Linfield, and that he would split the first one that tried to stop him. Old Joe Cooper ran for the rector, and my Daddy phoned for the police but they would not believe him. Shamus McCann ran after Barney and he and Dermot Ryan caught him at the bus stop. They told him that he was going the wrong way, that they were for Belfast too and would see him right. Dermot put his coat on him, and Barney let him, then they kept him safe until the doctor came in his car and took them all to the asylum. When Shamus and Dermot came back, they were not laughing. They said it was a pity of Barney, we might all end that way, and where was Old Joe Cooper.

With that, Old Joe Cooper came up the steps and asked them how Barney was, so they told him he was under a sedative, and Old Joe said he did not know what the world was coming to, and that Barney should have a bit of sense. It was funny to hear because Barney Hake is seventy-six but Old Joe is over ninety.

Mammy says Old Joe will never die because he is hand-made. One Saturday he ate six sausages for his tea and he was not well, so Mrs McFarland ran for Mammy as well as she was able, and Mammy ran for Mrs Conlan, and she phoned for the doctor.

It was Dr Emily who came and she said, 'Put him in the car and I'll take him to hospital just in case. Will you take your hand off my leg you saucy old man you before I belt you one,' and she drove off.

My mammy laughed so much she had an accident going up the steps. But Mrs Conlan did not think it was funny. Old Joe Cooper was none the worse and came back the next day on the bus and said they were good to him and the doctor had a grand chassy. Then he ate three more sausages, just to show them, he said.

That was last year, though. It was after that that he ran for the rector for Barney.

About Barney going to the asylum Old Joe said, 'What would you expect, the man lives on wee sups of tea and bread and jam and would not know a square male if he saw one. If we had him at Lady Smith or Maggers Fonteen he would have got a hungering that would have lasted him to this day. Dammit, I never pass a horse without wondering how it would eat if there was a sudden famine.'

'Tell your uncle Dan,' said Daddy to Dermot, 'to keep that brown horse of his well out of Joe's road, for he might just take a snap at it going past.'

They all laughed, but I was glad Barney was away because I was afraid of him. He followed Agnes and me down the Water Walks one day, and would not let us by him when we wanted to go home. I could have got by but Agnes would not have been fast enough.

I was so scared I was sick, but I shouted, 'There's my daddy!' He turned to see where and we ran past him, and ran and ran until we got to the open space past his cottage, and then we could not run anymore. Agnes started to laugh and I started to cry, but we did not know why we were so frightened. He did not do anything except stretch out his arms across the path, so as not to let us pass. We had to tell Mammy because she wanted to know what I was crying for. Then she said never to go near him, and to run if we saw him, and not to get cornered, and to jump in the river sooner then let him catch us.

'But we would drown,' said Agnes.

'I do not mean in the deep part,' said Mammy, 'just the stretch at his cottage. You could walk in the river from there to the rock at the back of Finlay's and it would not come over your shoulders unless there was a flood. But don't for God's sake go in anywhere else, especially below the Beetling-house for it is forty feet there. In fact don't go near the Beetling-house. I bathed in this river when I was not any bigger than you and I know every foot of it. I learned to swim here.'

'Why do you not swim yet?' asked Agnes.

'Have I time?' said Mammy.

It was now ten past three and still a mile to Arcady. I wondered had Mrs Conlan the car with her. I thought that if I offered to carry her books for her she might have offered us a lift, not all of us, just Agnes and me. The boys and the twins were already home, I saw them go.

There is no place at Mrs Conlan's bungalow where she can turn the car and if she drives into the garage the car will be facing the wrong way in the morning, so she usually drives down into Arcady and out again, and reverses into the garage. This is because she cannot reverse and make a turn coming into the garage from the Pack Bridge Road. I do not know why, she just can't.

Just then she came by, and, come here, she did offer us a lift.

'My mammy is not very well,' said I. 'We are very glad of a lift. Thank you very much, Mrs Conlan.'

'Indeed, I don't know how she manages with you all,' she said. 'Are you warm enough with that window open? Good gracious, you are like ice. Agnes, reach your sister that yellow cardigan from the back seat. You had better keep it, it suits you and it is too tight for me. It must have shrunk in the wash.'

The cardigan was very thick and fuzzy, it felt lovely on my arms. The school is warm enough, but short sleeves are no good to walk home in, even if it takes only twenty minutes. Mammy says it is only coming in out of the cold that makes me cough but Daddy says I need flannel on my chest, so the cardigan will do instead. It is the same colour as the kingcups at the side of the river in the month of May.

The new people were in the cottage. There was smoke coming from the chimney, it was like the one in Mervyn's new Reader. And a soldier was hagging sticks on the front path. But I had no time to stop. I was up the steps and into our house in a flash. Mammy was sitting at the fire, only the fire was out and Hector had knocked over the bucket, it was lying on its side and all he had done in it was soaking into the floor. Wee James was in his cot, trying to get out and crying.

'Where are the rest of you?' asked Mammy.

'They are coming,' I said, and grabbed a bucket and went for water. I had to scrub the floor at once, and get sticks too if I could. The floor-cloth was all holes and slimy, it was so skiddy that I could hardly wring it out and the smell was awful. The nurse wants us to let Hector go to the Hospital School. She says they could teach him to keep clean and we could see him once a week, but Mammy says she could not stand not knowing how he was getting on.

The pump has a handle on a wheel, and it took all my weight to swing it, it is more like a mangle than a pump.

When I got in again I threw my good yellow cardigan up on the high line in the kitchen, so that it would not get dirty, and washed and wiped at the floor till it was near dry. It is a wood floor and whatever is spilled on it sinks into it, the first hot fire we have will bring out the smell again.

Then we had to get sticks.

Mammy said she would not come with us because wee James was crying and Mria was coughing and Hector needed changing. I knew from Mammy's face that she had a headache. She gets real bad ones sometimes, fit to split a paving-stone, she says.

Harper's Planting is not far from the house, up the lane out of Arcady, and over to the right behind Mrs Conlan's bungalow, about half-way to the Pack Bridge Road. Mr Harper said we can take all we can get of the trees, even cut them down, because he wants to put cattle there and it is not safe for them until we have cleared out the dead branches and stumps. On fine evenings Daddy and Bertie take a bag and a saw and cut a bag of blocks. But Daddy won't let any of us have the saw if he is not there so on that day we were only able to get small stuff. There are still fifteen trees left, one very big and four medium, and ten little ones off which you can break bits if you are determined. The little trees will hardly burn at all though, they have smooth grey bark. The others have rough bark with grey moss on it and they burn like fun, but you would need the saw because they won't break.

Bertie is not as old as me or as big so he had to do what I said. He would have needed to, he would have got nothing done if he did not because he is as lazy as sheugh water.

At the last we had quite a big bunch of branches gathered and tied with an old bit of rope, and we were pulling and heaving this way and that way, trying to get it to the lane, but it was catching in all the stumps and snags hidden in the grass.

I would love to be rich and order in a load of coal like Mrs Conlan.

The coalman comes to the school and says, 'Any coal, mam?'

She gives him the key of her coalshed and says, 'You may put in a ton, Harry.'

So he puts it in and shoves the coalshed key through her letterbox, then she gets it when she goes home at three o'clock.

This time we had a long drag of it, because we had got all the near branches long ago. We had to go right to the back of the Planting and pull all we got right across it. It was nearly dark and the wee ones were on ahead with the twins, taking the little bits they got, but Bertie and Agnes and I could not get the bundle of branches over the ditch. Two men we don't know came by with guns.

One handed the other one his gun and said, 'Would you let me give you a hand with that or you will be here all night. Whose kids are you anyway?'

Bertie told him and he said nothing, just gave that big bunch of branches a heave. It flew over the ditch and hit the lane. The rope broke but he tied it again.

Then he said, 'Night, kids,' and went after the other man.

We were home in two minutes and Mammy had a wee fire going and the pan on. Fried bread is lovely when you are all cold and scratched. I could not wear my good yellow cardigan to get sticks, it would have got torn to bits on the branches.

'You got on well the night,' said Mammy. 'Where did yous get that lot? That'll keep the life in us a while longer.'

'That's the last,' said Bertie. 'Unless me and my da was to saw some. Maybe we could take a tree. It would last us a quare while.'

'Sure you could never take a tree! How would you get it sawed?' said my mammy.

'We could do it rightly,' said Bertie. 'But my da would have to cut it down first,' he added.

It was only to get using the saw and my daddy not there at the time, that was all that was in his head, for I know him. Once Bertie had the sawing of a tree he would lose notion of the job. He always does. But what's the use of talking.

And my daddy was not home yet.

I screwed my head round to see what time it was, because our clock does not go except when it is lying on its side. It was after six o'clock.

'Where in under God can he be?' said my mammy. 'And Mria worse, I wish he was here this minute to go for the doctor. Bertie, you'll have to go or we will miss the night surgery. Write this down,' she said to me, '"Mria has a bad throat and a cough and would you please come over after surgery, yours truly, Ethel."' She threw a coat over her head and shoulders, and said to Bertie, 'I'll convoy you across the Stick Bridge, then you run to the road, and don't stop to think. I want you to stop George Harvey's car and give him the note to give to Billy Wiseman to give to the doctor. If you miss him you may walk it, so shift yourself, I haven't the price of a bus after four loaves from Matt Edgar.'

When she had gone Agnes washed the dishes and I cleaned Hector. He had slobbered gravy all over his face and hands, sometimes I think he doesn't know the road to his mouth. The nappies on the high line were dry so I took them down, then washed out the four in the basin and rinsed them at the pump. I had to fetch more water too because Mammy would have to bath Hector and wee James when she got back. My hands were so cold I could hardly wring the nappies. She has a hard time of it with us all.

'Never marry,' she often says to me. 'It is cutting a stick to beat yourself with.'

'Come on, Ethel,' said my daddy once when he heard her say it, 'you enjoy yourself rightly at times.'

She started to laugh at him and said, 'Aye, so!' very sarcastically.

When I came back with the two buckets the wee ones were just ready to start a bit of codding, but I had to make them learn their lessons for the next day. Every night that week Bertie was away out to swing in an old tyre tied to a rope on Barney's tree, but he could not do that now even if he was back, for the cottage had people in it and they would not like it, forbye he would be looking in their windows and cheering and yelling. He is mad about aeroplanes and pretends he is flying one and shooting down Germans. Daddy was through the war and he says he never saw a German, only Italians. He says they ran as if they were reared on senna pods when they heard General Montgomery was coming with the deserts rats. He was a desert rat and he is proud of it.

Mammy came back, shivering and rubbing her arms. Her jersey has short sleeves now because it had big holes in the elbows so she cut off the sleeves just above the holes to make it look civilised.

'Is it dark?' asked George. He is like a wee old man. I do not think he knows what dark is.

'It's dark all right,' said Mammy. 'Dear but this is cosy now we have a bit of fire. I think it's freezing. The moon's all crined in wee, and you can hardly hear the river. It's very like a night you would have snow. Where the devil is your da and why isn't he home? I declare this is scandalous.'

'Is Bertie all right to come back by himself?' said I. 'Sure if he misses the Stick Bridge he'll be in the river before he knows.'

'Not him,' said Mammy, 'I tied my apron to the far end of the handrail. He's to gather it up and bring it with him when he's coming back. Take off that kettle, it's boiling. Where are the dishes, or did you do them when you got my back turned?'

'I did them,' said Agnes, 'I did the dishes and she did not.'

'Well she was not idle,' said my mammy to her, for she knew it was me did the nappies and fetched water and kept the fire up and started the wee ones at their lessons. 'Go on, ye boys ye!' she said to the wee ones. 'See who is finished first and I'll hear you your tables.'

'I haven't any tables,' said Mervyn.

'Never mind,' she said, 'I will teach you some and then you will be able for them when you do get them. It pays to be smart.'

It was time Agnes and I started our tables because we are learning hard ones. Agnes is at parts of a pound and I am at per cents. I would rather do per cents than parts of a pound for I have done them twice and I don't know yet what one eighth is, a twelfth, or a sixteenth.

'Hurry up you two,' said Mammy to us, 'and I will wash your hair and you can dry it at the fire. It's a wonder you're not lousy. You're for it the next time, Doreen, I think I'll cut yours and give you a with-it look.'

'I'm sure you'll not,' said Doreen.

'What did I hear you say?' asked Mammy.

'Nothing,' said Doreen.

'That would need to be the truth,' said Mammy. 'Do you think I need a licence to cut your hair, or maybe an Act of Parliament?'

Doreen said nothing and minded her business, Mammy was just waiting for the chance to clash her ears if she was cheeky.

Bertie came in with Mammy's apron all rolled up and threw it to her. 'I got him,' he said. 'Can I go round to Dennis Barkley's?'

'You can not,' said Mammy. 'Sit down and do your ecker, are you mad?'

She was asking Mervyn his spellings and I was asking Doreen hers, but Hector started to yell and shout. Mammy had to take him on her knee and hold him with one hand while she asked Mervyn his spellings, looking past Hector at the book in her other hand. Hector did not want her to do this and started to slap at her face, so that she had to twist her head away. The rest of us would not get away with what he gets away with, but Hector is not just right.

'Would one of you strip wee James,' she said, 'before he falls asleep in a heap like a wee pup.'

Wee James was as cross as a fitch and it had to be Bertie or nobody, he is Bertie's boy and Bertie could do rightly without him. But at last he was in his bed and everybody felt the relief, for he fell asleep the minute he was in. Mammy could start bathing Hector at the fire. Hector was well enough content because now she was attending to him and nobody else. Then she put him to bed too.

Bertie had to learn to spell expedition for the next day and he could not, he got it wrong every time.

Mammy asked him, 'What does it mean anyway?'

'Crossing the Stick Bridge in the dark,' he said, 'that's an expedition.'

We all laughed.

'You tell that to the master tomorrow,' said Mammy drily.

'It is a journey that is not too simple,' said Bertie. 'You might not make it.'

'Well, good for you,' she said. 'You deserve to know how to spell it. Come on and we'll have another bash at it, it can't be that hard if you know what it is.'

By the time she had finished with us we could all spell it, even Mervyn, by shouting it out in chorus. Of course I could spell it anyway. I was kept in for not knowing it last week, that's why. Mrs Conlan is brave and easy if you don't understand the sums, but she says any fool can spell. It is just learned off like a parrot, and if a parrot can, you can. We are all smarter than parrots except Hector, so we had it off in no time.

'Would you look out,' said Mammy, 'and see is your father coming at all, or is he staying the night with his rich friends.'

This is a joke. When he is late home he always says he was being entertained by his rich friends. It is just a saying. One night Mammy cried and said she would have the truth from him if she had to peel him like an onion, and he laughed so much he had to lie down. He woke us up twice that night, laughing at what she had said to him.

'What are you doing,' she said to him, and the clock struck four.

'Laughing, what else,' he said. 'It's a great life if you don't weaken.'

'You fool you,' said she.

12

When I opened the door to see if Daddy was coming there was a noise in the lane so I waited to see if it was the doctor's car, but it is bigger and had no lights. It came down as if the driver knew the place and it ran round the pump and swung till it was facing the mouth of the lane. I thought it was a lorry. A man jumped down out of the front and slammed the door, and here, wasn't it my daddy.

'You got it,' I said to him.

'I got it,' he said to me. 'There'll be no holding us now. Ethel,' he said, 'I got the truck, fifteen pounds and a jack thrown in. It's not much to look at but there's life in it yet, like somebody else I could name. Come out till yous see her.'

It was dark and cold but we all came out except Mria and Hector and wee James.

'Well, she needs new tyres but that's a detail,' said Daddy, kicking the wheels. 'Sure she's as sound as you like. I've a bargain here, she should have been eighty but he's going to Marrafelt and has no yard now to keep her in.'

With that the doctor drove up, and it was Dr John, not Dr Emily. Before he could speak my mammy had us all into the house, except Daddy, who wanted to fix something on the lorry.

'I thought there had been an accident,' said the doctor. 'Where is the invalid?'

'It's Mria,' said Mammy. 'She is in her bed. Where else would she be?'

'Missus, dear,' said Dr John, 'would you send a wheen of these wee weans to bed so that I can see the one that's not well.'

Well the boys went up, but Agnes and I could not because we sleep in the low back room with Mria.

I shouted out to Daddy, 'Do you want your tea?'

He said, 'You bet! So that's what's wrong with me!'

When he came in his hands were black with oil from the lorry, but luckily I had the kettle hot and he could have a wash. I had two big slices of fried bread for him and a cup of tea wet. There was not any milk left, but he never takes milk in it anyway.

'Keep her in bed,' said the doctor, 'and don't let the others near her. Have they had their diphtheria shots?'

'Why, has Mria got it?' asked Mammy, sounding scared.

'She's got a bad throat,' said the doctor, 'and that's one reason why.' He nodded at the bucket we have to have for Hector because he does not know the way down to the closet.

Till George started school he could take him down, but since then Hector will not go out of the house without Mammy, so she just has to let him do it in the bucket.

'Is that right?' said Mammy. 'Well, I do try and train him but he is very odd lately, he will not do anything he does not want to do. If the rest tried it I could skelp them, but what can I do with him? Lately he will not go out the door without a roaring match, even with the rest for company.'

'I have told you what you ought to do about it,' said Dr John. 'If you won't you won't, but you might think of the poor child. He will be warm and fed and kindly treated. You know quite well, Ethel, the Priory is not a jail, and he is such a risk to the others in this crowded house. Sore throats are the least part of it. Just think whiles who will look after him when you are not able to. Keep that Mria in bed and give her no food, only warm drinks. And get those tablets tonight, and see if she can't get some sleep.' And away he went.

'Have you two shillings?' asked Daddy.

'I have not,' said Mammy. 'Are you mad? Where would I get two shillings?'

'Singing in the Fair Hill,' said Daddy.

But Mammy did not laugh. 'I know you want it for the bus,' she said, 'but I have not got it, and that is God's honest truth.'

'Then the child'll get no tablets this night,' said Daddy. 'There is no use in walking in because the chemists will be shut by then,' and he ate up the rest of his fried bread.

I had hoped he would leave a bit because I was still hungry.

'Would you run up to Mrs Conlan's,' Mammy said to me, 'and ask her would she lend me two shillings.'

'Don't you dare,' said Daddy, 'I will ask Dermot in a minute. If I went down now I'd catch him in the middle of Z-Cars and he would not answer me till it was over, and then maybe say he hadn't it. . . No, it would be no use.'

14

'Away quick to Mrs Conlan's,' said Mammy to me. 'Tell her I'll pay her it back on Friday. Run or it will be too late for you to catch the bus.'

It was very dark in the lane and I was afraid to walk in case something caught my tail, so I ran all the way.

Her door is painted black with a shiny brass letterbox and knocker. I knocked and knocked before she heard me. She had the television on, for I could hear the voices in Z-Cars and Fancy Smith was talking. I love him.

At last she opened the door and said, 'Mercy me, is that you and I never heard you. What is it you want, child? Come in out of the cold this minute.'

Her living-room is lovely, with a green sweet of furniture and thick curtains and a television and a wee table with a big glass vase full of pompous grass and a green rug with a pattern on it at the fire, and the fire was piled up with big lumps of coal and plenty of slack. I could hardly tell her about the two shillings for looking at her pictures, one is the Virgin Mary because Mrs Conlan is a Catholic and the other is a woman in a long white dress and umbrella in a garden with flowerbeds.

In the middle of it Mrs Conlan gave a yell, 'My oven!' She ran into the kitchen, tore open the oven door, snatched out an oven soda, a little bit burnt, and an apple pie. A lovely smell of hot apples and sugar came out of the oven and she said to me: 'I suppose you would not say No to a piece of pie?'

'I would not, indeed, thank you very much, Mrs Conlan,' I said, 'but I have to go to the town for Mria's tablets, or none of us will get a wink of sleep. She has to have them and if I miss the bus the chemists will be shut by the time I have walked it.'

'Well, it's a mercy you came here,' she said, getting out a plate and a spoon, 'because I am going into the town in about ten minutes. You can come with me in the car. So you will still have time to eat your pie.'

'I have no prescription with me,' said I, 'I will run and get it.'

'Eat your pie,' she said. 'You can get it when I turn the car. You will have to take the bus home, dear, so here is the money.'

'Sure I might get a lift,' I said.

15

'Don't you dare,' she said, very seriously. 'You never know who is driving up that road at night. You are never to take a lift with anybody you don't know, do you hear?'

'That is what Mammy always says,' I told her.

Well, as soon as I had finished my share of the pie, she got the car out and we sailed down into Arcady in quare style. I got the prescription off Mammy, and we arrived in the town in just a minute or two. Mrs Conlan reached me a half-crown and told me to be sure and catch the bus, and not go roaming the town because it was coming on to snow and I had no coat with me.

Mrs Conlan knows rightly that I have no coat because I am the biggest and Agnes has mine and Doreen has Agnes's, but she lets on she doesn't know. I can get on the best without one. I would like one fine, but a coat costs pounds, and shoes are more important. Mammy says she will get me a coat the first chance she has, and I know she will. It will be easier now my daddy has got the lorry at last.

In the car I asked Mrs Conlan how you spell Shamus and it is not spelled like that at all, it is Seumas or Seamus, I forget which.

FEBRUARY

Daddy sawed plenty of sticks for a week or two after that, and then there came the week of the big storm.

It was absolutely wild.

We were all in school when it began.

The master came into our room at half past one o'clock and said to Mrs Conlan, 'We'll have to let them go home early, Mrs Conlan, it is beginning to drift already. I am going to take as many of the wee ones home as I can. Would you tick them off on the roll as they go.'

I could not see any sense in this but you could see it was not the time to be asking, so I kept quiet.

Mrs Conlan said that everybody with wee brothers or sisters in lower classes was to go and put on their coats and caps and bring them to the Primary One classroom. Anybody that had no wee one to look after was to go home right away.

After a while the master came back with his hat and overcoat. We sorted out a load of wee ones who had to go up the Belfast Road and he took them first. He was away over an hour, and said the main road was like a bottle because sleet had fallen first and it was freezing as it lay. We lived quite near but Mrs Conlan said we would get a lift with her, so we stayed and I helped with the wee ones who had nobody to help them with their coats. Nurse Gorman arrived in her car and said she had come for Vera, her niece, but she took Dennis Barkley and Elsie Morton and Doris Guy also. That was a lot for a bubble car but she said at least it would not capsize, how could it with that lot holding it down. She had something there. The master made four more trips and that cleared most of the others. But this time his car was covered with snow and he could not see out, so he got out and wiped the windscreen with some oily smelly stuff on a duster, and the

17

windscreen wipers stuck.

'I might have known it,' he said. 'It must be freezing pretty tight and this doesn't help much.

'I wish you would let me help,' said Mrs Conlan.

The master said, 'If you had a breakdown you might sit till the morning, you know the only repair you can do is change a wheel, but thanks for the offer anyway.'

Miss Carter gathered up all the remaining ones who lived on the Pack Bridge Road and set off with them, pushing her bicycle at the end of a long string of them. Miss Diamond did the same for the ones from the Back Road. She lives up in a big red house and her father is the rector, he is very cross. The master put the last of them in his car and drove off. Then Mrs Conlan locked the school door and put us in her car. We were like sardines in a tin, but she gave us a lift to her bungalow. She said we should hold hands in twos because the wind was screeching down the lane fit to blow you down, and to climb on the bank if we heard a car coming because with that slope and the snow the wheels would not grip even with the brakes on. The snow was blowing in our faces so hard that it hurt so we turned our backs and reversed into it. Bertie was the only one that had waders and we walked in his tracks as well as we could. Albert Dunwoody's Leghorn hens were blown about like bits of paper because they had not the sense to get in, either that or they could not get in because of the wind. I saw him out catching them.

He is a farmer but he has only one cow and some pigs and simply millions of hens. He has hens in cages and hens in deep litter and free-range hens and hens for eating. He hatches eggs in an ink-youbater, he has to look at them every night with a torch, it is crazy but that is what he does, because I have seen him doing it. I would not say he is a friend of ours, but he has not very much to say for himself anyway and if we want him we know where he is. He is a good man and bothers nobody. He is married, but his wife is very quiet too, if you said Hello so would she, but not unless you said it first.

By this time it was getting dark and I knew I would still have to go to Gorman's for our bread. The last time it snowed like this it was not nearly as bad, but the people in Arcady had to go to the Iron Bridge for their bread because the breadman could not cross the Stick Bridge. He just stopped at John Finlay's and blew a whistle until the people got the idea. Mammy was first across the Iron Bridge, which has no handrail but is wide enough to drive a car over if the driver knows his way and is careful. I was frightened she would fall into the river, for the water was within maybe six inches of the iron. But she came across all right with the bread in a bag on her back, and said she was going to join Duffy's Circus, she might as well, now she could walk the tightrope. But she was only joking.

When we came in, all out of breath from struggling with the storm, the bread was there, for the breadman had hurried up and got there early, and Mammy had run across the Stick Bridge and got it herself. Mria was not at school and she was able to keep an eye on Hector. She had got over her bad throat long ago, but this time she was off with a cold. It was funny going up the steps without being able to see where they were for the snow on them.

Daddy was away in the lorry, selling peats, Mammy said. She was sitting at the fire with Hector on her knee. He was asleep, that was a mercy, and wee James was beating on the floor with a stick and singing. Anyway he thought he was singing, the wee soul. There was a good fire on, and four bags of peats were neatly placed under the table. After a while Mammy got up and said she would make pancakes. We were all warm and cheerful by this time, but two of us had to go for buttermilk, so Agnes and I said we would. I put on my old coat that is now Agnes's, it was too wee, and Agnes took the one that is now Doreen's. Then we took the can and set off. Mammy did not like letting us go because of the snow, even though we had a flash-lamp.

We get our buttermilk from Maurice French's. He lives in a big white farmhouse at this end of the Iron Bridge, but most of his land is across the main road in two other townlands. We can only go to his place by the Water Walks, a lot of people use them but not at night unless they know them very well. The Water Walks are paths running along and across the river and the leats to the factory that this used to be, where they cross water it is usually by

19

wee stick bridges only wide enough for one person and with no handrails. The Stick Bridge between Arcady and the main road is the only one that has a handrail, it is wide enough for a lorry but not strong enough any more because the planks are rotten, and if there is a lot of water coming down the river you can stand on the Stick Bridge and feel it shake. The other stick bridges are in better repair but I don't much like crossing them if there is a flood on. They are over leats and sluices and as the factory has stopped working this long time most of them have filled up with silt and white stuff, I think it is lime. They are not very deep except in a few places we all know about.

I never go up the Water Walks to Maurice French's without thinking of wee Kathy Henessey. She was drowned on the Water Walks. Her mammy was dead and her daddy married again and her stepmammy wasn't nice to her and made her do messages and her only five years old. One night she sent her up the Water Walks for buttermilk, to Joe Morrison's because Maurice French was only a boy at the time, and never bothered herself. At six o'clock her daddy came in for his tea and asked, 'Where's Kathy?' and she said, 'She's not gone long, she went for a wee taste of buttermilk.' After a wee while he said, 'I don't like it, she is too long away. I will have to go and see where she is,' and he rose and went out. He found her lying against the roots of the big tree, she never even got the length of Morrison's, with the six-quart can clenched tight in her wee hand. After a while the stepmother wanted to adopt a child but he said, 'There'll be no wee girl in this house. I had only the one, and you drowned her on me.'

It was old Mrs French that told me that story, and it is every word true.

And that is why I do not like the Water Walks. Sometimes if I am there by myself I run like mad to get into the open, away from the trees, in case I see wee Kathy Henessey slipping down the path with her red knitted frock and her long fair curls, and the six-quart can in her hand.

Well, we were all eating pancakes when Daddy came back. He gave my mammy some money and said, 'Is that what you want, will it do for a time? I have to have a tyre fixed or she will be running on her rims like Katie Ganzie.'

My Mammy started to laugh and said, 'Katie Ganzie may be running on her rims but she knows a good man when she sees one.'

We all laughed at that.

One day Katie Ganzie was out in her back field scaling dung when the Duke of Edinburgh drove past on his way to Belfast.

She jumped on the dyke and waved the dung-fork and let a yell out of her, and here didn't the Duke wave at her, and she told everybody. But I think he was likely in stitches with laughing because Katie Ganzie is six-feet tall and has her hair in a bun, and she wears a berry on top of it, and a thin brown skirt and a thick jersey that comes down to her knees nearly, and nearly always a brown stocking and a black one, unless she is coming on her bike which has no tyres to put more money into the post office. She works about the farm in a pair of hob-nailed boots, size eleven, that belonged to her brother who is in Australia. Likely he went because she made him work far too hard and she would not give him enough to eat. Katie Ganzie will not spend a penny at all, and that is why they say she is rich. Her farm is a wee goldmine. She has pigs and sells them, and hens and sells them, and my daddy says that if there is a hen that can not produce either an egg or a good excuse, her days shall be short in the land which Katie giveth her, for Katie would wring her neck as soon as look at her, and sell her to the fowl-man. One day George asked Daddy what the fowl-man wanted all the hens for and Daddy said, 'Nothing, he just collects fowls because he is crazy about them.' George said that the last time the fowl-man was stopped at French's a lot of the hens stuck their necks out between the bars of the coop on the back of the truck and shouted, 'Help!' That was why he was worried. You dare not tell George that anything is going to be killed, he gets hysterical, he is so upset. The same boy likes a nice bit of fried bacon, but he does not know it is dead pig. We haven't told him.

After he ate his share of pancakes Daddy went out, and took

Bertie with him to help work on the lorry.

'Surely you didn't bring her down the hill,' said Bertie. 'You will never get her out, with the snow in the lane as slippy as a bottle.'

'I had to, son,' said Daddy. 'She was missing and I knew I'd have to strip her to see what the trouble was.'

'Would you shut that door,' said Mammy. 'You'd think the sun was splitting the slates, the way you leave the door open till we're all foundered.'

So I shut the door. We were all away to our beds before they came in but I heard them talking.

'There'll be a powerful frost this night,' said Daddy. 'Get all the stuff you can and cover up the bonnet, or the watertank will split when it thaws. Here's my greatcoat, take that, it's good for nothing else, and this old mat off the floor. There's a bit of lino in the Plantation, I know where it is, I'll get it. Don't you come after me for the drifts would go over your head.'

After a time they came back and Bertie was coughing.

'For Pete's sake, shut up,' said Daddy. 'Do you want to wake the house. The best cure for a cough is don't. Away you to your bed as soon as you're warm.'

I didn't sleep for a long time, with the wind screaming past the house and the whole of Arcady shaking as if the wind was hitting it thumps. I was scared, although I was inside and safe.

I must have fallen asleep because the next thing I heard was a great thud and then a clatter on the cement balcony. I jumped awake, and woke Agnes and Mria too.

'What is it?' said Agnes.

'What is it?' said Mria.

'I don't know,' said I, 'Mammy, what was that?'

'It's not our chimney anyway,' said Mammy. 'If it was, you would not be asking me. Maybe you'd better get under the bed.'

'It's too cold,' said Agnes.

Anyway we all lay down and cuddled in and slept till the morning.

We could not go to school, we could not even go to the top of the lane to Mrs Conlan's, we could hardly get to the pump.

Mammy looked out and said, 'Some of you will have to get the water, if I fell down the steps they would be ruined.'

We all laughed at that.

Agnes and Bertie and I happed ourselves up and went down the steps very carefully to get the water. Agnes dug out the steps with the fireshovel while we were trying to swing the pump. The pump was frozen, of course, and Mammy had to boil the kettle of water she keeps filled in case anybody takes bad in the night. Then who should we see stepping through the snow but Mrs Hanna, the soldier's wife from the cottage where Barney Blake used to live. We had not seen her close up before but we knew her. She has black hair and a lot of lipstick and a wee white face, it is pale white, Mammy says. I saw she was wearing a smock and was very fat so I guessed she was expecting. Likely Bertie and Agnes knew too, but they said nothing, that was a mercy. She did not know the pump was frozen and started to wind at it but it wouldn't move. Her feet slipped, she fell in the snow and hit her face on the cement in front of the pump. It all happened so fast we were still standing looking at her when Mammy came down in her slippers with the kettle. She would not trust us with it and it boiling. The soldier's wife was trying to struggle up, and she would not cry though her mouth pulled in all shapes. She is only a wee bit taller than me and it was funny to see how young she was under the lipstick. Maybe she is not twenty yet.

'My God,' said Mammy, 'are you hurt, Missus? Get in the house the lot of you, and take bread and jam, till I get the pump going and help Mrs Hanna into the house. Bertie, will you see if Hector's awake, and if he is give him a piece without jam, or he will have jam on the walls.'

Then she got down in the snow beside poor Mrs Hanna and talked quietly to her, and wiped the blood off her face. She had a wee cut outside her eyebrow. Mrs Hanna tried to get up but she was trembling all over, so Mammy helped her to the bench and brushed the snow off it. She made her sit down while she poured the kettle in at the top of the pump. She counted twenty, tried the handle, and gave it a swing till the muscles stood out on her arms. It moved, she gave it another swing, the handle went round once, and after that it was easy. The water came and she filled all the buckets, ours and Mrs Hanna's. (Daddy says Mammy is as strong as a blacksmith. 'That's right,' she says to him, 'turn up your feet till I see do you need shod.') Then Mammy walked Mrs Hanna to her own door, and Agnes and I came down and fetched in our water. I took over the other bucket for Mrs Hanna, but the door was shut so I left it on the step. The soldier had cleared the path to the cottage, and that was good going because he has to leave for the camp before it is light, a soldier can not be late for his work like another man.

'There'll be no school the day,' said Bertie, sawing a slice off the loaf. 'There'll be nobody able to make it through the snow but the Harpers, they'll likely get the milk-lorry.'

'What milk-lorry?' said I. 'They may take their tea black in London, for I have not heard a tanker this day.'

'I saw one on the main road,' said Bertie, 'but I hould you the hauliers won't get one down the Pack Bridge Road this week, if they do it will be a miracle. Come on and go to school just for the value, there will be hardly anybody there and we will get playing games and telling stories and shovelling snow.'

'If we get in,' said I. 'Maybe the master won't be there either.'

'Well, come on anyway,' said Bertie.

We put our lunches in our bags, happed ourselves up with scarves and put old socks on our hands, and Bertie and Agnes and Mria and I went to school. It was not so bad because Bertie had waders and went first so we all walked in his tracks. The lane was slippy slippy but we all took the bunker and we were at school before we knew. The wee Harpers were getting off a trailer that their daddy had brought them in. His tractor is a Fordson Major and it is nearly as big as an elephant and painted blue. It has a sort of cellophane shed for the driver. Bertie says it is not cellophane, it is talc, but I know better. Talc is what you put on babies.

With that, down came Artie Forbes on another tractor with a milk-can carrier bolted on to it, and Rosaleen and Joy and Ivor standing on it and gripping Artie. He is not their daddy. He is their big brother and will have the farm in the heel of the hunt.

'Thank you,' said Mrs Conlan to him. 'That was good of you, Artie.'

'I had to come anyway,' he said, 'to put out baled hay for the cattle on the other land. They haven't the brains to kick the snow off the grass and pick a mouthful. I wish they were reindeer.'

We laughed at the very notion. Wee Billy Harper said something and I could not make it out, but Aileen Harper told me that Billy had said it would be quare and handy for Santa if Artie had a reindeer farm, and would he not think it over. But Artie was already away.

The master had an awful job getting here. He had to take the bus because the car would not start, and when he got off he had to flounder through the snow to the Stick Bridge and cross it holding on to the railing, and then walk up through Arcady in our tracks. No wonder he was foundered.

The school was very cold and the radiators were only just warm, so the master went down and stoked the boilers and Mrs Conlan fetched all of us into the Primary One room where there is a big range we learn cooking on. She put a fire in it that would have toasted bread six feet away, and put the guard round it.

The school milk never came so at eleven o'clock Mrs Conlan said, 'Would anybody like soup? Now is the time to speak.'

We all said we would, so she fetched four tins of chicken broth and a big pot we use for cookery lessons, then made the soup and heard Bertie his tables at the same time. I never had chicken broth before. It was nice.

In the afternoon we all went home about half-two. Artie and Mr Harper came for the wee ones and the master and Mrs Conlan and the rest of us walked home. We left the master when he had to go on to the Stick Bridge. He went across very carefully because he did not know where the bad planks were.

As soon as I got in Mammy reached me Hector's bucket and said to empty it. I did that, and rinsed it with Jeyes. Bertie and Agnes pumped the water for drinking. Maurice French came down the Water Walks with a bale of hay to hap up the pump in case it froze again. He pulled the hay into long twists and made a sort of a rope of it, then wound it round and round the pump, except the wheel, until it was all covered up.

'Leave the rest of the hay lying,' he said to me, 'in case anybody else slips on the ice. That wee woman's lucky she's not dead.'

'Is she not all right?' I asked him.

'She's away to the hospital,' he said. 'They had to carry her on a stretcher down the Water Walks to the Iron Bridge. Mind those buckets in case you spill them, for it will be ice in the morning.'

Away he went and pumped four buckets of water for Mrs McFarland and Old Joe Cooper, because they should not be out in the snow, especially Mrs McFarland, she has a bad foot.

We were just sitting down to our tea when Daddy came in and said, 'We would need to get more peats for the fire, a bag lasts no time with the fire on all day. Who's game to come up to the Far Moss with me? The road's cleared and I hear there's less snow there.'

'Who else is coming?' Bertie wanted to know.

'Just me and as many of you as are able for it,' he said. 'It will be moonlight early.'

'Will we have to carry them?' I asked, for the Far Moss is three miles up the Pack Bridge Road.

'I got a sheet of tin off Maurice,' said Daddy. 'We could slide them home on it.'

'Then come on till we go,' said Bertie. He could hardly wait.

There is a roller from the old mill lying at the end of Arcady, so Daddy and Bertie took the sheet of tin over there and walloped it over the roller till it had a curve at one end. There were several ragged holes along that end. Daddy said it had once been on the roof of Maurice's Dutch barn but a storm blew it off, the holes were where the bolts had been. They were useful to put our clothesline through. Daddy said it was plastic with a wire core and would stand the abuse. When they had done working with the tin it was like a sleigh, and it slid very well.

We walked and walked and walked. Agnes and Mria said they were tired so Daddy let them ride on the tin sleigh, but a wee while did them for it was too cold on their legs. As last we got to the Moss and the moon came up, it was like a picture. The lane had a foot of snow but there was less on most of the bog.

'What stack is ours?' asked Bertie.

'Ach, take a wheen off them all,' said Daddy. 'I hid the bags in a hole in the hedge. Wait a minute till I get them. Stay off the snow,

26

you might go into water.'

We were running here and there in the moonlight, and the grass was as stiff as if it was starched. Agnes and Mria put the peats into the bags, and Daddy said to get as many in as they could for we only had six bags. Bertie and I gathered the peats off the stacks. It did not take us very long.

'We'll not rush,' said Daddy. 'It's a long road home and you will be tired enough at the end of it.'

'Will we sing?' asked Mria.

'Not while I have my health,' he said. 'You will need all your breath for walking. If a wheen of lorries hadn't come down here today you would be up to your waist in snow instead of stepping in their tracks.'

It was so quiet we could hear wee creatures in the hedges and the church clock in the town strike ten. A long way off somebody was swinging a tractor. And here, didn't we find a big hare lying dead on the road. I was afraid of it in case it would come to life again, but Bertie wasn't.

'A lorry hit it,' he said. 'Would you look at its head.'

Daddy picked it up and put it in amongst the bags of peats.

The sheet of tin was hard to pull when it was loaded, but Agnes and Mria pushed at the back until at last we were at the Arcady lane, and went up the wee hill to Mrs Conlan's.

'Now,' said Daddy, 'this is the difficult bit, if we let go of it we might kill somebody. Take the hare,' he said to me and reached it to me.

I had to take it by the hind paws. It was an awful weight and I was scared of it but I had to take it. It was not bad at all, only furry and dead and cold, poor thing. Daddy and Bertie wrestled the tin down the lane with only three bags on it and after a while they came back for the rest, but we didn't wait for them because it was too cold for standing. After they had got the rest of the peats down to the house, they took the tin up to Maurice's. We would have gone straight in but Old Joe Cooper shouted to us and we went down to see what he wanted.

'You poor wee cowld things,' he said. 'Come in and have a drink and then go straight home to your mammy.' And he gave us

27

each a wee taste of red stuff in the bottom of a glass, and poured hot water on it to fill the glasses.

I thought he was quare and mean with it till I tasted it. It tasted awful but strong, and we all took it as medicine, but we drank it up like good ones.

Old Joe began to laugh to himself and asked, 'Are you warm now, girls?'

We said we were.

'Well,' he said, 'tell your mammy you have been at the port-wine, it is gey wet but it has its uses,' and he opened the door.

We all thanked him and ran up home. Mria said her legs were dizzy but she was exaggerating as usual.

When we went in Mammy said, 'Are you foundered? I never should have let you go, you're only wee weans. Where's Bertie?'

We told her what Old Joe Cooper gave us and she was shocked, but she said it likely saved our lives. It was nearly twelve o'clock at night, and she had the wireless on for company. It was playing Irish dance music and Mria danced a bit to it to get warm. That was how Agnes and I knew her legs were none the worse for what we had got to drink. Mammy had soup for us and we told her about getting soup in school from Mrs Conlan.

'That one,' said Mammy. 'It's them that has none that knows how to rear them.'

But I didn't care, I like Mrs Conlan. I would have got my death if it was not for her yellow cardigan.

Daddy and Bertie came back and fetched in five bags of peats.

'I gave Maurice a bag,' said Daddy, 'for the lend of the tin. We never could have got them home without it.'

We were all clean done, and as soon as we went to bed we fell asleep. It was quiet compared with the night before. Mammy told us it was Lyle's chimney that had fallen and woken us up, but neither one of them got up to see.

The Lyles are both very odd. He is a wee man about as big as me. He has a yellow face, and his trousers are navy-blue and come right up to his oxters, you just see six inches of tie. Daddy says likely he heard that the Germans were coming and juked down into his trousers and never came out since. But that is only

28

Daddy's joke. Mr Lyle is not well. He never goes out of the flat and he has attacks in the night about three times a week. Mrs Lyle told Mammy that he had not let her get a full night's sleep in six years, that's how long he has been sick. Mrs Lyle is sick too, she has bad legs and her ankles are bigger than Mammy's knees, and she gets short of breath if she walks to the main road for the bus. She can't go out of Arcady by the lane at all, it would kill her to go up that hill, and sometimes the breadman gives her a lift up because he is sorry for her, but he might get the sack for it, you are not allowed to carry passengers in a bread-van.

Now I come to think of it, nearly everybody in Arcady is a bit odd, or else sick. Look at Old Joe Cooper, he is over ninety and has fish and chips and port wine for his supper, and music on the wireless when he likes, he is lucky to be so old and so healthy. And Mrs McFarland has a bad foot. She was born like that, but she got a man just the same, though he is dead now. She is over seventy, and she has a joke that she is courting strong with Joe Cooper, so maybe he will be her second. He enjoys this, and always tells people they are engaged. She is a nice old woman and keeps her house very tidy and has a canary she calls Peter Dick. She keeps herself to herself.

Well, Dermot Ryan is not odd, but he is sick. He hurt his back and had to have traction, but it was no good so he had to have an operation. He is out of hospital this long time but is not allowed to move hardly. He was swinging a tractor for his Uncle Dan Molloy when the tractor swung first and Dermot lit on his back in the yard. He is about twenty-eight or maybe older and he lives with his three sisters in the lower end of Arcady, next the water. His sisters all work in the town, two in the shirt factory and one is a shorthand-typist, so I hardly ever see them except on Sundays when they are going to Mass. They all dress very well but Bridie is the one you notice first, she is the eldest. They are all very religious and you see them setting out of a Saturday evening to go to Confession. I wonder what they confess for they never do anything wrong. I said that to Mammy and she said for me to mind my own business for a change.

Seumas McCann and his wife live in another one of the lower

flats, with Paul and Kevin, their two sons, who have a motor-bike and ride away on it to play hurling. They are always coming home late with bruises and cuts and sticking-plaster. Their mammy is convinced that one or both of them will be killed at hurling, but she can't stop them, they love it. Seumas McCann spends days and days in his pigeon-house and only comes out when it is time for supper or maybe Z-Cars. My Daddy says if he could live on maize he would never come out, sure he thinks he is a pigeon too. He is a quiet man, taller than my Daddy and thin. He works in the same place as John Finlay, only in the day time. They have their flat just lovely, with a real carpet in front of the fire and a TV set though you can only get the BBC on it. I heard Mrs McCann telling Fidelma Ryan that since they got the high aerial up they can get Tellyfish Eerian. I wish I knew what that was but I am mystified.

One flat at the other end of the balcony has the Pettigrews in it, but you would never know. They come and go because they both have jobs, but they speak to none of us because they think they are better than we are. They are saving for a shally bungalow and are living here because it is cheap and they can save faster. Mammy says they have neither in them nor on them. Their suppers for the week are five tins of spaghetti and a pound of sausages. You just could not believe that unless you knew them. Between them and the Lyles there is an empty flat, which is just as well for they do not like noise in the night and Mr Lyle makes plenty when he is having an attack. In fact less would do. Mrs Lyle says he is not in any pain but he feels frightened that every time will be the last.

'How is the soldier's wife, Mammy?' I suddenly remembered to ask in the morning.

Mammy said, 'Not very good, the poor wee thing. They had to take her into hospital and phone him at the camp.'

'Will she die?' I asked.

'I hope not,' said Mammy, and gave me a look to shut up because the rest were listening.

All the week the snow lasted. Then it started to thaw and the whole place was mud. My daddy sold forty-six bags of peats that week and got me and Agnes and Mria waders apiece because we hadn't a dry foot among the three of us from Monday to Friday. And he got Mammy a new sweater, a big woolly red one.

'You fool you,' said Mammy, 'sure if I had the wool I could knit one and it would not cost half what you paid for that. Where did you get it? Maybe I could change it for wool.'

'If you did you would knit something for the weans with it,' said Daddy. 'I know you. Your arms were that cold last night I dreamed I was catched by an anaconda in the jungles of the Upper Amazon.'

'My word,' said Mammy, 'you were far from home. How did you get back safe?'

'I just groped my way.'

They both burst out laughing.

Well, the snow melted, and we got to school the next week without any trouble in our new waders, and then the master was off with a cold. Miss Diamond and Mrs Conlan and Miss Carter divided up his class and took a third each. After a while we heard noise in Miss Diamond's room, it is next to our classroom. All the girls were crying, you would have thought, and the wee ones shouting Oh-HO! and the big ones from the master's class muttering. Mrs Conlan went to see what was wrong, and there was Miss Diamond on the floor. Mrs Conlan thought she had fainted, but Dennis Barclay said she had opened the top cupboard and looked in, but whatever she wanted was not there so she bent down and looked in the low cupboard, and she had not shut the top cupboard door properly so that when she stood up she hit her head an awful whack on its lower edge. With that, Miss Diamond opened her eyes and was mad when she found she was on the floor and a whole fuss was being made about her.

'Let me up,' she said, 'I am not dead yet.'

Mrs Conlan got her into her chair and sent Mary Cosgrove for a glass of water for her. I will never forget Miss Diamond's face. It was perfectly white. I never saw anyone like that before. She had two black eyes the next day but she had put make-up over them and you would hardly know.

31

Then one day we came home and saw the soldier's wife again. She looked thin and ill, and she hurried in when she saw us. Likely she was shy because we had seen her fall.

When the rest had gone out except Hector and George and wee James, I asked Mammy about the soldier's wife. I did not like to ask about the baby, but Mammy told me that the baby was born too soon and it was dead, and the soldier was awfully upset because he could have got the water and he forgot, he was used to the town where they have taps in their houses.

'She is upset too,' I said, 'expecting a baby and getting a dead one.'

'It happens,' said Mammy. 'You have just to stiffen your lip and go on. But she'll have a sore heart this long time, the poor wee girl. She is only seventeen and thinks it is the end of the world.'

'Will I be married when I am seventeen?' I asked.

'Not if you have any sense,' said Mammy. 'Leave it till you are thirty, that's time enough and you'll be better able to size up your chances. Seventeen's too young to have to start saying "yes dear" and rearing a big family. What are you talking about, you're not thirteen yet, have you your eye on somebody?'

'I have not,' I replied, 'I was only asking.'

'Well ask me again in five years,' said Mammy. 'Here, away over the Stick Bridge to Gorman's and get four loaves and a bottle of tomato sauce. And be quick about it, I hear the lorry coming and there's no tea made yet.'

MARCH

March comes in like a lion and goes out like a lamb, they say. That was not true this year anyway. This March was as quiet and as cold as anything, till we thought the winter would never end.

Mammy took sick with the flu and had to go to her bed. She could not look after Hector, so it was either Daddy or me for it, but Daddy had a job hauling baled hay from Ballytasket to Richard Johnston's big field, and he be't to keep at it or he would lose the chance of the job, so I had to stay off school. Mammy was awfully ill and the doctor wanted her to go into hospital.

She said, 'Would you have a taste of sense, doctor, if I was to buy all I would need to go into hospital it would have to come out of the weans' mouths. So I can't go and that's that. Just give me whatever you think and I'll do the best I can on it. Where there is life there is hope.'

'Well, Ethel,' said Dr John, 'I wish the half of them had your spirit,' and he gave her antibiotics.

She was much better in a week, she is as strong as a horse. But Daddy says she is not.

'For dear sakes, would you stay in and give yourself a chance Ethel,' he said.

She was sick for three weeks and two days and Hector and wee James were harder to look after. The weather was that bad I could not let them out, and Hector was very dirty. I wish Mammy would let them take him to the Priory, they would look after him there. I was thinking who would look after him if Mammy died and it would have to be me. There is nobody else because now Daddy is working every day with the lorry and he is not back any night till seven because he does his own loading and unloading.

And I can't look after Hector very well because now he is getting so big. He is huge for his age and fat with it, and if he is in

33

a temper the first thing you know he hits you. He is not bad, but he does not know any better. Wee James is not bad either, but he is that fast on his feet you could not watch him. I thought he was in the river twice while Mammy was lying in bed. I think if he had fallen in she would have thrown me after him for letting him. He would need a string tied on to him, so that you would know what way he went, then you could either follow him or reel him in the way Joe Cooper does when he is catching fish.

One thing is, we have plenty of everything these days for Daddy brings home the money all right, the lorry made a world of difference. I have a coat at last, a dark blue one, and Mammy got tartan and made me a warm pleated skirt.

I don't know yet if Agnes and I have passed the Qualifying, but if we have we will need school uniforms in September. Mammy says she has laid by money for that when the time comes. I do not care if we have not passed for we will be going to the Secondary Modern if we have not and I would rather go there than to the Grammar School. The Grammar School is twelve miles away and the other one is only two, we could walk to it the very best. But I will be sorry to leave Mrs Conlan, she is a great teacher.

And Daddy bought jerseys for us all, including himself and Mammy. She still has her red one but Daddy says she would need to wear the two of them and look after herself. It was double pneumonia she had, I can spell that because Daddy bet me it began with p and I bet it did not and I lost.

We have not been up in the Plantation this long time, but Daddy said this morning we would need to go up and get that tree out, and he knows how it could be done, tie it to the lorry. So this evening we are going to do it. He has taken the saw to be sharpened and will be back early to finish the job in daylight.

Well, we should have let the tree alone, for it fell on us and if it was not for Paul and Kevin I think we might be dead by this time.

It happened like this.

Daddy came home at two. He told Mammy what we were going to do and told her to gather up the wee ones and keep them in the house because he did not want them among our feet while we were cutting down a tree. This was one of the smooth trees in Harper's Plantation and it was dead. He just took Bertie and Agnes and me, and the saw, and a piece of wire rope he borrowed off Mr Harper, and away we went.

I don't know what we did wrong, but this was the idea. He and Bertie took turns and sawed more than half through the tree from the far side, then tied the wire rope round the trunk as high up as they could reach, reversed the lorry up the lane and tied the other end of the wire rope to the thing at the back that you put the spare wheel in, only our lorry has no spare wheel. The lorry was sitting on the top of the high hill in the Arcady lane, pointing into Arcady, with the brakes on. Bertie got into the cab, waited till Daddy said the word, and then took the handbrake off. Daddy expected that the lorry would go quite slowly down the hill because he thought the lorry did not weigh much more than the tree.

Agnes and I were standing on top of the bank between the lane and the Plantation, a wee bit behind the lorry, and Daddy was standing in the lane a bit ahead of the lorry on the other side, ready to get in the minute the lorry started to move. The far door was open, ready.

Well, when Bertie took off the brake a lot of things happened.

There was a terrible crack from the tree, it jumped up in the air and came straight at us, branches first. Agnes started to run but tripped and fell into the lane. That is what saved her. Before I could run something hit me a thump on the back, I fell into the lane on my arm and it was all twisted under me. The whole tree came sailing over the bank into the lane and turned completely over and went down the hill after the lorry. I was lying on my mouth and nose, not able to move, but it missed me and Agnes. I had to laugh at her, because she started to get up but when she saw the tree coming she lay down again quick. Then I saw Daddy lying down the lane a piece.

The lorry stopped and the tree slid on over the top of it and broke the little window at the back of the cab. This was down on the nearly level place in front of Old Joe Cooper's. Bertie hopped down out of the cab and stuck two big stones in front of the wheels in case the brakes did not hold too well. He went staggering over to Joe's bench at the pump. He sat down and laughed till I thought he would die. All the time Daddy never moved. Agnes started to cry as if she was half-killed, and it turned out she was the only one who was not hurt at all. My left arm hurt so much I wanted to give wee meeows of pain, but it looked as if Daddy was worse than any of us.

Then Paul and Kevin came running up and said, 'Here, what's the damage?' and ran to pick me up, I was still sitting on the ground. Paul said, 'You poor wee creature, that arm's broken.'

I said, 'My daddy's dead!'

Kevin said, 'He is not, the divil looks after his own. Come on, man, look alive!'

Paul carried me to the bank, to be out of the road because the breadman was coming in with the van. The breadman stuck his head out of his cab and asked, 'What's wrong, is it an accident?'

'An accident, is it?' said Kevin, 'It's a disaster, one dead, two injured, and a nervous breakdown. Come out of that and we'll see if we can't get them into the house. I doubt he's got a bad touch.'

The breadman got down and said, 'Is he dead? Are you codding?'

'I wish I was,' said Kevin. 'You take his feet and I'll take his head, and Paul, would you bring in the wee girl? I hope to God he does not come round till we get a bed under him. What in thunder happened?'

'We pulled a tree out of the Plantin' with the lorry,' said Bertie.

'Who was driving the lorry?' asked Paul. 'Here's your father, lying here, and yonder's the lorry!'

'I was,' said Bertie.

'What did you think when the branch of the tree came into the cab?' asked the breadman.

'What branch?' asked Bertie. He looked. 'What odds,' he said, 'it missed me.'

'You're a cool one,' said Kevin, 'to run over your daddy and drive on like Stirling Moss!'

'Sure the tree was pushing the lorry in front of it,' said Bertie. 'I told my daddy the handbrake would never hold her and the tree both.'

At this, Daddy started to groan so they hurried up the steps, took him into our house and laid him on the couch. Mammy stood and looked at him, and then at me as Paul carried me in and put me on the edge of the table. He had set me in a pool of tea where Hector had spilled his cup and my knickers were just wringing, but I was too shy to say. Agnes came in roaring and crying.

Bertie said, 'Mammy, my hand's cut,' and showed it to her.

'Never mind your hand,' she said to him, very quiet. 'What's happened to your daddy?'

'Get the doctor,' said Daddy. 'Dr John, mind. The wee girl's hurt too, the tree hit her off the top of the bank.'

I couldn't see him because Paul was standing between us, holding me on the table because I was awfully dizzy.

Old Mrs McFarland came to the foot of the steps and called up, 'Send the weans down, Ethel. You have your hands full. I will give them their tea and keep them for a while.'

Mammy reached Agnes a loaf and a bag of sugar and Mria a new pot of jam off the shelf. 'Go on away down to Mrs McFarland's,' she said, 'the lot of you except Hector and Bertie and Frances.' She whipped a clean nappie off the high line and wrapped it tightly around Bertie's cut hand, it was bleeding all over the floor. 'You go too, till the doctor comes,' she said to him.

'But Ma,' he said.

But she pushed him out and shut the door.

'Now,' she said. 'what is wrong?'

'I'll go on,' said the breadman. 'How much will I leave you?'

'Four,' said Mammy. 'Thanks for helping. And thank God it was a Wednesday or there would have been nobody fit to carry them in. Kevin, would you ring Dr John, and tell him come quick. Oh my God, is that one killed as well?'

Up till then I do not think that Mammy knew I was hurt.

'She's broken her left arm,' said Paul, 'that's one thing I am sure of. They were lying hither and thither in the lane when we ran up. She should not be moved, the poor wee creature.'

Well, that was the last I knew till I woke up in hospital, and my left arm was all cold and parcelled up in thick white stuff like bandages and cement. The nurse was all clean and tidy. She was kind to me and got me a drink of orange juice. She said my daddy was not dead, and my mammy was sitting with him until he came round.

'Did he have an operation?' I asked.

'Why no,' she said, 'we were able to help him without.'

There were three other girls in the ward and they were all sitting up looking at me.

'I had my appendix out,' said one. 'What happened to you?'

'I had my tonsils out,' said the second. 'What happened to you?'

The big one did not say what she had out, she just asked, 'What happened to you?'

'I was hit by a galloping tree,' I said, and fell asleep.

I will say one thing for the hospital, they feed you well. And I am the girl that can eat all I get.

They let me go home at the end of the week, and one of the doctors told me it was not lucky to have trees fall on you, as if I didn't know. When I came out of hospital Bertie had to go in, the glass the branch broke had stuck in his hand and the doctor said he had blood poisoning. They had to give him penicillin but he came out in a rash so they had to stop it and give him something mice-in, that is what he says, but I don't believe it, there isn't any such thing, he must have made it up.

But he is in the same ward as Daddy, so they can keep each other company, and the one lot of visiting does. It would need to for the sick money has not come through yet and Mammy can hardly manage. The forms came all right and she filled them in, that was on Tuesday, but she could not get to Daddy to sign them until the Saturday, and then when she posted them they would not be lifted till the Monday.

I am back at school unless Mammy needs me. I have not been at school much all through March because of Mammy's illness and then the accident, so I know the attendance woman will be after me, so she will. That was why I went back with my arm in plaster and all, even if our Agnes has to go to the closet with me to make sure I am respectable before I come out. Because I have no strength in my left hand.

And the tree is still lying in our yard, tied on to the lorry, the way Bertie left it. He can't saw it with his bad hand, and Mammy can't, Dr Emily forbid it. Likely it will lie there until Daddy comes out of hospital, but they say he won't be right for a brave while, he says it was the door of the truck that hit him as it went by. So I don't know what will happen.

And I have just remembered our saw is lying out in the plantation, likely it will be all rusty by now.

The last of March is stormy stormy, and it is all we can do to struggle against the wind on our way home from school. In fact it is against us no matter which way we go, for in the morning it blows in our faces, and changes in the afternoon and blows in our faces again.

Wee James was out in the yard, playing at Joe Cooper's door, when a tin basin Mrs McCann has for her hens flew round the corner and hit him and scared him nearly to death. Mrs McFarland had to give him a jam piece to quiet him. Agnes was getting the clothes off the line when a sheet caught the wind and nearly took her into the river, only the soldier's wife was there and caught her and pulled her down on her hunkers. She said something but Agnes did not know what it was. We can't make out a word she says, though Mammy can.

The soldier's wife is all right again now, and they are supposed to be getting a house on the camp. She puts an awful lot of detergent in her washing, and the grating over the drain is always filled with a big puff of white suds on a Monday. Now that it is windy this is flying about in lumps and sticks to the bushes round about. Mammy says if she had what some people could do without she could do a better job with Hector's nappies. Wee James is trained now and Hector is the only one still wearing them. Mammy says she has not had her hands out of water for thirteen years.

Paul and Kevin have just come in, pushing the motor-bike. If it is too rough for those two it must be bad, they would face anything.

39

Lyle's chimney is fixed at last.

They told the landlord, and he said he would send a man. But he sent no man. So they told him again, but he said, 'That's strange,' and sent no man. Then Mr Lyle made Mrs Lyle go in the bus and tell a solisitor. The solisitor wrote a letter to the landlord, so he sent a man out the next day and had the chimney fixed. Mrs Lyle told Mrs McFarland that they could lie in their bed at night and look at the bare sky and stars through the hole in the slates that the chimney made when it fell, and the rain was running down their bedroom walls and all the paper was peeling off. I would not like that at all. Our house is not very grand but it is dry enough.

But I wonder what sort of letter the solisitor wrote, it must have been powerful altogether.

Bridie Ryan is engaged to be married to a publican. In the Bible that is a tax-collector but now it means a man who has a pub. His name is Mr Feeny. I thought he would be nice-looking, like the soldier or Kevin McCann, but he is not. He is an old man, bigger than Daddy, and cross, in fact I would nearly say he looks feroshus. I was down with Mrs McFarland when I heard the news. Mrs McFarland is not pleased about it at all, although it is none of her business. She likes all the Ryans and says, 'They are the best of neighbours, but you daren't speak, you daren't speak.'

She said to Mrs Lyle, 'Could a lovely girl like Bridie not have got somebody nearer her own age than yon oul' fella? He must be near sixty, and drinks like a fish.'

And Mrs Lyle said, 'Houl' your tongue, Lizzie, isn't she getting two pubs in the centre of the town, and a lovely big house and a maid if she wants one. Sure by the time they have a family he'll be dead!'

Mrs McFarland said, 'I am not so sure of that, he's the sort that would live just to spite her. I just can't understand it. If that is love you may give me the other.'

'Here, here,' said Mrs Lyle, 'she is a fine girl but she must be near forty, likely there'll be no family.'

'Is your head cut?' said Mrs McFarland. 'Sure I was in it the night she was born, she won't be thirty-five till Christmas!'

'Well, I thought she'd be more than that,' said Mrs Lyle, all disappointed, 'I thought she was the oldest.'

'Not at all,' said Mrs McFarland. 'There were Paddy and Dan and Michael and Eileen all before her. But they are all away now.'

They talked on but it was just a lot of old blether about ones they used to know when Arcady was a factory and the ruins on the hill were Workmen's Row. In those days where Mrs Conlan's bungalow is now there were another two rows of cottages, I had seen the old walls at the end of Mrs Conlan's garden but I did not know that they had been cottages. And I found out something that I never knew before, Mrs McFarland and Mrs Lyle and Mammy's mother, Mrs Skeffington, used to work in Arcady then, along with Bridie Ryan's mother, in the dyeing department, at the jigs. This is not dancing and they could not explain what it was they did, but they were helping the dyers.

Later on in the week I was with Mrs McFarland again and said, 'My mammy says Bridie is the same age as she is, and she is nearly thirty-nine.'

'Wheesht!' she said. 'I would not tell Maggie Lyle to please her. Let that just be a wee secret between us. Poor Bridie has enough to contend with, without Maggie Lyle telling everybody she is near forty. Bridie's mammy was my mate at the jigs for thirteen years before she was married, and a good mate she was too.'

'Is she dead?' I asked.

'Not a bit of her,' said Mrs McFarland, 'she is living in Portadown with her married daughter Eileen. How is your daddy? And wee Bertie? I declare my heart stopped when I saw the boys bringing you down that day, forbye I thought the lorry was coming in through the side of my kitchen!'

I told her that Bertie was all right and that my daddy was coming home any day, and went up home for my tea.

The fish man had come and we all got yellow haddie. Bertie likes it fried but this time my mammy had enough margarine so she cooked it in the big black iron skillet and it was lovely, I could have eaten my share twice. But Hector did not like it.

He does not like anything except jam pieces, and we have to

watch him when he gets one because he would rub it on the wall as soon as not. Mammy is at her wit's end to get food smuggled into him to keep him healthy. If he is not healthy the nurse can get him taken away to the Priory in spite of what Mammy says, and we are all trying to get Hector to eat. It was the time she was sick that made him like this. The doctor said he could not be in the room with Mammy or he would take sick too, and he just stood at the door and wheenged. He does not know enough to turn the handle, so it was easy enough to keep him away from her, but he would not eat. Mammy says God knows if he understands anything, but he seemed to know that she was not with him, and he wanted her back and he knew where she was. That was a whole lot for Hector to know at one time for he is not like the rest of us.

There is a friend of Mammy's who had a spastic baby at the same time as she had Hector, and he goes to the Priory every day for his lessons. Mammy said she would love to go and have a chat with his mammy for she would tell her the truth.

But Daddy said, 'For God's sake, Ethel, how could anybody take Hector in the bus? Sure you know he's like nothing human.' And she said that was true, but she would not let Hector go until she saw for herself what good the Priory could do.

I asked, 'Mammy, what is a spastic? Mrs Conlan says we have to help research to help the spastics.'

Mammy said, 'A spastic is a child that can't move right or maybe talk right. They are just not perfect, and they won't be any better, but they can learn to use what wits they have.'

Well, it surprised me the way she reeled it all off. Mammy knows a lot that would surprise you, but not that kind of thing, so I think she and Daddy have been talking about Hector and perhaps the doctor has been advising her again. Dr Emily says it is a shame that a bonny boy like Hector could not learn to be clean, at least, and feed himself, and wash. Mammy does her best with him but he spoils all he wears and you daren't give him anything to eat by himself, he would rub it on the ground and eat it dirt and all, and even wee James knows not to do that. I am awfully worried about Hector myself, because when Mammy was sick I could not make him mind me at all, and I just could not watch him because he would do things wee James knows not to do like pulling the tablecloth or trying to catch the steam coming out of the kettle. It is no use being good to him. He will have to learn for himself if there is anything in him to learn with, and the way he missed Mammy when she was sick shows he knows *something*.

The last day of March we got reading library books in the afternoon at school, because Mrs Conlan was doing the returns for the master. She is very quick and quiet and can add two columns of figures at once, like eighteen and thirteen are thirty-one and sixteen is forty-seven and twenty-five is seventy-two. I wish I could.

I was reading a book I had not had out before, but I forget what it was called. It was about a rich boy who smoked cigars. He was on a ship and fell overboard and a man in a rowing-boat saved his life and took him to a fishing-boat and the captain hit him on the nose because he said some of them stole two hundred dollars off him. That was as far as I got before Mrs Conlan started us at Geography. I used to call it Jography but she made me stop it. Some words don't look like what they are, but if they are odd it helps you to remember them. If they were spelled right, you wouldn't.

When we came home there was a strange woman with Mammy, and a wee boy on her knee. He had on grey trousers and pullover, and socks, and black shoes and a wee red blazer. He was as clean as anything, you would think he was just unwrapped brand new.

'Martin,' said the lady, 'say hello to the children.'

He said hello and shook hands with me and Bertie.

'Hello, Martin,' we said.

He was kicking with his feet but his mammy never said and she never slapped him, she just let him kick. Mammy and she were having cups of tea apiece, so Bertie and I gave each other a look and went out to fetch in sticks. The big tree had been sawed at last because the soldier did some, and so did Maurice French, but not so much, he has no time. Only the trunk is left to be cut.

'Who is that woman?' I asked Bertie.

43

'That is Margaret Halliday,' he said. 'That is the spastic wee boy, I used to see them at the bus-stop before they flitted to Ballycromkeen. He can't keep his feet still but he can talk all right.'

When we came back with the sticks they were away, and so was Mammy. When she came back she said she had to convoy them to the Iron Bridge because the wee lad was unsteady on his feet and they would never have got across the Stick Bridge.

'You should not be doing that with your arm,' she said to me. 'Don't do a turn till I tell you, you've done your share. Sit down and read a book or hear the wee ones their reading.'

'Our good saw is out in the Planting,' I said.

'It is not,' she said. 'The night you and your daddy got killed, Maurice French came down and asked could he do anything and I said, "Find the saw or we're all sunk," so he found it. I greased it and kept it on the high shelf until the soldier came and asked could he saw sticks for me. He is a lovely boy, that soldier.'

'Mammy,' I said, 'was that wee boy the spastic?'

'He was,' she said, 'but dear knows I don't like the thought of the Priory. Hector would have to go and stay if he goes at all, and we'd only get to see him once a week or that, the poor wee soul. But I'll tell your daddy and see what he thinks, it'll not be long till he's home.'

But it was late when he came home from the hospital, and all the wee ones were in bed. Mammy was brushing my hair, because I could not with my one hand, when we heard feet on the steps and it was him and John Finlay. John Finlay is the night-shift man who lives in a red brick cottage at the Iron Bridge.

'Hi, Ethel, I have a surprise for you,' he said from outside.

'You have not!' said Mammy. 'What size is it?'

'About five-foot-eight by eighteen inches,' said Daddy, and he pushed open the door and came in.

'What were they thinking of to let you out?' said Mammy. 'Sure I thought they were going to have you stuffed and put on exhibition.'

'God, Ethel, you're a turn,' said John Finlay. 'I'll away and

44

leave you,' and away he went, laughing.

Mammy said to Daddy, 'Are you really all right?'

'I'll last a while longer, with care and wee bits of fadge. It is not everyone who is hit by a galloping tree and lives to tell the tale. Is my tea ready, I'm dying with hunger.'

All the haddie had been eaten so Mammy made him egg and chips.

'Oh boy,' he said. 'That puts the strain on my stitches but it is worth it. Ethel, I thought I would never see home again. Who was at the tree, it is all sawed but the trunk.'

'For once,' said Mammy. 'It was your rich friends. I mean the soldier and Maurice French.'

'And there's my eldest, armed to the teeth,' he said. 'If anybody looks the part, she does. What do you mean by going about with an offensive weapon?'

'What weapon?' I asked.

'That thing on your arm,' he said. 'One good clout with that would settle any sort of an argument.'

'I never thought of that,' I said.

'What's that writing?' he asked.

'It says, "Do not touch",' I said. 'That is what the black doctor at the hospital put on it the last time I was there. I am not allowed to get it wet.'

'Did they hurt you, love?'

'No,' I said, 'I like them. The black doctor was the best. He has a lovely smile but I can't make out what he says. The nurse had to tell me.'

'He's got the right idea,' said Daddy. 'When do you have to go back?'

'On the fourteenth of April.'

'So do I. Let's go in the lorry, if she'll move, hey?'

I would like that because I have never been for a ride in the lorry yet. Bertie has, when Daddy was delivering peats, but I haven't.

But Mammy never said anything that night about Martin Halliday.

45

APRIL

I thought that when Daddy came home from hospital he would be able to work, but he is not. He can not even fix the lorry and it needs fixing, the time it ran down the hill something broke.

Whatever it is will be hard to mend. Daddy says it is a plug, but that because it is a very old lorry he can not get the sort he wants. He was in the town today till half-six, he had tried every garage in the place and could not get one. He says he is very depressed because the lorry will maybe never run again, what we did to her with the tree was bad for her.

The tree was still tied to the back of the lorry so he went out after teatime and got the wire rope off, then coiled it, took it back to Mr Harper, and apologised for keeping it so long. Mr Harper said that was all right, he had not needed it and he knew it was safe enough. I went with him because Mammy said I had to. I know rightly why she made me go, it was in case he stayed out too late. Mammy is smart. If she told him to be sure and come home at nine he wouldn't, just to spite her, but if I was with him and my arm in plaster he would come home without being told in case I would catch a chill or something. Mammy thought he had done enough for one day.

The Harpers were all at home. Mrs Harper's brother, Gilbert Taylor from Ballycromkeen, was there and he asked Daddy if he was all right again because he wanted some manure shifted and the tractors were busy. He has a very big place and grows barley and keeps sheep and cattle and is making money hand over fist, if you are out at six in the morning and hear a tractor it is likely one of his, he never stops working. He was the first one in this district to get in a harvest by floodlights to beat a storm. Daddy says he would run over broken glass in his bare feet sooner than let a chance of money go by him. He is a hard big man with a red face,

46

and he carries a stick all the time because one time he met a bad bull and he had no stick and the bull got him down and tried to kneel on him. His wife had the tea ready, so she went to where she thought he was, but he wasn't there. She searched and found him. Then she caught the bull by the ring in its nose, pulled its head up, yelled and scolded at it, took it into the byre and chained it up. She was a town girl just come to live in the country and she didn't know a bull from a cow hardly, that was why she hadn't the sense to be frightened. Gilbert Taylor was a bit squashed and he thought he was killed, but he wasn't and one week in hospital did him, but after that he always carried a stick.

But Daddy had to say he was not all right, he could not load or unload yet because of his stitches, and Gilbert Taylor said, 'Oh,' and that was that.

When we left to go home it was pitch dark and Daddy said to me, 'I think we should take the short cut tonight.'

'What short cut?' I asked.

'Oh now,' said Daddy.

We went up the back lane out of Harper's and into Albert Dunwoody's back lane. It was longer than the Arcady lane and full of big pot-holes. I was glad I had my waders on. It was so cold that putting my hands in my sleeves did no good at all, they got numb just the same. I was sure we were for Albert Dunwoody's for we took the left fork at the river. The house is down in a hollow out of sight but there is a big shed made of zinc about fifty yards this side of it. The shed is just full of machinery and balers and a chainsaw, and there a truck with a wooden body and a wooden roof made out of an old Austin car, that Albert Dunwoody takes pigs to market in.

'Hold your tongue,' said Daddy, 'and don't move till I tell you,' and he went up to the shed door. He listened for about three minutes, then opened the door and went in, closing the door after him.

Well, he was in there for ages. I started to tremble with cold but I stayed where I was. I was under the big lilac tree and all I could smell was pigs, I wished the lilac was coming into bloom because it would have drowned the smell of the pigs.

Then Daddy came out of the shed and shut the door. After a minute or two he came back and I saw he was wearing an old pair of grey woollen gloves of Mammy's. By this time the clouds were leaving the moon and he nodded to me to take to the field. I went over a gate and so did he. But first he pinned the gloves inside his coat with a big nappy-pin. I still said nothing and neither did he.

'Come on across to Gorman's,' he said when we were at the Stick Bridge, 'and I'll get you a bar of chocolate. But don't go handing it round, the weans will get theirs another day.'

So we went to Gorman's and he bought a peppermint Aero bar for me and ten cigarettes for himself and Mammy, then we went back home over the Stick Bridge.

'So it's you,' said Mammy, 'I thought you two had eloped to England. Sit down till I make a taste of tea.'

Daddy reached her the cigarettes and she said, 'Oh ho! Oh ho!' but lit one just the same, then made us French toast and it was lovely. Wee James woke up and started to cry so she went to turn him over, and quick as a flash Daddy had the grey woollen gloves under the kettle and a peat on top of them, and the pin in the cushion, and the long screwdriver up on the high self. The gloves burned like mad, and I smelt car oil, but I never said anything. Mammy came down and never noticed, and I washed myself and went to my bed.

I had to go for another check-up because the first time they would not take the plaster off and said to come back in three weeks. I did not see the black doctor I liked, but an Indian lady and I understood her talk. She had a gold earring in her nose, and a red silk dress down to the floor but with a white coat on over it. I asked Mrs Conlan if the Indian lady knew she had a dab of lipstick on her forehead, but Mrs Conlan told me that the Indian doctor must be a high-caste Hindu and the mark on her forehead was the sign. I never knew before. 'Was the black doctor an Indian too?' I asked. No, said Mrs Conlan, he was from Gyanna. I can't spell that but it is on top of South America, I can find it on the map.

Mrs Conlan took me in the car for the check-up because she was going to the library anyway to pick books for the school library. Mrs Conlan always picks them herself and we get good ones, but Miss Diamond always picks ones about doggies and pussies and rabbits wearing clothes, and I don't like them because they are not true but Mervyn and Doreen and Alec do.

Anyway, when we came back to Arcady I was nearly crying because they never took the plaster off my arm. I just thanked her and went into our closet in the yard, shut the door and I cried till Mammy shouted down.

'Are you asleep in there or what? Come out at once and let your Daddy get in.'

So I wiped my face on the lining of an old coat of Mammy's hanging behind the door, and came out.

But that was two weeks ago and sure I soon got over it.

Mr Lyle had two attacks in the last week and poor Mrs Lyle was crying from Tuesday to Friday. Mammy says it is a shame the way he torments her, and her not well at all, in fact she might be the first to go. She is very short of breath and our Agnes is fetching water from the pump for her. Off her own bat, nobody asked her to, it is so strange of Agnes not to wait to be asked I can hardly believe it yet. And Maurice French calls every day to see if Mrs Lyle wants anything fetched.

The morning after we came back the long way from Harper's Daddy was out first thing in the morning, working at the lorry with a big file he has, it made a noise that gave me the toothache at once. Bertie wanted to stay off school to help him but Daddy would not let him.

And an awful thing happened.

Mrs McFarland was coming over the Stick Bridge from Gorman's and there is a hole in the planks. She tripped and put her foot in the hole, she could not help it. She fell on the Stick Bridge and cut her face and when Mrs McCann and Fidelma Ryan ran to pick her up she took a weak turn. They carried her in and Old Joe Cooper got her a wee taste of port wine.

She came to and started to cry and said, 'I have lost my pension, it fell in the river and the book with it.'

49

Well, Seumas McCann was at home, it was his half-day, so he put on his fishing-waders and went into the river with a net and fished downstream until he got her pension book. It was in a bright yellow cardboard wallet or he would never have laid eyes on it under the water. The book and the four pound notes in it were all wet, but they got it dried for her.

She said to Seumas McCann, 'God bless ye and may ye aye hae plenty!'

Mrs McCann and Fidelma were afraid to leave her so they told Mammy what had happened and she said she would look in a time or two to make sure she was all right. Fidelma could not stay any longer for she was on her lunch hour, it was lucky she was there at all. (She went out to shake the hall mat and there was Mrs McFarland on her mouth and nose on the Stick Bridge, she says she will not be better of the sight for a while.)

So Mrs McFarland has a black eye and her face is all swelled but she is getting all right now.

I caught the cold the night I was out with Daddy and I had a cough, so Mrs McFarland asked Mammy if I could come down and sit with her for a while to keep her from thinking long. She could not go out, she was shy because of her black eye and everybody asking her what happened. Luckily she did not hurt her bad foot at all, so she could do her turns in the house.

Mrs Conlan says if she can do her turns she must be a star performer in a circus. She says if I mean she can do her housework I had better write that, and not the other.

I have not been to school for two weeks, my arm does not hinder me but the cough does. Mammy has tried everything but I still have it. Daddy says he can not get peace to sleep with the Lyles arguing half the night and me coughing for the other half.

'Child,' said Mrs McFarland to me this evening, 'can you keep a wee secret?'

'Try me,' I said.

'I'm for giving you a drink every night,' she said, 'before you go up home. It is not wine or anything bad, and it will do your cough good.'

She made me a drink of dark red stuff and hot water. It tasted nice.

50

'What is it?' I asked.

'It's medsin,' she said. 'But do not let on to the rest of them, it's just for yourself.'

'I'll not let on,' I said.

It stands to reason. The rest have not got coughs.

'Will you be fit for school on Monday?' she asked me.

'I will certainly try,' I said, 'God willing.'

'Why did you say that?' she asked.

'Say what?' I asked.

'God willing,' she said. 'You do not know what it means.'

'I do so,' I said. 'It is what Mammy says when she is up against a stone wall. Like when she is ashamed to go into Gorman's because it is the end of the week and she can not clear the account. But it always does get cleared, God willing.'

Mrs McFarland gave me a funny sort of look.

I thought she might be going to kiss me and I would not like it, so I just said, 'Thank you for the nice drink, Mrs McFarland, it was delicious,' and I bid her good-night and left, quick.

And every night this week I got another drink so my cough is not half as bad.

Daddy helped too because he said to Mammy, 'For God's sake, Ethel, lay off the bread and get beef and spuds for a while, even if it's only a cow's tail.'

'Go into the town, you, and get the beef yourself,' said Mammy. 'You know Henry Connolly never has a thing in the van I could buy. And bring a cow's tail if you dare, sure it is all bones.'

'Well, I will then,' said Daddy, and away he went across the Stick Bridge and got a lift on a trailer of peats at that very moment.

I could see him sailing along backwards about level with the top of the hedge until he was out of sight.

When he came back he had a parcel with him.

'Good for you,' said Mammy, when she had it opened. 'Lamb, no less, and I thought you were a poor man! Away out till I get a fire on. Sure we'll have a feast.'

'What is it?' asked wee James, trying to see over the edge of the table.

Mammy gathered it up and made a face at us not to tell him,

51

and none of us did.

'Mammy,' asked George, 'what is it?'

'Away out and play,' said Mammy, 'I can't walk for the crowd round me. I'll give you a shout when it's ready. Bertie, will you take the hatchet and see if you can get more wood chopped.'

Bertie went, and Alec and Mervyn went with him. But George stood on.

'But what *is* it made of, Mammy?' he asked.

'Did you hear your mammy tell you to go?' roared Daddy and jumped at him.

Away went George with a yell, and Daddy and Doreen and wee James after him.

'Where are Agnes and Mria?' I asked.

'Up at Maurice French's with a message,' said Mammy. 'If you are going to stay you might as well help. Take Hector for a walk or something, he wouldn't go out all day and I could yell, in fact I could squeal.'

'Come on, Hector,' I said, 'till we see the wee fish.'

I took his hand in my good one because I thought I would have to pull him, but he came. Mammy had just washed him and cleaned him up and put a pair of Mervyn's old trousers on him, but his nose was running and I wiped it, he let me.

'Now where are you going?' asked Mammy. 'Don't be staying out till dark, mind.'

'Up past the Iron Bridge,' I said, 'Hector likes that way.'

Daddy came in as we were going, and out again with him to file at the lorry's engine with the file off the high shelf. Up in the Plantation I could hear Bertie hagging wood.

I took Hector along the path past the soldier's cottage. He pulled next the water and I held on tight and he had to wait till we had gone on a bit, up near Maurice French's. I could hear our Mria laughing and then Mrs French laughed too.

If you did not know it was Mrs French laughing you would think it was a wee hoarse dog barking. She is not very old but she is very wee, she only comes up to the V of Maurice's pullover, but let me tell you this, she is the boss. She has another farm over the river with no house on it, but they keep all their sheep and bullocks there. Where the house is they only have the cows and the hens and five wee pigs. They have the pigs in an old byre that is cleaned out, with a board across the door about a foot high. When Maurice clatters the bucket to feed them, they come lepping over the board like hurdlers to get to the troch first. Our George is clean daft about them.

Well, we went over the Iron Bridge and Hector stood a good while at the rails looking down but he could not see the fish. We went on by Henessey's and Mrs Henessey, his second wife, was baking. She shouted us in and gave us soda scones with her homemade butter. The butter was half-melted. I needn't tell you what Hector was like when he had done, and I wasn't much better. He was creesh to the ears and I had to clean him with the tail of my tartan skirt, I had nothing else.

They say Mrs Henessey didn't care a docken about wee Kathy, but she is kind to us. Maybe she is trying to make folks think she was kind to Kathy too. But I know one thing, our wee George is only five too, and if you told him to do something he would forget in the time you would clap your hands. Maybe Mrs Henessey told wee Kathy to stay on the path and she didn't. You would never know. If she had stayed on the path she would be living yet, and older than me. She had long curls and a wee red knitted frock. I wonder what she would be like now.

When Hector had seen the fish we came back. Monica and Fidelma were putting out their washing. It was as white as an advertisement but all they use is yellow soap. I know because Monica keeps it in a cracked saucer on their scullery window-sill. They do the washing after work, and Bridie does the cooking. They will miss her when she goes, but perhaps she will not go yet. There is no more word of her wedding and all the talk has died down. I wonder if she is going to get married at all.

Mammy had the lamb cooked. That stew was wonderful, I can tell you. There were meat and potatoes and leeks and swedes in it, and plenty of salt, and I put pepper in mine as well.

'Would you go easy on the pepper,' said Daddy, 'or you'll have us in convulsions. I say, Ethel, this is the life, hey?'

'I haven't any hay,' said Mammy. 'Eat what's in front of you, or they will all be asking for hay.'

'I am just in the mood for hay,' said Daddy. 'How about it Ethel?'

'Would you take a running jump,' said Mammy. 'Have you got that thing working yet, I mean the lorry?'

'It's a good job you said that last bit,' said Daddy. 'I was nearly going to tell you. Bertie, will you come out again and file till I tell you to leave off. If I've tried that thing once I have tried it fifty times and it still won't fit,' and he looked at Mammy.

She said, 'If you don't get the lorry fixed you may just get a job with Doonan, his driver's left to get a job in the Co.'

Daddy was away out of the door like a rocket.

'Where are you going?' Mammy screamed after him.

'To Doonan's, where else?' he roared, and ran over the Stick Bridge and out of sight.

He never came back till it was five past ten and they were all in bed but Bertie and Agnes and Mammy and me.

'Starting tomorrow,' he said. 'Driving for Doonan.'

'You're not!' said Mammy. She looked worried.

'I am so,' he said. 'You need not look like that, I will be careful. Come on, you,' he said to Bertie, 'bring the file.'

They went out and we could hear them filing away like mad. Daddy kept going on at Bertie, but all Bertie ever said was Yes. Then the engine coughed and stopped. Then it coughed again twice and stopped. I could hear Daddy saying, 'Will you let the choke in slower, you fool.'

And with that the truck started and kept right on till Daddy stopped it. We had gone out on the balcony to see.

He came running up to us and said, 'See that, Ethel? I'm a genius!'

'Wouldn't you know it,' said Mammy.

Then we all went in to bed.

MAY

The very first Wednesday after the lorry was fixed Daddy took me to the hospital to get the plaster off my arm. By this time the plaster was all cracked and mouldering away around my hand because I could not help getting it wet sometimes. Aha, I thought, now I will be able to go to the toilet without anybody, but I was wrong. It was the high-caste Indian doctor and she said it was all right to take the plaster off but that I must have fizzio-therapy for some weeks.

That is how it sounded but I could not spell it if you paid me.

She had a beautiful green frock on, down to the ground, with a gold stripe around the hem. Her feet are so wee I think she could wear size two shoes, I wear size four and she made me feel like a Clydesdale horse.

The nurses cut the plaster off with a big thing like what Maurice French cuts dead branches out of the hedge with, it had two blades like a parrot's beak nearly, and it made short work of the plaster. But my arm was all thin and the skin was off it in places. I could hardly move it. I could have cried.

'There,' said Sister Morton, 'that's the first step.'

'The bone has healed quite well,' said the doctor. 'Come back every Wednesday and Friday for treatment. Sister will tell you the times. Is your mother here?'

'My daddy is outside,' I said.

She went out to speak to Daddy and his eyes stuck out when he saw her, he had not seen her before.

When we were driving home he said, 'What an eyeful! What are the Indians thinking about?'

'I don't know,' I replied, 'I would need to ask one.'

'You are a card,' said Daddy. 'Is your arm sore?'

'No,' I replied, 'but it is awfully weak, I don't think I could even brush my hair.'

The next day at school I wasn't a bit better off, our Agnes still had to go out with me.

'How did you go to the hospital, dear?' Mrs Conlan asked me.

'Daddy took me in our lorry,' I said.

'It is not his lorry at all,' said George Brady, behind me. 'He only borrows it from his work.'

'It is so our lorry,' said Mria.

(We were doing painting and Bertie and Agnes and Mria come into our class for that.)

'It's Doonan's,' said George Brady.

'It is not,' said our Bertie.

'This has gone on long enough,' said Mrs Conlan. 'You had no need to speak, George.' With that she looked up and saw that he had dropped a blot on his drawing. 'What are you going to do with that?' she asked.

So he drew wings and a tail and a neck on it and said it was a wild duck.

'Good,' said Mrs Conlan. 'Now kindly don't interrupt again.'

And then she asked me about my arm and the hospital and my cough.

It was raining at three o'clock so she drove us all home.

It was raining on the Friday too, so she both took us and fetched us, but it cleared unexpectedly about twenty past three and Mammy asked me to take Hector for a walk for he had been in all day as usual. So I took him by the hand and we went up the Water Walks past Henessey's, then on over the Plank Bridge and along the path under the trees. Mria and Agnes and Mervyn and George were coming along but they were a good bit behind us because Hector was anxious to get on and walked fast. Mammy had him clean to go out but he was never clean for very long. You could not help talking to him as if he was a wee baby just learning, when I saw a bird I told him what it was and he pounced and missed it by a yard and it flew away. On this side of the river the path is farther from the water, but I did not let go of Hector any more than I could help. When he wanted me to let go he knew to twist his hand around so that I could not get a good grip of it. He did this several times but I always got a hold of him again. It was a long distance to the other Plank Bridge, I am sure we were twenty minutes getting there, but when Hector saw it he would not cross over it. If he had, we would have been on our own side of the river again and nearer home, but he wouldn't cross and I just had to give up. I was scared to push him over the Plank Bridge because it is so narrow and has no railing at all, and he would likely have fallen in to annoy me.

'Walk him round Burnt Island,' shouted Mria, 'and maybe he won't know it again.'

So I did. That was what the bit in the middle of the river was called. The big river split in two and ran round both sides of it, under five Plank Bridges altogether, and then joined together and ran under the Iron Bridge at the Belfast Road.

Hector did not know the Plank Bridge when we got to it the second time, but the others were away ahead of us, past the ruins of the Beetling House. The current was very fast and there was a lot of water in the river. Two or three of Henessey's ducks were diving in a sort of still place where the bank had fallen down to make a little bay, and before I could move to stop him Hector just jumped in among them. He was in shallow water up to his knees because he lit standing, but then he slipped. I don't know what I did. I must have jumped in after him because I got hold of his coat by the pocket, but he was in the deep water and I could not pull him out. He did not even yell and I was too busy. I got hold of a branch on the bank but my bad hand would not hold it and I felt myself going and yelled, and then my eyes and nose and mouth and ears were full of water and we were drowning. I was still gripping Hector's pocket when something hit me a great crash. I must have let go for I knew no more of anything till I was lying on grass and somebody was kneeling on my back, that's what it felt like. I looked round to see and I vomited till I could not speak, but I saw it was a policeman and he was not kneeling on me at all.

'Where's Hector?' I said. 'Is he drowned? Have you got him?'

I had an awful headache and I did not know where I was. There was an iron bridge near but it was not the same bridge as I know. A man in waders was down in the river. It was Seumas McCann and he had his long gaff with him. If the policeman sees that, I thought, he will summons him sure, a blind goat would know that that is for taking salmon.

'Lie still,' said the policeman to me, 'till I tie up that cut. You must have a hard head, young lady.' He tied his handkerchief over my forehead and went to the river.

I struggled up on my hands and knees and I saw a woman come up out of the water with Hector in her arms. He was too heavy for her, I could see that, and she was wet to the skin and her clothes stuck to her, and her hair was all soaking tails.

'Have you got him?' asked the policeman, and climbed down the bank and took Hector from her.

'I got him,' she said, 'but I doubt I was not quick enough.'

'Is there life in him?' asked Seumas.

'You're joking!' said the policeman. 'Look at that.'

'That was the rock at the big bend,' said the woman. She was not crying out loud but the tears were blinding her and she was still standing up to her knees in the river.

'God save us, Mrs Henessey,' said Seumas, 'don't upset yourself, sure you did your best, and nobody can do more without a miracle. Give us your hand and come out of the water before you get your death.'

'Will you take the lady home,' said the policeman. 'I never saw a braver action than yours, missus. Into nine feet of water, you that can't swim!'

'*A child was drowning!*' said Mrs Henessey. 'I will go home by myself, thank you. You help the child.' And away she went up the river path, half running and sobbing.

Seumas looked at Hector and I knew when he said a Catholic prayer that Hector must be dead. He picked up Hector and the policeman picked me up and they set off for home.

'Before we go,' said the policeman, 'stick that thing down your boot and keep your mouth shut. If you had not had it she would be gone too, so this time I never saw it.'

I was glad because the policeman was being decent to Seumas who had saved me. But I was too far through to say anything. I just remember seeing Maurice French's house when my head hurt so much I shut my eyes and never knew another thing until I was

58

in my bed. Mammy was crying with her head down on the side of the bed and I started to cry too. I thought my head would split with pain.

Mammy was talking to herself, or else praying. 'Oh, God,' she said, 'I am a wicked bitch, not to take better care of that poor witless wean.'

'Oh, Mammy,' I cried, 'I tried to get him out but the river was too strong. He went in after Henessey's ducks before I could stop him, and Mrs Henessey went in to save him but she could not get him, he hit the big rock at the bend.'

But Mammy only cried sore and said, 'Oh God, oh God, oh God!' and bit her hand and held it over her mouth as if to hold in what she might say next.

It was awful to see Mammy like this, I never saw her like it before, even when we were nearly killed by the tree.

After a while she stopped crying and just lay there holding my hand. A while after that she said, 'And the tea's to get, just the same.' She got up and dried her eyes on her apron, then went out into the kitchen and shut the door.

I could smell wood burning so I thought that Agnes or Mria would be trying to make the tea. Mammy fetched me some and I drank about two swallows and fell asleep.

When I woke up I heard talk. It was the middle of the night, Agnes and Mria were sound but Doreen was snoring, as usual. One voice was Daddy's and the other was a strange man's.

'He wasn't babtized, said Daddy. 'In fact none of them are. The last man would not allow it.'

'Well I see no need to discriminate against the children,' said the man. 'I will christen them if you will send them to church. I will see if you can't get the ground you want.' And he made a short prayer and went away.

Daddy shut the door and said something under his breath.

Mammy said, 'Shush, some of them might be awake, you never know.'

'If it wasn't for the row there'd be,' said Daddy, 'I would bury him myself in Albert Dunwoody's meadow. You know yourself, Ethel, that this talk about consecrated ground is only a mockery

59

to make money. What about them that got blown to hell in the War? You're not goin' to tell me that God'll turn on them because we couldn't find enough to bury and couldn't put a name to it when we had it scraped up. Forbye we had precious little time for a prayer at such times. I've seen four boys fried with flame-throwers, do you think God is going to ask were they buried in holy ground?'

'This isn't the desert,' said Mammy. 'This is the North of Ireland, and this day it feels like the north side of Hell. You've to starve the living to bury your dead it seems. How much will it leave us?'

'Enough to get by,' said Daddy, 'If the minister speaks for us. And why should he? He never saw us till tonight, but I'll houl' ye he's heard plenty. He could hardly wait to get out. Are you comin' to bed?

'I might as well,' said Mammy. She came in and kneeled down beside me, then went stiff all over and cried and cried and cried. The pillow was soaking and she shivered every two or three minutes.

'Get up, Mammy,' I whispered, 'and come into bed or you will get a cold.'

'How is your head?' she whispered. But she got up.

'It is all right,' I said. It was not all right but it had to do till the morning.

Hector was buried on the Monday but only Daddy and Bertie went to the funeral. The rest did not go to school and I was still sick in bed. They had to get Dr John to me on Saturday. He said it was shock. I started to laugh and cry at the same time. He said 'Stop it,' in a loud voice and I stopped.

I was off school again for a week, but Mammy did not stay at home, she got a job doing cleaning at the Yankee woman's at Castle Gaul. It is a big grey old castle and you can see the tops of the towers from the Back Road. This Yankee woman has bought the place but she is not here yet, and Davina Campbell came up to see if Mammy would go and scrub for four shillings an hour. That is better than you would get about here for scrubbing so Mammy took it. She went every day at nine and came back at six or half-past. I minded wee James. He was as good as gold.

When I had to go to the hospital I took wee James down to Mrs McFarland, and she gave him a toffee and asked him would he be her boy. He said he would if she would give him another toffee.

'He's no dozer,' said Mrs McFarland. 'Your daddy will never be dead while wee James is alive.'

I went to the hospital on the bus. When I came back it was teatime and Daddy was frying sausages. He was covered in white dust from the meal in Doonan's Mill and tired out from unloading bags.

'Is your mammy never back?' he says. 'Home's not home without Ethel. Away and see is she coming, a wheen of you.'

He cut bread and went out to dust himself on the balcony, so I fried the bread and took off the kettle to make the tea. We have a trivet but even so an open grate is not much use to cook on, a hob itself would be a great blessing.

Mammy came in and said, 'One half doesn't know how the other half lives. Davina gets ten pounds a week and that's more than you'll ever see. I know rightly what Doonan's paying you and I know why too. Would you not look for something else not in the driving line, that's too dangerous with the sort of licence you have now.'

'There's only that and the bleachwork at the Broke,' said Daddy, 'and you know what that did to me.'

'God Aye!' said Mammy. 'I never saw the like of it. Leprosy wasn't in it. And the worst of it was, it looked catching.'

'If that was all!' said Daddy. 'I think if I had it much longer I'd have tore the meat off my bones and thrown it away to get peace from the itching. Ethel, I will work as hard as I am able, but please don't mention the bleachworks.'

'I won't,' said Mammy. 'Sit down and take your tea. I'll try and find out do they want a man for the garden. The grass is up to my oxters and you would hardly know where the drive was. There's nobody laid a hand on it since the old cornel's time.'

(Mrs Conlan said the word is spelled colonel, but that was later, when I had asked her.)

'Is Tom Lamont still there?' asked Daddy.

'He is,' said Mammy. 'In the wee cottage the Finnegans left. He has his army pension and all his orders, and cooks for himself. He does a bit of weeding when he has the heart for it, but he can't dig or scythe so there's your chance. Will I ask? Davina's in charge and they would take her word.'

'Aye, well,' said Daddy, and got up.

'Where are you for now?' asked Mammy.

'To Davina Campbell's,' said Daddy. '"Work, for the night is coming,"' he sang, and away out with him, still singing.

'His head's away,' said Mammy. 'Would you do a message?'

'Who, me?' I asked.

'Who else? Away up to Maurice French's for a can of buttermilk and I'll bake. A soda scone would do you no harm, and I've to go to Castle Gaul the half-day tomorrow.' She looked tired and up her arms was black because she had been scrubbing floors. She had washed her arms up to the elbows but the dirt was farther up than she had washed.

I told her.

She said, for a joke, 'Don't let on to your daddy, he doesn't know!' Then she poured out some hot water and washed properly.

I had my coat on and money in my pocket and the can in my good hand.

She said, 'Hold on a minute, I'll go with you. James, love, you stay with Bertie.'

They all went out to play in the yard and Mammy and I set off up the Water Walks. She said nothing and neither did I. We came back the same way, with nothing to say. I was tired and sat in the corner learning my poetry for Monday.

At last she said, 'If you know that I'll hear you it.'

So I said it and got it right the first time, then went out and sat on the steps for a while. The soldier and his wife came in by the lane. He is tall and she is little. They are very fond of each other. He has yellow hair, always short and neat, and blue eyes and a mouth that goes up at one side when he laughs. She is just like a doll, she is so perfect and tidy. She has the highest heels and the tightest wee skirt you ever saw, and she dresses very smartly. It must be lovely to be married to somebody like the soldier or my daddy. But I would not marry the like of Mr Lyle or Mr Feeny for any money.

Wee James was up in the lorry tooting the horn till Mervyn and George got up and made him stop it. George said he was scaring the wee birds and Mervyn said he was running down the battery. He does not know that for himself but he heard Bertie say it.

They never miss Hector at all. Mammy threw out the bucket and washed all his clothes and laid them by for wee James. His shoes were not up to much so she burned them, and a wee wooden doll he used to play with. She never said he was gone, and after the funeral neither did Daddy nor any of us.

I was still sitting when the soldier and his wife came out again. He went the other way but she came past me and asked if I would come with her to Gorman's because her groceries would be awkward to carry over the Stick Bridge. I said I would certainly. When I had carried back a basket for her she gave me a bar of chocolate. The cottage is lovely. The soldier painted the inside yellow and the cheeks of the door green, and the sides of the fireplace are grey, and they have a wee black stove with knock-kneed legs and a pipe going into the wall at the back. That bit of wall is blackleaded and so is the stove, it is just shining. It is such a change from our rusted old open grate with a hook screwed into the low side of the mantelpiece to hang pots and the griddle. It is no sort of a way to cook, the heat goes up the chimney and the ashes go everywhere but into the ash-pit. The soldier's wife has a red woolly rug in front of the fire, and a table with a red tartan plastic cloth, and a sort of silver holder for the pepper and salt pots. She has a sewing machine on a wee table at the back window and the pieces of a skirt are on it, not finished. There is a picture on the wall of a flower lying on steps, and Barney Hake's grandfather clock. It has not been going these fifteen years, Mammy says, because Barney had the floor cemented and the clock was too tall to be raised so he cemented it in. They could have raised it easily if they had taken two big wooden curls off the top, but that is men for you, they are stupid.

When I went back to our house Mammy had finished baking

and there were two rows of soda scones sitting on their edges on the griddle by the hearth.

'Would you shout Bertie in to get me four buckets of water,' said Mammy. 'I have to start in to the sheets.'

'Mammy,' I asked, 'what does a sewing machine cost?'

'Twelve pounds at the very least,' said Mammy, just like that. 'Where did you see one?'

'The soldier's wife has one,' I said. 'She is making a skirt for herself.' Then I shouted to Bertie.

'Wouldn't you know it,' said Mammy, 'she is the handy wee girl. If I had one of those we would not be long in getting new sheets. I could make them out of flour bags. Mrs McFarland has hundreds laid by and, she would be glad of four bob apiece of them. Look, if you hear of a second-hand machine, run home and tell me. It would be the best thing I could buy.'

After eight o'clock Daddy came home and said Davina would ask for a job for him, and I was glad.

'Did she need coaxing?' asked Mammy.

'Did she not!' said Daddy. 'But if I get in, there will be nothing go but what is supposed to go, that I will swear. I have not got a good record in that line, Ethel, but you know how it has been.'

'Times will improve, please God. I jump yet if I hear peats mentioned.'

'That will do,' said Daddy. 'It is Albert Dunwoody I owe it to and we will see he gets all back as soon as I have a foot under me and money coming in.'

'He in cleaning out the deep-litter houses this minute,' said Mammy.

'Do you tell me that!' said Daddy, then picked up the spade and went out.

He was not back until ten to twelve and he was clean beat but he looked happy.

I suppose they thought nobody would understand what they were on about, but they were wrong. I did. Daddy meant that the time he was collecting peats on the Far Moss and selling them in the town they were not his peats. They were Albert Dunwoody's, but Albert Dunwoody did not know it, for he does not go to his moss very often. Sometimes it is months from when he wins peats till he draws them home. In fact, it was stealing. And that is why Daddy means to pay Albert Dunwoody. And I know what it was he went into the machinery shed for the night we were coming back from Harper's. He took the plug and the petrol feed out of Albert Dunwoody's old truck and put them in ours, it was the petrol feed that had to be filed to fit. I know that because Bertie told me. He did not know where Daddy got them, but I do. Albert Dunwoody has a great big farm and all the style you could name, and an MG car and carpet in the kitchen, but it was still stealing for Daddy to take his peats and the things from his truck. I don't think that he took them because Albert Dunwoody has plenty and we have nothing, especially when he took them. It was just that he had all of us to feed and no money and some of us were sick and he got desperate. But I wish he had not done it. I would hate Albert Dunwoody to find out that my daddy is nothing but a thief. Meaning to pay later is not good enough. But I would not like to be the one to tell that to my daddy.

JUNE

Well, a lot happened in the last two weeks.

It is the month of June now and Daddy is still working at Doonan's but this is his last day. It is a Saturday. On Monday he starts at Castle Gaul, clearing the garden at nine pounds and eighteen shillings a week. He was only getting seven pounds fifteen shillings a week at Doonan's because there is something wrong with his licence so if he is caught driving for anybody he might get jail and Mr Doonan would get taken to Court too, I think. I don't understand it myself, but anyway he is glad to be out of Doonan's.

Mammy thought the cleaning at the castle would be finished but it isn't, she has to go back to polish the floors and clean the windows. At the castle there are bare wood floors with rugs on them. So that will be another bit of money for us. Mammy says she will be paying income tax if this goes on much longer. She let the family allowance lie for two weeks and now she can let it lie for another week, so it will be eleven pounds and fourteen pence, and that it is nearly the price of a sewing-machine.

Agnes and I will have to go to the Intermediate School, but I don't want to go. I like the master and Mrs Conlan. We will have to have jimfrocks, they cost three pounds and ten pence, and a blazer is more. And raincoats. I don't know if books are free.

After dinnertime Mammy came in and washed her arms, and asked if Daddy was back yet. He was not, but just with that he arrived and he was raging because Mr Doonan only gave him seven pounds ten, he said he had made a mistake with his insurance stamps and Daddy said he had not, it should have been seven fifteen clear. So they had a row and Mr Doonan said he would see the day when he would give Daddy a job again.

Daddy ate his dinner and went down to Seumas McCann at the pigeon-house to calm himself. I do not know where you would get anybody calmer than Seumas McCann.

The Welfare Nurse came up to see Mr Lyle, he has been ill for two weeks and Mrs Lyle is not well either. Mammy says they will finish up in a home because there is nobody to look after them. They were to have got a bungalow on the new estate out near Katie Ganzie's, but they never got it and now I don't think they will. The new bungalows have gardens and Mr and Mrs Lyle would not be fit to cut the grass in theirs, and I hear you have to.

When the Welfare Nurse drove off it was still only three o'clock and I thought I would go over to Gorman's for sweets or crisps. I do not have money of my own very often but yesterday the master asked for volunteers to clean out the big cupboard in his class-room at dinnertime, so Sadie Millar and I stayed in and did it and he gave us a shilling each. It was worth a shilling because the bottom shelf had a glass vase in it and it had got broken, the shelf was full of glass splinters and we had to take great care.

I called in to Mammy where I was going and she said all right. Away I went, running, but I had to stop because Dermot Ryan and Old Joe Cooper were on their knees on the Stick Bridge, nailing pieces of tin over the holes in the planks. One piece of tin was a five-gallon oil drum hammered flat, and they put it over the hole that Mrs McFarland fell through. They stopped to let me by. Then they returned to their hammering.

I had to wait to cross the main road because there were cars and buses coming and there is no zebra. The Belfast Road is not like the Pack Bridge Road or the Back Road. I know nearly everybody that goes up and down them but it is all strangers here, even the bus drivers are strangers.

Eventually I reached Gorman's but I had to stand for a good while because Mrs Gorman was out at the back getting oil and Vera's dog was sitting on the stairs watching me. It was a white and black spaniel, and they have a white and black cat too. If I could have a dog or a cat I would have a cat, and if I had any choice I would have a marmalade one like the Harper's. They have this great big orange tom cat, he can kill rabbits and fetch them home. From the look on his face you would know he was not a pet cat, but a hunting cat. Aileen Harper says he would take the hand off you if you tried to as much as stroke him.

I had no time to think any more because Mrs Gorman came back with Edie Russell's oil. Edie paid her and went to go out, but first another woman came in. She was tall and slim and had a black pleated skirt and a yellow blouse and a yellow bando on her hair. I did not know her.

Edie Russell turned and said, 'Hallo, Mary! I never knew you standing there, are you still nursing?'

'I am at the Free,' said Mary in a made-up voice. 'But I am at Uncle Albert's for a few days holiday.'

I was glad to see from Edie Russell's face that Edie did not like her for I didn't either. I had only seen her two minutes earlier but you can always tell. The accent took me to the fair. She was trying to talk like Sally Ogle on the TV, and she couldn't. I was in first but she just ignored me and started buying enough stuff for a cruise to Greenland. When she had done, it would not go into the two baskets she had with her.

'I may go back for the car,' she said.

Mrs Gorman hastily said, 'No, I will lend you another basket.'

I saw she did not want her back in, so maybe she did not like her either.

'I could carry it for you,' I said, 'I am doing nothing at the moment anyway.'

'Oh would you?' said Mary, all pleased. 'I'd be glad if you would for I am in a bit if a hurry.'

She was in no hurry. She was just saying that to impress us. I dared not look at Mrs Gorman or I would have laughed out.

Vera's mammy will stand no nonsense off people that owe her money but she is fond of a joke too. She has dark hair and a pale face and wears a royal-blue nylon coat-overall in the shop. In fact she looks just as smart as Mary, only Mary thinks there is nothing like herself in the Six Counties. Mrs Gorman fetched another basket and packed in everything that would not go into the other two, I am sure she did not waste a cubic inch. I took the basket, it was brave and heavy but I thought I could manage it.

We went over the road again and down the path and over the Stick Bridge, with the older tin patches rusting already where the paint is worn off the oil-drums it is patched with. There are too many patches in that sentence, I will have to sort it out later.

When we turned right at the far side of the river I knew that Mary's uncle must be Albert Dunwoody, and I could not imagine how he came to have such a niece. I still did not know her other name, so I was no wiser whether she was his sister's or brother's daughter, or his wife's sister's or brother's daughter, not that it mattered a hoot to me. I changed hands on the basket, but I could only carry it five steps with my bad hand, so I had to change it back and say nothing. Mary walked on ahead in the centre of the lane and never once looked to see if I was coming. Her heels were so high she could hardly walk at all. When she reached the door I was nearly ready to drop the basket because my arm was so sore. I set it down on the step while she went in and put her baskets on the table. Then she came out and took Mrs Gorman's basket. After a minute she brought it back out to me emptied and said 'thank you, dear,' and closed the door in my face.

I just could not believe that she was not going to give me anything for helping her. There is not one person in Arcady who would get you to do a message for them and give you nothing at all. We don't ask but they have not the face to take something for nothing. The soldier's wife does not give me chocolate all the time, but if she misses a time or two there is something good the next time, and Old Joe Cooper and Mrs McFarland pay Agnes to fetch water, and Maurice French pays the boys for doing wee jobs for him, and Mrs Conlan and the master never let you do anything for nothing. Mrs Henessey lost four of her ducks and when our Bertie and George got them for her she gave them a big lump of currant cake apiece, and that was nothing compared to carrying a heavy basket! Do you know, I was so angry I could have squealed.

But at least I still had my own shilling, and I could get the crisps when I returned the basket.

I was passing the end of the machinery shed when I heard a shout, 'Is that you, Mary?' Come in a minute!'

'It is not Mary,' I shouted. 'It is me.'

Albert Dunwoody came out. His hands were all oily and he had a blue can in one, like a gun. 'You'll do just as well,' he said. 'Come in and see if you can get a taste of oil into this.'

Well, you never saw such a sight in your life! He had enough machinery for a show at Balmoral Showgrounds. I do not mean cars or tractors, although he has both this is not where he keeps them, but just machinery. He had two dustbins big enough to put me in and shut the lid, and the blades of a horse reaper, and the blades of a tractor-disk, and two harrows, a rusty one and a good one stood on their edges against the combine. He had two wee oil-stoves, and a motor-mower for the lawns, and an ordinary mower like Mrs Conlan's, and two hoses, and a scythe, and a spare blade for it, and a slasher for hedging and ditching. He had a big circular saw and a wee circular saw with the guards down over the blades, but I knew what they were. Lying on the bench were two things with copper hairs around them in a fancy pattern, only the hairs were wire, I have no notion what they were. Two big squirts were hanging on the wall, and the barrels of a gun, and a hay rake. A big black machine stood in the corner, with belts from it running up into the roof, and another sort of engine was sitting on bricks on an old oil-stained wooden table at the side of the shed, with screws and things all round it. A glass-fronted book-case was full of tools, and a sweep's brush was hanging from a hook on the roof. Hanging from the roof too were the catch-'em-alive rat trap and the wire cage Albert Dunwoody keeps the clocking hens in till they learn sense. Only of course when the hens are in it, it is not tied to the roof, it is outside. Just below the wire cage was a window without glass, I do not mean the shed window, but a new one made to go in a wall somewhere else, and not painted yet. It was leaning against an old dirty dusty pedal sewing machine without any cover.

Albert Dunwoody took me over to the big black machine with the belts and said, 'Here, see if you can get in at the back of it. It can't start by itself so you are safe enough. But keep well away from the belt and the wheel. Are you right?'

I got in with no trouble at all. I could see what his problem was. He is a very big man so he could not get in where I could, and if he

70

leaned over to reach he would touch the belt and the wheel so the machine might start and if it did he would be minced.

'What do you want me to do?' I asked.

'See if you can find a wee round hole in the casing,' he said.

I looked and found three. He reached me the blue oil-can and told me to put three good squirts of oil in each hole, so I did that. I only lost one drip of oil from squeezing the trigger of the oil-can too soon. I liked working it and was sorry when I had to stop. I gave it back to him and squirmed out at his feet and asked, 'Is that your machine over there behind the window?'

'It is,' he said.

'Would you sell it?' I asked.

'Who wants it?' he asked. 'Sure it maybe doesn't work. It has been there for four months.'

'I do,' I said. 'I would like to buy it if I could afford it.'

His face went all straight and serious. He lifted the window and set it to one side, then wiped the dust off the machine, and saw it had no needle. 'Away up to the house,' he said, 'and tell Mary I need a sewing-machine needle.'

'*A sewing-machine needle?*' said Mary, as if she did not believe her ears. 'Who wants one?'

'Mr Dunwoody does,' I said. 'He shouted out of the machinery shed.' She left me on the step but after a while she came out and said, 'Here.'

'This is a sewing-needle,' I said. 'Mr Dunwoody wants a machine needle.' I was exasperated. Who wouldn't be.

She gave me a look and snapped it from me. It was stuck in a piece of cloth. She was a good while coming back again, and then she gave me a machine needle stuck in an old sock. 'Tell Uncle his tea is ready,' she said, and shut the door.

To look at her you would think she was a lady, but she does not act like one. She has no manners. She is no more like the Welfare nurse than chalk is like cheese. It is not how you shape your mouth that makes you a lady, it is what you are thinking.

Mr Dunwoody was sitting on a box in front of the machine, oiling and pedalling it. It was going like the wind, very nearly silently. His feet looked funny pedalling in wellingtons, big thick

71

khaki ones like tractor tyres.

'So here you are,' he said, 'I thought you were away to Belfast for one. Give me it, please.' He had it in the machine and threaded with a dirty blue spool he found in the machine drawer before you could say knife. 'Reach me that duster.'

I handed him the sleeve of an old shirt that he had been cleaning pistons with, there were two pistons lying on it to prove it. He slapped it down under the foot of the machine and sewed down it and the machine sewed beautifully.

'There,' he said, 'how's that?'

'Oh, Mr Dunwoody,' I cried, 'would you really sell it to me?' I was hoping he would say something less than twelve pounds because that was all Mammy had at the minute.

'Try me!' he said.

'My Mammy needs one badly,' I said, 'but they are very expensive.'

'Sit down and see if you can sew with it,' he said.

I did, and the pedal went flipping up and down at the least touch. I sewed better than I ever did on the one we have in Mrs Conlan's class at school.

'Go home and ask your mammy would she take it. It is only taking up room in here, for I am not a sewing man. Tell her if she does not want the machine it will go in the Quarry Pond, for I soon won't be fit to get into the shed for junk.'

'How much is it?' I asked. 'She will want to know before she says.'

'It is a present,' he said. 'It is in my way, and you could be using it.'

'She will be mad,' I said. 'She would want to pay for it.'

'Then I will give it to you,' he replied. 'You tell her it is yours, if she will let you have it. Go on, don't stand there.'

'Oh, thank you, Mr Dunwoody,' I cried, and ran all the way home.

Mammy had the sheets washed out and on the line and was sitting on Old Joe Cooper's bench starting navy-blue knitting. I sat down beside her, all out of breath, and she grinned at me and went on knitting. Wee James was sitting on the river-bank about

72

two feet from the water, and the boys were away up the lane in a body. Wee James made a nice picture in his grey trousers and blue shirt, the water beyond him was silver and his hair was gold.

'Will wee James be safe there?' I asked.

'He's tied,' said Mammy, 'I've the house clothesline through the X of his braces and the other end tied to the lilac tree. He can't fall in even if he wants to.'

'Mr Dunwoody has a sewing-machine in his big shed,' I told her. 'He wants to give it to me, if you will agree. He says the shed is getting too full and he will have to throw it out soon. Would you let me get it?'

'Wait a minute,' she said. 'Get my purse.'

'Where is it?'

'In the knife-drawer,' she told me.

I got it. She looked inside. There was a pound note wadded up on one side and some more on the other. It was nice to see so much in it, all last winter I don't think I ever saw more than the family allowances in it, and that was never for very long.

She took a comb out of her pocket, did her hair and then put her knitting on the window-sill. After that she took the odd pound out of her purse and give it to me. 'I will come with you in case he wants a lift with it,' she said. 'But you are to say, "This is a pound and I hope it will cover the damage," and thank him for the machine.'

'I will indeed,' I said.

So we went down to the big shed. Mary was out on the step calling, 'Uncle, Uncle, your tea's ready.'

But Mammy was able for her. 'Hullo, Mary,' she said. 'What a big girl you have got to be, you will have to be careful or you will get fat. What on earth have you done to your hair? It was a lovely colour when you were at school.'

Mary went in as if she was scalded, and that was that.

Mammy and Mr Dunwoody lifted the machine into his big wooden barrow and they tied it in with a wire aerial Mr Dunwoody snatched off a hook.

Mammy said, 'I'll wheel her up.'

'You'll wheel none of her,' he said. 'She's too heavy for you.

73

Stand back!' He spat on his hands and heaved up the handles and ran with the barrow. We ran after him. I knew why he ran. The lane was full of potholes and if he went slowly the barrow might have cowped with him. There was nobody about when we arrived in Arcady, so himself and Mammy just hurried the machine into our house, then he went thundering back at the gallop with the barrow.

I had to run after him with the aerial and the pound note, and I caught up with him just as he was closing the shed door. He took the money and listened to what I had to say. He knew what it meant and so did I. Mammy had found out somehow about Daddy taking bits from Mr Dunwoody's truck to make our lorry go, it was that she was paying for and not the sewing-machine. But he never let on and neither did I. He would not take the aerial back, for he said he does not use that sort of aerial now.

'What am I to do with it?' I asked, perplexed.

'Give it to your Mammy.'

'What could she do with it?'

She could knit potscrubbers,' he said, and went in laughing to get his tea.

Mr Dunwoody is a good man. I love him best after Daddy and Mammy and Mrs Conlan and the master.

That was the third Saturday in June and I will never forget it, it was a memorable day.

On the Monday after that I was out at the pump getting water before school when the postman came into Arcady and asked me if Miss Ethel Skeffington lived here.

'No, she doesn't,' I said.

He gave me a funny look. 'What's your Mammy's name then?' he asked.

'Ethel Brody,' I said.

'Here,' he said, 'give her this and ask her if it is for her. It has your house number on it and all.'

I took it to Mammy.

She turned three colours, tore it open and said, 'God, it's from my mother.'

74

'Is it for you at all?' I asked. 'The postman is waiting to hear.'

'Yes it is,' she said, 'he knows rightly that it is.'

Mammy was still reading the letter when I came back, and when she had finished she folded it and put it on the high shelf. None of us except her and Daddy can reach it. They keep anything valuable or dangerous or private up there where we can not get it, like money or tools or papers in a tin box, and the green and red delf parrot Mammy's Aunt Minnie gave her for a wedding present.

'Is there any news?' asked Daddy. 'You would think she would give you your right name after all this time, Ethel, that was vicious.'

'It was,' said Mammy. 'But what else can I expect. She had her beliefs, and what can I do about it? Rita's had enough too, she is marrying a sailor, a petty-officer.'

'About time,' said Daddy. 'She's gathering dust this ten years. There is something wrong with beliefs that make a bright lively lass like Rita into a dour-mouthed targe before her time.'

'At least she'll be able to call herself Mrs,' said Mammy, very nastily. 'That was the particular point of the letter. Rita was a good girl and waited till God sent her a Believer. That was the message.'

'Sure the man's only wasting his time,' said Daddy.

'I wish to God *you* were,' said Mammy. 'I have lost count, is this eleven or twelve?'

'How should I know,' said Daddy, 'I only swing the starting-handle.'

Mammy laughed till she nearly had an accident, and Daddy laughed too.

'Rita can have her Believer every time,' she said, still laughing, 'I would not swop for you any day, you are a card. Come on or we will both be late.'

The two of them tore out of the door and away down the Water Walks, with Mammy's coat flying behind her because she had not got the time to put her arms in the sleeves.

JULY

I have been going to the hospital twice a week for a long time and my arm is nearly all right again. The high-caste doctor says she is very pleased with me as it was a bad break, only she did not tell me at the time. On this occasion she was wearing a dark yellow silk robe with silver lines at the hem and a little thin silver necklace. Her hands are very little and her hair is very black. She told me to take her hand with my bad one and pull hard but I did not like to in case I hurt her, so she told me to take the black doctor's hand and pull, and I did.

He said, 'Not bad, not bad at all. What are you doing with that hand now?'

'I am pulling,' I said.

'No,' he said, 'I mean at home.'

I told him I was making a jimfrock on the sewing-machine and he asked if it was a machine I had to wind by hand.

I knew the kind he meant so I said, 'No, I put the cloth in and hold it straight and pedal like mad, and the machine sews by itself. With both hands I am preparing the cloth to go under the foot where the needle is jumping up and down.'

'Can you carry anything with your arm yet?' he asked.

He is only a young man but he is a doctor already. Mrs Conlan says he is reckoned very clever and will be a great loss when he goes back to Gyanna, if that is how it is spelled. I can't spell everything right all the time, or I would never be out of the dictionary. But I hope to improve.

'I can carry a basket with not very much in it,' I said. 'But my arm gets tired before I am home from Gorman's shop. It is a brave bit although you are in sight of our house all the time.'

They looked at each other and they were baffled.

'How far is a brave bit?' asked the black doctor.

'It is along the lane to the river and over the Stick Bridge and out to the main road, and across the main road and into Gorman's,' I said. 'It might be half a mile if you were able to straighten it out and measure it.'

'Thank you,' said the Indian doctor. 'You explain very well. We think your arm is much better, and you need not come back for the exercises any more, unless it becomes painful again. If it does, you must see your own doctor and tell him.'

I thought I should thank them for they had taken an awful lot of trouble with me, so I did, and went home in the bus, sort of sorry it was the last time. But I did not like the exercises so that was all to the good too.

There were three girls and a woman in the bus, they were sitting whispering and tittering and I was sure it was about me. I could not think what was wrong with me. I had on my green frock that Mammy made for me and sandals on my bare feet. There was nothing odd about that. My lace collar was sprent clean too, I had washed it myself. I thought maybe they had never seen a human being before.

The oldest one said to the others, 'That is one of them, I would know the breed anywhere.'

They got out of the bus at the same stop as me, and followed me up the road to the Iron Bridge and over it. I thought they might be going to visit friends on the Back Road because that would be the best way in from the main road, but they missed the turn for Burnt Island and followed me on up past the soldier's cottage. The soldier's wife was taking in the washing and I went to help her. She had baked fairy cakes and gave me two. They were a bit burnt but very tasty and I finished them before I knew. It was sad that Hector was not there to get his share.

Mammy was sitting out knitting when I came up. Her job at the castle is finished for the time being. She had done a big wash and the sheets were flipping lazily back and forth on the line in our garden. There were four sheets and a lot of small things. She has got flour bags off Mrs McFarland and washed the names off them with yellow soap and patience, and made sheets on my machine.

'How did you get on?' she asked me.

'I haven't to go again,' I said, and sat down beside her.

'Away and get wee James,' she told me. 'He went up the lane after Joe Cooper and Joe is going a brave bit, to the Cottages, and wee James won't be able for it.'

Wee James was coming back when I found him. Old Joe Cooper had persuaded him to turn. He took my hand and marched along very solemnly to Mammy.

'Where are the rest?' I asked Mammy.

'Albert Dunwoody gave Bertie two big cases, some machines came in them, and they are all down fetching them. We will have a dressing-table yet.'

All this time the woman and the three girls were having a discussion down just this side of the soldier's cottage.

Mrs McFarland came hirpling up and I arose to make room for her. She was eating dulse out of a paper bag, and gave me some. It was very salty but I had to let on I liked it. Wee James saw Paul and Kevin coming. They were not at work because their boss's father died so the works are closed for the funeral. Kevin broke two fingers last Sunday in a hurling-match but he says they don't interfere with business. They are not in plaster but in a shiny plastic splint. I have never described Paul and Kevin because I have had no time, but they are both dark and good-looking with brown eyes. Paul has a capped tooth in the front that he broke playing hurley against Leinster last year. I always thought they were twins but Mammy told me they have three years between them. There is a terrible scandal in their family, their sister Nuala married a Protestant. Mammy told me in case I was talking to them and mentioned mixed marriages, she says I would talk about anything.

Well, there was a far worse scandal waiting to burst on us, if only I had known it.

No sooner was wee James caught up with Paul and Kevin, than Mrs McFarland said to Mammy, 'Who's yon?'

Mammy looked round and said, 'I might have known. It is Martha and the girls.'

I was mystified. I knew Mammy had just the one sister, Rita.

'Away and see are the rest coming with the cases,' said Mammy to me.

I did not want to go, but I went.

The cases were about three feet square and too heavy to carry so they were trundling them. Bertie as usual was not doing much, but he had Mria and Mervyn and Alec and George at one, and himself and Agnes and Doreen at the other. They would push the top of a case till it cowped forward, and push it again till it cowped, and they were laughing so much that they were coming with no speed.

I thought if I had our inside clothes line we could tie it round a case and slide it home, so I went back to get it. There is a big bend in Albert Dunwoody's lane as it runs to the Stick Bridge, but there is a hole in the hedge for a short cut, and that was the way I went, up about ten or twelve feet of bank. Then I suddenly heard Mammy say something and I stayed where I was, with just my eyes looking over the top of the bank through the hedge stems.

Mammy was sitting with Mrs McFarland, and the woman and three girls were standing in front of her.

The strange woman said to Mammy, 'You are nothing but a big fat brazen hoor, marriage is for life and death and all eternity. You may call yourself Brody but you are Ethel Skeffington and always will be, and you are living with my husband in sin these fourteen years. It is a miracle God does not strike you dead.'

I was horrified to hear anybody speak to my mammy like that, but what could I do about it? And I was amazed. Then at what Mammy said next I nearly fell through the ground with shock.

Said Mammy, 'You are an ignorant bitch and no wonder he left you, with all the arguing and barging he had to put up with! I suppose you know no better, how could you with the rearing you got.'

Mrs McFarland kept saying, 'Oh now, oh now!' but neither of them let on they heard her. Mammy was red in the face and knitting at ninety miles an hour, she does if she is mad.

The woman said, 'Well, I don't know when I ever heard worse, you sitting there in your shame, talking like this to a respectable married woman!'

Mammy gave a loud scornful snort and said, 'Where is she?'

Mrs McFarland was in agony in case there would be a fight, and said, 'Oh now, oh now!' but it was no use.

Mammy looked up and saw the youngest girl sneering and said, 'I'll bet your mammy has not told you who *you* are, dear, so I might as well. There was a Yankee evangelist here the year before you came on the scene, and your mammy's husband came home to find the blinds down and the pastor in with your mammy, making a very long prayer. He might have believed it only her knickers were hanging on the pump in the scullery. So now you know, dear. And the best of British luck.'

The woman gave a loud scream, clapped her hand over her mouth and turned three colours.

The eldest girl seemed to be upset and said, 'Come on home, Ma, you are only making a show of us all.'

'Mind your own business,' said the woman. 'Do you think I am going to put up with Ethel Skeffington sitting there in her grandeur when I have to work my fingers to the bone for my two wee girls?'

'They should be working, the useless lumps,' said Mammy in a passion, knitting faster than ever. 'Music lessons your arse and parsley!' she said. 'When I was their age I had fifty pounds saved from working in the mill! You would save yourself trouble if you put them out. The eldest seems a nice girl but then I know who *she* is, and she is welcome any time she cares to call. Her daddy would be glad to see her.'

'You and your fifty pounds!' said the woman. 'You just decoyed him away from me.'

Mammy gave another loud snort. 'I had no need,' she said. 'After what he had been through, he came running. Take a look at yourself some time. It was bad enough when you took every penny he had to get a piano you couldn't play, but when you joined the Peculiars and wouldn't let him live with you any more, let you take what you got! If he'd met with any kindness he would have stayed. He's no chancer. He's stayed with me and done his best for us and worked hard and sore every chance he has had from the very first. And it has not been easy, we have had our hard times too. You don't want a man, Martha, you want a wee bullied crawling slave in the day-time and damn all at night-time, even if you weren't past it!'

'Missus,' said the woman, 'if you want a bat on the mouth just say that again! That is all I am saying!'

'It better be,' said Mammy, 'or I will stick my feet in you, you long-nosed greedy targe. If you come here again I will make an example of you, you won't like. You had a man and you lost him because you would neither be a mother to his weans nor feed him without a lot of preaching and abuse. He's not told me, but the neighbours have. They heard you through two stone walls. The man's not a fool. If you'd kept your mouth shut you might have him yet. But not you!'

By this time the woman and the girls were away up the Arcady lane like hares.

'They're going the wrong way for the bus,' said Mrs McFarland.

'Let them!' said Mammy. She was just raging.

'Come down till I make you a cup of tea,' said Mrs McFarland. 'That was a terrible shock you had, Ethel.'

'As long as it has not harmed wee Seumas,' said Mammy, and put her hand on her stomach.

'When's it to be?' asked Mrs McFarland.

'January, God help the wee thing,' said Mammy. 'We might call it Hector.'

'Oh, no, no, no,' cried Mrs McFarland. 'You never had luck with that name, Ethel, promise me you will call it something else.'

I was still lying on my face in the hole in the hedge. I had heard an awful lot that was not my business and I was all bothered about it because I could not understand it all.

When Mammy and Mrs McFarland went in I got the skipping-rope, and the inside clothes line as well, and we did what I said. We were able to pull the boxes right to the end of the lane. When we had the two of them about level with Mrs McFarland's door Mammy came out. She sent Mria and Agnes to Gorman's for the groceries, and the bread, and they weren't at the Stick Bridge till Daddy was in, asking if it was a flitting.

'Away for the hammer,' said Mammy, 'and take the sides out of both of these, or we will not get them in.'

'What are you going to do with them, Ethel?' asked Daddy.

'I will have a dressing-table or bust,' said Mammy grimly.

'You have all the bust you can handle,' said Daddy.

But she did not laugh.

'Are you all right?' he asked.

'I am fine. And put the pan on.'

The pan hung on bulls from a screw under the mantel-shelf. I knew she was still mad because of the visitors, but I could not let on myself. She would have killed me with the brush if I had told her that I was in the hedge and heard all.

But I wonder what hoor means, I never heard that word before. I will ask Mrs Conlan.

Well, after the tea was cleared away Daddy and Bertie and I went out. Daddy knocked a side out of each case, but still could not get them into the house, so he knocked off the bottoms as well. The lids were separate anyhow. Bertie and Mria carried in one case and Daddy and I carried the other. Mammy and Mervyn fetched the lids and sides and bottoms as best they could. George and wee James gathered up the nails.

I hardly knew our upstairs because Mammy had pushed the beds one on each side of the window in the big room, and there was space enough on the far wall for the two cases. Daddy put the bottoms back on them and stood them up. Each had a lid, two sides and a back, and there was a space between them. Over this space he made a bridge with one of the lids and nailed it on. The sides he had taken off were in planks so he took four of these planks and nailed two on each side, inside each case, level, about a foot and three feet from the bottom. Then he joined some more of the planks together and made two shelves to rest on the nailed bits. With the still unused planks and lid there was enough wood and to spare for a counter on each side of the bridge.

'There,' he said, 'does that suit your ladyship's conveniences?'

'It does that,' said Mammy. 'Come on and help me.'

We have not got a lot of clothes. Our winter jerseys were packed in the polythene bags the potatoes come in so we arranged them neatly on the first shelf. Mammy put her two dresses, a cardigan, her good slippers and a nightgown for the hospital on the shelves. I put my yellow cardigan, my wellingtons and my coat. Agnes and Mria and Doreen and I had all got tartan skirts since Mammy got the machine, it is far too warm for them now but she got the stuff in a sale and made them too big for us, so all those went on the shelves. The boys had wellingtons and their other trousers to put in the dressing-table. Daddy got his old leather jacket and put it in too, and his other shoes. They are very worn now.

Mammy asked suddenly, 'Where would I get some heavy polythene? I could make them raincoats.'

'Ethel, you're a genius,' said Daddy admiringly. 'I will get you some if I can. A lick of paint would do this no harm. It looks a bit raw.'

'How are you Burke!' said Mammy, and went downstairs.

The kettle for the dishes had boiled over on the fire and the kitchen was full of steam.

Just before the holidays we were all together in Mrs Conlan's class while the master was doing the roll-books. Jim Getty was telling Mrs Conlan that his uncle George was home from England.

'Is he still in the Air Force, Jim?' asked Mrs Conlan.

'He is that,' said Jim Getty. 'He is a Warrant Officer One now.'

'That's fine, Jim,' replied Mrs Conlan, and went on writing on the board.

'Mrs Conlan, please,' I said, 'what does hoor mean?'

'Oh dear, don't ask me just now,' she said. 'Wait till I get this finished.'

But school ended and she still had not finished, so I stayed behind and asked her again.

'It is not a very nice word,' she said. 'Don't ever say it in school. It means a badly-behaved woman. Wherever did you hear it?'

'It was a woman who came to see Mammy. She did not mean it to be nice. Mrs Conlan, Mammy is going to have a baby in January.'

'How do you know?' she asked, surprised.

'I heard her say to Mrs McFarland.'

'If your Mammy wanted me to know, she would tell me herself,' said Mrs Conlan.

I felt as if I was getting smaller and smaller. I was so ashamed I could have cried. It was an awful day. Mrs Conlan never scolded me but I would have felt better if she had.

On the Twelfth of July my daddy carried a banner and got a pound note. We all went to the Twelfth Field but it was no good, Mervyn wanted to hear the bands but it was not music, it was a lot of speeches and sermons and we did not enjoy ourselves. Doreen got a bit of currant cake and a drink of lemonade from Ray Hilton's mammy, and about half an hour after it she was sick. Mammy had to sit down on the ditch and hold her head.

Ray Hilton's mammy laughed and said, 'Well, it had to happen, Ethel, sure she will be none the worse.'

Mammy said, 'Not a bit, it will be a lesson to her.'

George and Mervyn and wee James went down the Field and disappeared, but after a while wee James came back and told me a garbled tale. All I could make out was that something awful had happened. I went to look and a turkey was chasing them. I picked a stick in the hedge and said to see James, 'Stay you here!' and went to save them. I am not scared of turkeys because Mrs Henessey had some last Christmas. It was funny to see them because Mervyn was first and George was next and the turkey came in third.

'It is a good job that wasn't a gander,' said a voice, and it was Old Joe Cooper.

We hardly knew him. He was not wearing his tweed coat with the pleated pockets, but a good navy blue suit and a bowler hat and white gloves and an orange collarette with a gold fringe. He had a raincoat on his arm and a stick.

Another old man, with a big white moustache, was with him. He was a stranger, but Bertie had heard that this was the master's father. He thought he must be a hundred. He was a master at our school when Daddy was a wee boy, and one day he gave all the boys eight slaps each for mitching the day before to follow the hunt coming past in the lunch hour. When they saw the hounds and the horses and the red coats, the boys just took off and forgot all about school. Daddy says he ran nine miles that day and came home about half-eight not able to play ploit. His mother said she knew rightly where he was so she was not worried.

It was past teatime when we all got home except Daddy. Mammy sent us to bed early and we were all agreeable to go because we were clean beat. She said she would wait up for Daddy. So we all fell asleep.

After a while I dreamed I heard a thump and woke up and heard Daddy singing.

'Will you give over,' said Mammy in a loud whisper. 'You will wake the whole of them.'

'What odds!' he said. 'I will sing them a wee song.'

'You'll sing no wee song,' said Mammy. 'Come here and wash your face. Where in under God have you been?'

'Fishing,' said Daddy, and something thumped on the table.

'Where is the gaff?' she asked.

'Wrapped in some oul' bags under the pigeonhouse,' he said. 'Am I drunk?'

'You are,' said Mammy.

'Well, don't look at me like that,' he said.

'I'm not,' she said. 'It would be a quare thing if you could not get drunk on a holiday and enjoy yourself.'

I could hear Daddy keeping quiet. I knew he had expected Mammy would be cross with him because she usually is if he comes home drunk on a Saturday, but when she was not cross he did not know what to do.

'I'll get a job on Monday,' he said.

'You would need to,' said Mammy. 'The winter's coming and it has never been a bed of roses yet, in fact I don't know yet how we came through the last one. It's a miracle you would not get a piece of bog and cut peats.'

That was the first time I knew we had no bog. For sure, I mean. The other time it was mentioned, I had found out that Daddy had been stealing and selling Albert Dunwoody's peats. That was bad enough because Albert Dunwoody was always awfully good to us.

'It would be handy,' said Daddy. 'I'll see Thomas McManus

while I have the price of a lease. It will be no great sum, for Cranee Moss is abandoned this long time. And we need petrol and oil.'

He did not sound drunk any more, only tired.

After a while they came to bed. On the way Daddy said something very softly at the foot of the stairs.

And Mammy said, 'Well, it's done now, you may like it or lump it. Paugh! what a smell of drink, if I didn't love you I'd be clean scunnered at you.'

I heard no more for that was when I fell asleep again.

Daddy was working at the Buroo so the only day we could go away was on a Sunday.

He had come in on Saturday and said he had got a piece of Cranee Moss and bought a spade to cut peats, and the petrol and oil he needed. He said Mammy was to make four loaves of sandwiches and get extra milk because we would go for a picnic on Sunday.

That was a lightsome change from Mammy teaching us our catechism and hymns and verses from the Bible. I liked that, but going away was nicer.

Mammy sent Agnes and Mria over to Gorman's for the bread, eleven apples, a pound of margarine, a tin of pilchards, a pound of onions and a dozen eggs. We made two kinds of sandwiches, pilchard and egg-and-onion. Wee James had to have special ones, egg with no onion.

'You never got me the polythene,' said Mammy. 'And if it's a bad day they'll be lost, the wee things.'

'We can't manage it now,' said Daddy. 'How much money have you?'

'Not near enough I am sure,' she said. 'How much would it cost?'

'It's not dear. I will do what I can for a pound. There is a sort they put on floors in the decorating business, to keep the splashes off. Sure it would do rightly. Have you thread?'

'I have,' said Mammy.

So he went over the Stick Bridge and got a lift. When he came back he had this big bale of colourless stuff with him.

86

But it was away past three o'clock.

Mammy said to me, 'Away and get my old coat from the back of the closet door.'

I did that.

Mammy then laid it out on a newspaper and said, 'Cut round it.'

So I cut. She showed me where.

'Now for the sleeve,' she said.

It had an odd kind of a sleeve in it, that you would not think was the shape of a shoulder until there was a shoulder in it. It was not like the sleeve Mrs Conlan showed us in school. That was rounded on top and this came nearly to a point.

When we had finished copying the shape of Mammy's old coat we had a sleeve front and a sleeve back, half a coat front and half a coat back.

'Now,' she said, 'to the divil with buttons, I would need over thirty and it is impossible. We will have them slip over your heads like ponchos. Ponchos are the very latest thing anyway, with hoods on them. Yours first.' She seized me, put the pattern against me and folded up the hem, then slashed out a front and a back and two sleeves, that she gave me to hold. 'If you leave down the bits before I tell you, I'll kill you!' she said. 'For then I won't know one coat from the other till they are sewed up.'

Then she measured the pattern on Bertie, but she had to turn it up farther, and fold a bit across in the front and crease the length he would need the sleeves, before she could cut out a coat for him. She did the same for the others until there was none of the stuff left but a lot of tartles of rags, but there was no coat made for herself, and none for Daddy, and none for wee James. She said it did not matter because they could shelter in the cab of the lorry. It was after five o'clock and not a stitch put in one of them, I did not know how she could have them made in the time.

She said to me, 'You are going to begin to sew them, and I will show you how. There is nothing to it really. You sew the sleeve back armhole to the coat back armhole, and the sleeve front armhole to the coat front armhole. When you have done that, tell me and I will show you what to do then.'

'I will ask if I am stuck,' I said, and lengthened the stitches and began to sew.

Mammy got the tea ready and I sewed away until I was ready for help.

Mammy said to sew the sleeve seams from the armhole to the cuff, and the coat side seams from the armhole to the hem. So I did that, and here wasn't the coat finished! I was amazed. By that time Mammy had eaten something so she brought her cup of tea with her, set it on the machine and sat down to sew while I would have my tea. I just snapped up a slice of bread and buttered it, watching Mammy so that I would miss nothing, took another slice and jammed it, then drank my tea. I would not have noticed if it had tasted salt. By the time I had finished she had sewed Agnes's and Bertie's coats and was started on Mria's. She was a stitcher at the Broke Mill before she married Daddy so she can sew like the hammers, you never saw anything like the way the polythene streamed in under the needle and came out sewed.

After we had washed the dishes and put on water for our wash, Mammy told me to take the remains and cut out eight stripes about an inch wide and as long as I could get them. Agnes held the stuff because it was very slippery to cut.

Said Mammy, 'Don't think I want to do you out of the sewing, but I can still sew faster than you and we are in an awful hurry, as you know. It is a mercy I served my time at the stitching or I would not know where to start making eight raincoats.' And she began to sing:

Cold stone dead in de market,
Cold stone dead in de market,
Cold stone dead in de market
I shot nobody but my husband!

'God save us, Ethel,' said Daddy, all alarmed, pretending to believe her and making for the door, 'whatever did you shoot him with?'

'With the dishcloth,' she said, pedalling furiously.

About ten to eight she stopped and lined us up. She made the ponchos go over our heads by cutting a very slight V in the front of the neck. She let me sew the hoods, they had only one seam each. About seven inches below the point of each hood I sewed on a long stripe by its middle, I had to go over that three times to make sure it stayed sewed.

'This is like blinkers,' said George.

'You can see through it,' said Mervyn.

Mammy tied the loose ends of the strips under their chins. The ends of the hoods came down over the necks of the coats and overlapped in the front under where the strips tied.

'There,' she said, 'no extra charge for the fashion show. I did not know I had it in me, but you never know what you can do till you try.'

They were every bit as good as plastic coats at nine and eleven each. They would certainly keep the rain out. I was proud of them.

'Now,' said Mammy, "to save any rows I will put your initials on them.'

'But mine are the same as Alec's,' said Agnes, 'and Mria's are the same as Mervyn's.'

'Then I will put your names on them,' she said, 'at the tail. You will know where to look yourselves but nobody else will ever know.' She climbed on a chair and from the high shelf she got down the pencil that Henry Connolly dropped the last time he was in Arcady. It had a thick black lead in it and she printed our first names inside the tails of our coats with it. It wrote on the polythene as if it was paper, it was no ordinary pencil I can tell you.

Mammy was tired so I put the machine away and cleared up the mess. We were up over the shoe-mouth in polythene clippings.

'Who will go to Maurice French's for buttermilk?' asked Mammy.

We all knew that meant she was going to make pancakes. Doreen said she would go, so she fetched the can and Mammy gave her sixpence and a toffee. She was back with the buttermilk before the pan was hot because she ran both ways. We were eating pancakes out on the balcony when Dr John came by and said a bit less noise would be appreciated because Mr Lyle was having an attack, so we shut up and went in because Dr John would warm your ear in a minute if you were not careful.

There is a girl at our school who had a gumboil and when her mammy called in the doctor to see it the girl would not stand still to let him look at it. He told her twice and she would not, so he put her over his knee and after that he had no bother. It was a lesson for her, forbye nobody ever hit her before, especially on the backside. Mammy said when she heard it that she had it coming to her, standing there girning and wasting the doctor's time, as if he had nothing to do but coax her. Anyway I am glad it did not happen to me.

Sunday was a lovely day.

We left before nine and never even stopped to wash any dishes except the cups we were taking with us. Mammy took a knife and a box of matches and a newspaper and a can of paraffin oil and four bottles of milk and a taste of tea and sugar and the three-quart can and three towels and a bag stuffed with things she might need in an emergency, such as her purse and I don't know what else. She climbed up into the cab and Daddy handed wee James and George and Mervyn up to her, then shut the door and locked it in case one of them opened it. He helped the rest of us into the back of the lorry and told us to hap ourselves up in the tarp because it would be cold. Then he got in and drove off.

Bertie and Mria and Agnes and Doreen and Alec and I were wrapped in the tarp like fish in a parcel. Sometimes we had our heads out and sometimes we had our heads in but it was warmer than you would expect. After a while I put my head out and saw the sea. I never saw it before but it looked just the way it did in pictures. A wave rolled in and broke, and I understood at once how a wave is made. Mrs Conlan had explained it of course, but seeing a wave was the best way. I heard a noise I could have sworn was a cat, but it was a seagull. There were only a few of them but it was enough, they did not sound at all cheerful.

We came to a wee road and went down it, and out on to the sand and up to the right as far as some rocks, and stopped. I got down and so did Bertie, and we helped the others. The lorry had made tracks on the sand but our feet did not because it was pretty hard. There was nothing on it but bits of seaweed like giant's dulse, and some bits of wood and an old shoe and a whin bush. There was a wind blowing but the sun was brave and hot.

'There!' said Daddy. 'Away you go and see where we are. And don't jump in to see how deep it is.'

We went to the rocks and passed them. Beyond we were in a bay with white cliffs like a picture-book. Some of them were split and the splits went a long way back, like caves. I did not fancy the look of them. They put me in mind of the sort of place an octopus would live in, or crabs.

With that, wee James came roaring after us so Bertie took his hand for safety's sake. Agnes found a shell almost at once. It was pink and silver. I have seen common snail-shells before but this was so nice it was a strain to believe that a snail made it all by itself. We took off our sandals and went in paddling, and after the first splash we never noticed that the water was cold at all. Then we went down to the end of the bay and turned the corner. There we found a deep hole in the sand at the foot of the cliffs, full of pale green water, with just a narrow place left to get by, so we went very carefully because none of us can swim. After that it got very rocky and the rocks were all slippery, so we got out of there and went back to the pool and walked around it to find out if there was any place it was shallow. Mervyn bet George that the far end was, and he was right. I waded in carefully to see, in six steps the water was nearly up to my pants so I came out. The bottom was sandy and there was only a wee taste of weed on the sides, like wet green fur. That was how it looked, and when I stroked it it even felt like wet fur.

In the afternoon Daddy took Bertie and Alec and Mervyn and George in for a swim in the pool. They could not swim so he said he would teach them, but he nearly taught them to drown. He got very excited, pulled George out and put Mervyn in the shallow end, then swam after Bertie, who was away like a motor-boat in twelve feet of water.

'Come on ye boy ye!' roared Daddy.

Bertie stopped swimming, said, 'What?' and sank.

I could see him sprauchling all the way to the bottom.

Daddy fetched him out and said, 'You'll do, you can swim like a duck. Now swim out.'

And Bertie did.

'There's no need to drink it,' said Daddy. 'If you do that you can *walk* out.'

Then he went back for Alec, who had gone lashing to the edge but could not get out because that side was too steep. I do believe Alec swam, but nobody noticed because Daddy was so excited about the other three. He had us laughing all the time.

'Where's Mammy?' I asked.

'Langwishing in her boodwor,' said Daddy.

With that she came round the corner in a bathing suit, and jumped in and swam to the shallow end. I wished I could do that. She swam back again and touched the rock at the deep end, then turned and swam to the shallow end and waded out.

'Come on, you,' she said to me, 'in you go next.'

We changed in below the lorry. Mammy pulled the tarp down nearly to the ground on one side so we were screened off. She got dressed and I put on her wet suit. It was awfully cold and the straps were far too long, but she hoisted them up to my ears and put knots in them.

I was scared to go into the pool but I went in. Daddy walked me in from the shallow end. I put my arms the way Mammy did and swam six strokes, but then Daddy had to save me.

He said, 'For two pins I would let you sink.'

And I said, 'Aha, but I have not two pins, you will have to save me.'

He was only joking, of course he would not let me sink. He made me try to swim twice more, and then he took Mria. I had to dress myself and give Mria Mammy's bathing suit.

By dinnertime we had all had a bathe, even wee James. He went in his bare skin, riding on Daddy's back while Daddy swam once down the pool. He put me in mind of Tom the Water Baby that was in my Primary Three Reader.

We were all mad with hunger, so Mammy dried and dressed wee James while Daddy was dressing, and the rest of us ran about trying to find stuff for a fire. We made a hollow on the sand and rolled some big stones around it, then put the things we found in the middle with some newspaper and a slosh of oil, and up it went. Mammy reached me the three-quart can and told me to fetch water.

'Where from?' I asked. 'The sea is salt.'

'Honestly?' asked Mammy, all surprised.

Bertie and Mria laughed at me. They knew she was only pretending.

'There is a spring in the biggest cave,' said Daddy. 'Just set the can under the drips and wait for it to fill.'

I did not want to go into the cave because it would be dark, but in I went. The walls were white rock and the floor was sand with lots of big round stones. It was very slippery everywhere because it was dripping with water, and as cold as the inside of a refrigerator. (No wonder I can spell that, there is a shop full of them beside the town bus stop and there is nothing else to look at.) It was too wet to sit down in the cave and I had a busy time keeping out from under the drips from above. I stuck the can under the biggest trickle and it was not too long until it was filled.

Mammy boiled it and made tea. It was the oddest way to be making tea but it tasted all right. I could not describe what we ate, it was so much mixed up. Then we dried our hair if it was still wet, and rested, and played tig. Mammy did not play tig but Daddy did, until Mervyn fell on his mouth and nose and his glasses fell off. Then Mammy said that was quite enough, we should settle ourselves. The tide was beginning to come in so Daddy shifted the lorry, and shifted us too in case it would catch us, he said he has seen a car caught by the tide on the strand up the coast. He said it was only God's mercy that a gang of young fellows came with a rope and pulled her up, or she would have been under water and good for nothing when the tide went down.

'Ethel,' he said then, 'if that is not rain coming, what is?'

We looked out over the sea and saw a beautiful sight. Clouds had come up over the sea and there was a hole in them. You could not see the sun but it was shining through the crack, in a slant on the sea. It became very windy, and the sand blew about and stung our legs. The waves dashed in, and the sky darkened.

'Put on your raincoats,' said Mammy.

She grabbed wee James, put him in the cab of the lorry and climbed in after him. Daddy went in under the lorry and lay down with his chin on his arms. We scrambled into our homemade raincoats not a second too soon. I was tying the strings of George's hood when the rain came down. It did not stop to fall, it was like standing under a spout. We had not our shoes on, so we just danced along the sand seeing who could hop farthest and skip farthest, and other things like that till the rain ceased.

Rain on the sea makes a noise I never heard before. I will have to think how I could describe it.

At teatime we could not have a fire but we ate all that was left and drank milk. Then Daddy said he would drive home another way and take his time, so we packed ourselves back into the tarp and called it a day.

We reached home very late, and stiff. It was still daylight, but only just.

We were so stiff we simply creaked up the steps, and Old Joe Cooper said we should keep as quiet as we could because Mr Lyle was dead and Mrs Lyle was taken bad and was away to the hospital. The ambulance came for her but Barney McConnell's hearse was coming for him as soon as it was dark.

So we went and made chips. Then we went to bed. I licked my hand and I tasted salt, I was still the flavour of the sea. We listened for the hearse until it came, and afterwards until it went, and then we fell asleep.

AUGUST

The beginning of August was thundery and once or twice we had storms with lightning. Mammy was always afraid it would strike our chimney, but it didn't. It hit a tree in the Plantation instead, and split it in two and set it on fire, but it rained so hard, immediately after, that the fire was put out. Daddy and Bertie were up in the Plantation for five evenings, sawing and chopping at that tree, until the saw was blunt and the head came off the hatchet. The flying head just missed Doreen, who was bringing them chocolate.

Mammy finished my navy jersey and I finished my gymfrock. (Mrs Conlan says that is how it is spelled. Till she told me how, I could not see any sense in such a word myself.) I herringboned the whole hem my own self, it took days because I am not very good at herringboning. Mammy was very particular and made me rip it out again if it was not small enough, I did not like this but it was good for my herringboning. Mammy has got our new socks and shoes for the Intermediate School laid by under the dressing-table so if we had blazers and raincoats I think we would do. But I don't like to say it to Mammy because she has worked so hard all this summer to get our things. Maybe she will be asked to go back to the castle when the American woman comes.

That woman has owned the castle since May but has never set foot in it yet. It is well for some people that have a castle to live in and cannot be bothered to come and see it even. Davina Campbell is getting ten pounds a week because she is in charge of it all until the owner comes, but even she does not know when that will be. She says she expects she will get a telegram any day or hour. Agnes Turtle works there too. She is about twenty-six and has no nonsense about her and I like her. The day we did in the grizzly bear I was over there helping Mammy when I cut my hand on a knife I did not know was in the knife-drawer. I bled all over the green lining but Agnes said not to bother, she would clean it up, then she tied up my hand in a bandage. I was scared Mammy would send me home if she knew, but I did not tell her and neither did Agnes. When Mammy did find out it was too late to be worth her while to send me home.

The way we did in the grizzly bear was like this.

The American woman's solisitor wrote to Davina Campbell and told her to clear out anything with moth or woodworm and burn it, and make the rest as presentable as possible. So she had an inspection when she and Mammy and Agnes had taken four coats of dirt off everything. Except for Tom Lamont the caretaker, the castle had been deserted since ever I mind. They started to throw out an old wardrobe but the back fell off before they got it out of the hall, it hit the stuffed bear that stood there with a tray in its paws, and about a dozen wee moths flew out of him.

Davina Campbell said to the bear, 'You're for the high jump!'

But he was not for any high jump. Mammy and I trailed him out into the backyard, away from the house and the stables, then she sent me for the oil and the matches, and never noticed I had my hand tied up. When I came out again Mammy was stroking the bear and saying, 'You poor thing, you poor thing.' She made me laugh. Davina Campbell came out and laughed too, she says Mammy could make her laugh if she was dying.

She does not laugh very much because she is sad. She is a widow-woman. She is tall and thin and kind of fair, and very strong. She is kind to me, not like Mary. She never had any children and she says she would have liked some rightly but it was not to be. Mammy says she will always like Davina because it was Alec Campbell who spoke for us and got us the flat in Arcady when we had not got a house.

I was only a wee girl not started school and Bertie was walking and Agnes creeping and Mria was just a wee wean in Mammy's arms, not even getting her teeth. If I think I can just remember where we lived then. It was a thatched cottage beside a burn. There were rats, they came to play in our yard. I sat and watched them and was not scared, I did not know I should be. I could see they were having fun with each other and finding things to eat. Daddy had a terrier dog then and it used to chase them if it was at home. But it stayed nearly all day up with the dogs at Thomas Hugh Archer's, he had four collies, and a boxer with a nasty face, and a black poodle, it was a fool and still is.

Well, here, Mammy was frightened that the rats would bite us, so she got Daddy to fetch a man in from the Council Offices. He came and he saw for himself but he did nothing.

Mammy went to the Council Offices herself and said, 'I will camp at the roadside if you do not get us a house. If one of the weans gets bit with a rat I will take you to court.'

He still did nothing, he just said the council was building houses about a mile up the Belfast Road.

Mammy said, 'Aye! At two pounds a week rent. I would rather have less and be able to pay for it, and nobody telling me my rent was sending their rates up.'

But it was no use. I can remember that because Mammy talks of it yet, and keeps me reminded. One day she had been to the doctor's and was waiting for the bus in the town when Alec Campbell came by pushing his bike and asked her how she was doing, so she told him where we were living.

He said, 'Did you not know the Arcady Factory is in flats now? It is not near full, I will put in a word for you with the manager.' And he did.

We flitted soon after that and have lived in Arcady ever since. It is a good thing we came, I could never have gone to school from the cottage because it was in the middle of a maze of leats and I would have lost my way for sure. That was at the back of another factory away down the Belfast Road, miles, I think, I have never been back to see.

We babtized the bear with a good dose of oil.

Then Davina said, 'Would you like the teeth and claws? They would only be destroyed in the fire.'

I was delighted. If there was one thing I would like to have it was a necklace of claws. When I looked at the claws I rued it, because they were too big for that, but I was glad of them anyway. I have them in a tin box on the high shelf, and it is the first thing of mine that has been put up there. Davina said they would serve to remind me of the day we did in the grizzly bear. Then we put a match to him and up he went in flames. If you want to see something different, try frying a dead grizzly. It was something.

It was no use telling them at school, it would only have made me look a liar. Some truth is like that. No matter how you tell it, it sounds too much to believe. Besides, after he was burnt I found the plate from the thing he stood on, and it said 'Pyrenean Brown Bear, 1856'.

I would hate to be dead and stuffed, would you not?

Daddy got a job digging drains for Archie Agnew.

Archie is the man who bought the farm below Albert Dunwoody's and he is going to show them a thing or two. He was at college he says, and they learn how to farm scientifically there. Albert Dunwoody was at Greenmount College when he was young and Artie Forbes left last year, but they never let on, they just let him talk. He wants drains put in his two low fields and my Daddy is the boy to dig them, he understands field drains because two years ago he did the same job for Mr Harper that lets us get sticks in his plantation. Daddy did not know a thing about drains when he began, so Mr Harper taught him.

Mammy had been trying to get a job too and the first one she did get was at the egg factory. She had to crack eggs and smell them. That was all. But she only stuck it for the one week, the smell of the eggs made her sick, her stomach turned at them and stayed turned for a week after she left. That was because she had got two rotten ones on her first day. She says she has smelled bad eggs before but those two were perfectly stinking. But she was not beaten. On the Saturday she was much better, or said she was, and went and got another job on the two-to-ten shift at the Imperial Hotel, working in the kitchen. It is only four pounds a week and her tea but she says she will have to stick it until Daddy gets another job for the Family Allowances would never keep us. She is getting fat, and she gets distracted at the least little thing, and her hands and ankles are swollen.

Daddy said to her several times, 'Are you sure you are all right, Ethel? It was never as hard on you before.'

98

She said, 'I am older now and that is all there is to it. God, send this one all right and make it the last. You may go to Cranee and get cracking. If you don't sell peats or haul something the weans will be at Barnardo's for Christmas.'

Daddy said, very low, 'I have ruined your life, Ethel, one way and another, in fact I ruin all I lay hand to. I will not come back till I get work. And for God's sake don't lift anything heavy, you might hurt yourself.'

Well, he went out and was away until after dark. When he came back he said he had got a job with Thomas Hugh Archer for the time being, helping with the harvest. And he said he had asked Davina Campbell, and she had got word that the American woman would come in October. That is one month and eighteen days to go.

Bertie helped Seumas McCann to clean out the pigeon-house and got half a crown. He went over to Gorman's and got seven bags of crisps and shared them with Agnes and Mria. If he had not they would have told Mammy how he spent the half-crown. I did not know until after the deed was done.

I had not seen Mrs Conlan for ages because she was away in Rome for her holidays, but she sent word with Matt Edgar the breadman that she wanted to see me. I had the dinner to make or I would have gone at once. Afterwards I washed the dishes, and washed my face and hands, and combed my hair. I left Agnes in charge of the wee ones because Mammy was just getting up to go to work.

Mrs Conlan said she was glad to see me looking so well, and I had to say the same to her. She was all sunburned and looked years younger and had green earrings in. She said she was up to her ears in work as she had not had a clear-out for some time, but that if she did not clear out some stuff she would need new cupboards. She said I could take anything I liked because Hallowe'en was coming and we would want to be dressing up.

I never saw such a lot of stuff in my life. There was a pile of newspapers, and an old burst chair with two legs falling off it, and a good polythene bucket with a hole in it and no handle.

'Please, Mrs Conlan,' I said, 'could I have that bucket? My

99

Daddy could put a wire handle on it.'

'Certainly,' she said, 'you might as well.' She threw down a pile of clothes on the back lawn and said, 'You can keep anything you want,' and went into the house.

I went through them and right enough there was a lot of rubbish which I put on the fire, but there was a green coat that would wrap around me three times, it wasn't Mrs Conlan's I'm sure. It had no buttons on it and the pocket was torn, but there was nothing else wrong with it so I set it by to take to Mammy. There was a fur collar full of moths so I burned that, and some old torn skirts, but I tore the zips out first. And then there were two good skirts as big as the coat I had saved.

Mrs Conlan came back with an armful of old shoes and threw them down. 'Some of this stuff is my sister Monica's,' she said. 'It must have been here for years because Gerard is six and he is the youngest.'

'Where is your sister now, Mrs Conlan?' I asked.

'In America,' she said. 'She wrote to me to throw these out. When first she went she didn't like it. I thought she might come back, but she likes it very well, now.'

'You are throwing away a good pattern, Mrs Conlan,' I said. 'There is one here for a blouse, size thirty-two.'

'It would be too small for me now,' she said. 'But that is about a size bigger than you would need. Maybe you could make one, now you have a pattern.'

I was going to say I had no stuff, but then I thought that it would sound just like begging, so I thanked her for the pattern.

I threw some torn and dirty old net curtains on the fire, they did not burn but melted into a black cake. An old brush head was next, it had more hairs on it than ours so I laid it by. Mrs Conlan was in the bungalow collecting stuff while I sorted through the shoes carefully. There was a red pair, size six, that needed heeling, and a pair of good suede boots with a zip and a fur lining. I did not know what size they were but they looked to be the same as the shoes. I saw a pair of brown shoes with pointy toes that I remembered Mrs Conlan wearing last summer, but the heel was entirely missing from one so into the fire they went.

And with that Mrs Conlan stumbled across and threw down a big bale of what looked like heavy curtains, all colours. 'The most of them are rotted with the sun,' she said to me. 'And the velvet ones are all faded, I could never put them up again.'

I dragged them away from the fire and spread them out to see if they were any good. The pink and silvery ones were rotten all right, and so were the green silky ones. But the velvet ones were only faded badly, they were an awful colour at the edges but they were quite strong and the lining, a fawn stuff, was good. The other pair were all blue with white lining, the blue was rotten but the lining was not. I did not burn the velvet ones nor the blue ones. The fire was hot so my face was all scorched and my eyes smarted with the smoke. The stuffings of the chair smelled the worst. Sparks flew up in the air when I poked the fire with a long stick.

'You were a great help,' said Mrs Conlan, when we had raked the fire into one last wee heap. 'I just do not know how I could have done it in the time without your help. You must stay for tea.'

'Oh, is that the time it is?' I cried. 'I was to make the wee ones their tea! But thank you just the same, Mrs Conlan.'

I gathered up the coat and the red shoes and the two skirts and I was so loaded I could hardly travel. Luckily the rest were down at Maurice's when I got back. I could hear them shouting. I put the things in Mammy's room under the dressing-table and went back. Mrs Conlan had put the brush-head and the pattern and the boots into the bucket, so I put it on my hip and held it to me while I picked up the blue curtains. When I had left them down home I went back a third time for the rest of the curtains. The velvet curtains must have been lovely once, dark green with coloured stuff on the pelmet. They were enormous, it was all I could do to make my arms meet round them.

It was teatime but I would not make any till the rest came in, so I got myself a jam piece and put the kettle on and made up the fire and set the table, then there was still time to spare so I went out to empty the ashes. The soldier's wife called me across and asked me would I go to Gorman's for her. She is scared to cross the Stick Bridge in case she takes a dizzy turn and falls into the river. She gave me a list and a pound note and away I went.

101

'Is this for your mammy?' asked Mrs Gorman.

'No,' I replied. 'It is for the soldier's wife.'

'Tell your mammy I would need to see her soon,' she said.

I knew what about, and it was not very nice. That is what she always says when Mammy owes her money. There was nobody in the shop only her and me, but I was ashamed. Mammy could not help it.

Mrs Gorman put a pound of sausages and a dozen of eggs in the basket, and weighed a pound of tomatoes, and half a pound of the good bacon, and four soda-scones in a crisp white paper bag, and a packet of biscuits, and a bottle of cordial, and a bar of chocolate, and gave me twopence change. She had marked the price of everything on the list and added it up for the soldier's wife to see. Mrs Gorman always does that when we fetch the things for anybody, even Mammy. I do not know if it is to keep us from taking the change, as if we did not know better, or to let them see that the change is right because there are the groceries and there are the prices.

On the Stick Bridge I met Dennis Barkley, who is in my class at school, and he would not let me by.

'I will tell my daddy,' I said. 'And he will give you a warm ear. And so will Corporal Hanna if you make me drop these things in the river.'

Dennis said he was not afraid of my oul' da.

So I said, 'Well, he will have to give you lessons, he frightened Rommel, he would not find it hard to terrify you or the like of you!'

'Him,' said Dennis, 'he was never in the Army, he was in jail for bigamy.'

And with that I hit him a good poke in the stomach with the bottle of cordial, and he came at me to hit me but tripped and nearly went into the river, and I passed him running and got away.

The soldier's wife said, 'I thought you would fall in. Who is that boy? I will tell his mother. That was very dangerous even if it was all in fun.'

I nearly said, 'All in fun your Granny!' but I didn't. I said, 'You can't tell his mammy, she is in England with another man and he

102

lives with his Aunt Margaret and he is ruined.'

'Well, I will tell his aunt then,' said the soldier's wife. 'He might have put you in the river.'

'Ha!' I said. 'Let him try it.'

She gave me the bar of chocolate, then I thanked her and went up home.

I took the head off our brush, it was easy. I stood on the head of it and pulled the shaft left and right, time about, as hard as I could till it came off. It was loose before anyway.

Bertie came in with the rest at the back of him. A wasp had stung Mria, isn't she unfortunate, and Mrs French had slabbered washing-blue on her leg till you would have thought she was wearing a stocking. George had found three hens for Mrs Henessey and he had an egg with him that she gave him, so I scrambled it for him in a wee taste of margarine while Bertie put the new head on the brush. The hammer was on the high shelf so he hit the nail in with a stone from the yard, sure it did rightly. Agnes had a can of buttermilk with her and said Mrs French told her to say that the sixpence would do the next time Mammy sees her.

I made pancakes for the tea. I did not think they were very good but the rest ate them just the same. It was nearly seven o'clock so I captured wee James, washed him and put him to bed. He had a long serious talk with himself before he fell asleep.

Waiting till Daddy or Mammy would be home made it a very long day. After a while, when it was getting cold, the rest came in and I remembered the stuff Mrs Conlan had given me, and thought they had no need to know where it came from. It was none of their business anyway. Agnes would have been asking questions till the morning if she had seen it.

Mammy was back at a quarter to eleven. She sat down and put her head in her hands, so I made her a cup of tea and a bit of toast. While she was eating it she heard all about the stuff so she cheered up and said it was just like Mrs Conlan. She crept upstairs to where the boys were sleeping and examined the curtains under the dressing-table with our torch, and crept down and said the white lining would make grand school blouses for Agnes and me to wear

103

to the Intermediate School, when it was washed and starched and ironed. Daddy came in and she told him, but I could see he was not too well pleased.

Mammy said, 'The velvet will be warm dresses for the girls this winter. If I boil it carefully, the faded bits will be re-dyed. I have seen it done so's you would never know.'

'I would have got you a warm coat, Ethel,' said Daddy.

'I know,' she said. 'But this one will do fine for now. You will need money for petrol when you start selling peats, until you are on your feet. We would need to go to Cranee and get on with the cutting, we have left it late enough as it is.'

We went to bed, but I thought that Mammy looked awfully tired, I am sure it is not good for her to have to work so hard. These last two days I am nearly sure her face is swelled, too, her eyes look funny because they are so wee.

We have been in Cranee Moss all this week. We go up first thing after school, in the lorry, our lunches and a taste of tea and sugar and milk with us, and we stay till dark. Daddy takes Bertie and Agnes and Mria and Doreen and Alec and me. Agnes and I have our old spade and a spade Seumas McCann lent us. They are not peat spades but they have to do. I do not know if the way we cut peats is the right way but it is the way we do it. Daddy showed us how to pare off the top of the bank and this is not particular work, so we take turns at it. But it is hard. About fifteen minutes of it does me. When we have a bit pared, Daddy cuts peats from it, then Doreen and Alec stand them in threes or fours on their ends to dry. We work two hours and stop for fifteen minutes. That way, Daddy says, we will not get exhausted too soon. Lying resting is pleasant. The bog smells nice and is full of trees and bushes and the tweetings of birds, so that it is not silent the way it was when it was winter. I never noticed so many different birds before. Now I know a bluetit and a sparrow and a swallow and a thrush and a blackbird and a crow and a cock pheasant.

The cock pheasant came walking out of a bush, scratched his beak with his toe, as bold as brass, then gave a loud cry and flew off.

'Would you look at that!' cried Bertie. 'Hasn't he got cheek!'

I was lying in the heath at the time, and it was all springy like a mattress. The sky looked very high from there, like a great big blue bowl upside down, deep blue right above me and lighter blue around the sides. Cranee is very high up and if you were standing on top of the highest bank you would see the hills in County Derry, but from where I was the horizon was all leaves and grass. The heath had flowers on it the same colour as Mrs Conlan's marking pencil, a sort of purply red, and when I shook them they tinkled like wee bells.

We have cut and stacked peats in threes until we are all tired out, you would not have to sing us a tune to put us to sleep. Daddy is not working at the Buroo any more. He said he would rather get peats than work at both and get jail.

Our bit of the Moss is black with peats sitting getting dry. If it does not rain Daddy will be able to sell them when they are dry, and then cut more for us in the evenings and weekends until the dark comes too early. He says there is lots to be done yet at Castle Gaul and Tom Lamont can't do it. Daddy has Davina to put in a word for him, but she daren't hire him until the owner comes.

And she is not coming till October. It would be awful if she took a notion and did not come then either.

Mammy washed and starched the lining of the blue curtains and made Agnes and me two school blouses each off the pattern Mrs Conlan gave me. They will do no matter what school we go to, and they are not much too big after all. She just took the lining out of the velvet curtains and washed it, then laid them by till she has the time to work with them. She has had to arrange for wee James to stay with Mrs McFarland every day from one to four, because we are going to our old school here until the new term starts in the Intermediate, and the holidays are over now. Mammy has to be at work from two and we don't get home till ten or twenty past three, but Mrs McFarland says wee James is no trouble at all, and comes in when he is bid and chats away by the hour. Mammy has to give Mrs McFarland something for looking after him, and it is not easy, but she would not let her do it just for nothing.

On about the twenty-third of August Daddy got a job driving a tractor for Gilbert Taylor. He has a hundred and forty acres in barley because there is a subsidy for barley, the government pays him to put it in, and he is a bit behind with the harvest. It put a stop to us getting peats because Daddy will have to stay as long as he is wanted and does not get home till dark because Ballycromkeen, where the barley is, is a long way off, one and ten return in the bus. But the pay is good.

Mammy says it is a great relief.

Well Bridie Ryan was married this morning in the chapel and I heard the style was crushing but she did not look very happy. Fidelma and Monica were telling everybody what a lovely home she will have, and letting on they were jealous but I am sure they were not. Mammy said one look at Mr Feeny's face on a pillow would give her the dry bokes and what did Bridie do it for at all? But there was no answer to that one. Daddy said she did not want to die ignorant.

But Mammy said to him, 'Would you have a bit of wit.' Then she saw I was there and had heard them so she said, 'Not a word of this will you ever come over!'

I said I would not repeat it. But I agreed with Mammy that I would not marry Mr Feeny if he was the last man left alive, he looks as if he would beat you if you took the notion. But maybe he was all that was for Bridie, they say that what is yours knows your face when you come along.

I looked up bigamy in Mrs Conlan's big dictionary and now I know. It is having two wives at the one time.

I wonder, the woman who came to see Mammy, is she Daddy's other wife? I would like to know but he would be mad at me, and Mammy would tell me to mind my own affairs. And Mrs Conlan would say the same.

Well, if Daddy has two wives, it is all right, so had nearly everybody in the Old Testament.

So there.

SEPTEMBER

Mammy took Agnes and me into the town in the bus to get Agnes the rest of her school uniform. She has made Agnes's gymfrock already, and she knitted her a navy cardigan the same as mine because she can't afford blazers for us.

The raincoats were an awful price, over six pounds for mine and over five for Agnes's. But Mammy had enough money for them, she had let the Family Allowances lie as long as she could and then put this week's wages to it. I did not know they would be so dear. I will tell you here and now that somebody is making too much profit, for Mammy made us eight coats out of polythene for twenty-three shillings, that is under three shillings each, and they kept the rain out better than wool gabardine. If our new ones were even three pounds each it would be reasonable, but six pounds for a coat is daylight robbery.

It was the day before we went to the Intermediate, Mammy had kept me and Agnes at home from the other school. She has left her job because Doctor Emily told her she would have to go into the hospital if she did not. She had been told to rest and there she was, working away and paying no heed to the doctor. I was afraid that that was how it would end because she has been awfully sick every morning. I know this is not good because it is the wrong time for her to be sick. I know what it is like because Mammy was very sensible and never let on to me that she was not expecting when she was, and she was never as sick as this with any of them. I am worried in case she will not be all right. And the baby is not due for ages yet, it will be January the fifteenth before it puts in an appearance, she told me.

We were on our way home in the bus with our two big parcels when who did we see but Bridie Ryan, I mean Mrs Feeny. She had on a fur jacket and a wee red hat and she looked just lovely. Her shoes and gloves were the same red as her hat and dress but her bag was a great big crinkly leather black one, as big as Dr John's.

We all got seats together at the back of the bus. Mammy told her she was looking grand and asked her where she was for her honeymoon.

'We went to Spain,' said Bridie. 'But sure it was that hot it would have killed you. It is lovely, the sky and sea the bluest blue, but hot.'

'Were you in swimming?' asked Mammy.

'I was not!' said Bridie, all shocked. 'You don't mean to say you still go in, Ethel?'

'I do, surely,' said Mammy. 'I was in this year.'

'You were not!' said Bridie. She was scandalised.

'I love the sea,' said Mammy. 'It feels fresher than the river any day. Did you never face it, then?'

'No, indeed,' said Bridie. 'There was a girl arrested for wearing a bikini, she should have worn more in her own house with the door shut and the blinds down!'

'Now I daren't wear a bikini,' said Mammy, thoughtfully. 'You know who would do himself an injury laughing at me if I did.'

I tried to think of Mammy in a bikini, and I could not. It was too much to think of at once.

Bridie got out at our stop and came carefully across the Stick Bridge with us, taking care not to cut her high heels on the tin patches. The whole Stick Bridge has been patched at different times. The biggest patches are Castrol drums Kevin gets from his work, and the rustiest is a big tin advertisement that Ezekiel Orr, who used to own Gorman's shop, gave Seumas McCann to patch the Bridge when Paul and Kevin were just wee boys and they lived in one of the cottages there used to be on the left of the Arcady lane.

Fidelma was out beating a mat with an old bent badminton racket. She saw Bridie and said, 'God save Ireland, it's the bad penny. And how are you, *Mrs Feeny*?' Then she grabbed Bridie, hugged her and said, 'Oh, Bridie, I'm that glad to see you!' and they went in together.

'I'm glad to see that,' said Mammy. 'Fidelma was the one that thought she should give Feeny a miss.'

'Why is everybody against Mr Feeny?' demanded Agnes.

'Because,' I said.

We started school at the Intermediate the next day.

It is an enormous school of twenty-eight rooms and lots that are not for the pupils to go into. I have been there four days. There are splendid kitchens for us to learn to cook in, but they are called a domestic science unit. There is a wireless and television for teaching programmes. Agnes is not in my class. My teacher is Mrs Carpenter, and hers is Mrs Magee. They are both young and pretty and I do not think I will like Mrs Carpenter as much as I like Mrs Conlan. Mrs Carpenter has a far bigger class and I can see she does not have the time to be bothered with questions, unlike Mrs Conlan. Many a time Mrs Conlan had not the time to be bothered either but she would answer questions when she had the time. And she would stand no nonsense either.

We are not all the same age in our class. Aileen Dawson is fourteen and Emily Stevens is only eleven. Aileen did the Qualifying and she got it well enough to go to Grammar School, but then she was sick for two years with TB so she has forgotten all she had learned. She says she did lessons in hospital but they did not care if you did not do well because your health was more important. Emily passed well enough for Grammar School but there were no places left at the one her mother wanted her to go to. She could have gone to the convent instead but her mother said that was no use because she could only do Senior at Ordinary Level there. I do not know what all that means, but Emily does. Her mother is sending her here till her father comes home, he is on an oil tanker, and then likely she will go to a school in Belfast, even if it means staying with her auntie on the Cliftonville Road. Emily is not very big but she talks loudly. Mrs Carpenter has already told her to have less to say for herself, but it is no use.

Those are the only two I know yet.

The first day they did not know what to do with us, so they told us to write a composition on any subject we chose. I wrote about Mrs Conlan. I suppose I should not. If she knew she might be angry with me. And then I was afraid that Mrs Carpenter would think I was right cheeky, writing about my last teacher. If she knows Mrs Conlan, she might tell her. But the only thing she said was that I ought to use more full stops, she says I have no idea of punctuation. She is right, I have not, but I will learn. Mrs Conlan used to tell me I was in such a hurry to get it all written that I went on like Young Lochinvar, and it is true. Now I am at another school, I will have to slow up and do it better or I will be affronting Mrs Conlan every time I make a silly error. It will be hard.

Daddy is still working at Gilbert Taylor's and the first week he was never once back before ten o'clock at night, so naturally he got a lot of overtime pay. Daddy says there is one thing about Gilbert Taylor, he works you like a slave but he is not afraid to pay you. There is none of this nonsense about 'I have no money on me', or 'See me on Saturday in the town', or 'Ask the wife where she put it', or 'Will you take a cheque?'

I am glad that Daddy is working for a good man after all the mean things bosses have done on him. He said at the time that Fergus Doonan will need the five shillings he took before we will. But we could do with it just the same.

Daddy comes home too tired to speak, nearly, and Mammy says we are not to bother him at all, it is hard enough for him without us codding with him.

On the Saturday Bertie asked him were we going to Cranee Moss in the afternoon, but he said he could not get off. So that was another Saturday gone and no peats in. Mammy said nothing but we all know that our peats are nearly done and coal is out of the question, it is over fourteen shillings a bag.

Bertie said to me, 'We should make a move because the peats will be dry and if wet weather comes they will be useless. But what can we do, none of us can drive the lorry.'

Mammy is very little better and I do not want to worry her. Maybe we could go up ourselves and get some peats down, even it is only a bag or two. But fetching them is impossible. If somebody was going that way we might get a lift, but it is a place there would not be six vehicles pass it in a day.

We have a lot of homework compared with what we are used to. I do not know how we can get peats down, but it looks as if we will have to. If we had some sort of barrow it would be possible, but we have not. And Bertie is no use, he and Alec have been down at Maurice French's all this week, I do not know what they are doing but I am sure it is nothing good. I have had to get all the water myself, because Agnes gets it for Old Joe Cooper and Mrs McFarland for sixpence a week each. They wanted to give her a shilling each but I am glad to say she would not take it, she is not so bad after all. Anyway, I do not mind getting the water because my arm is strong again. The only thing is, they will have to watch what they say in front of her because she will repeat it all, she always does. I tell Mammy most things, but not anyone else. I would get no thanks for telling Mrs Conlan. I have not told anything to the master since one day last spring when I was telling him something and he asked did I know the brook.

'What brook?' I asked him.

'Men may come and men may go, but I go on for ever,' he said, looking at me.

I understood that he meant me so I shut up. I could feel my face go very red. I did not mean to go for ever, only until I had finished what I was telling him, but a nod is as good as a wink to a blind horse, so I stopped in the middle and not telling him the finish nearly killed me.

A story is a funny thing. If it is about somebody you know it is generally gossip unless you saw it happen yourself. If it is not about somebody you know, it is likely a lie. If it is about some-body you invented, it is a fairy-tale. Miss Diamond calls lies fairy-tales. Now I think of it, I would rather she called lies lies. I have no patience with fairy-tales myself. The people in them are not very sensible. For instance if Cinderella spent her life brushing up cinders, how did she know to do an old-fashioned waltz at the ball? And if the Ugly Sister really cut off her big toe she would have bled to death. You have an artery in your big toe, that's why.

On Friday I went to see Artie Forbes but he said he had no errand up to Cranee. I had to let it go at that. Not many people take the Cranee Road nowadays because it runs off the Pack

Bridge Road and runs on to it again about six miles farther on. There is not even a house on it, so even the breadmen never go that way, nor the creamery lorries, and it is not a short cut to anywhere. It is a hard place to get to. I suppose that is why nobody digs peats there any more, except us. It is too hard to fetch them in.

On Saturday I had to get messages in Gorman's for Mammy. I had a couple of pounds and a list. Mria came and helped me to carry all the things, so they were not any more difficult to carry than to remember. Doreen had been crying from six in the morning with a gumboil, Mammy was nearly distracted because nothing she gave her did any good. She told me she would have to take her to the dentist and that I was to make the tea. Away the two of them went, Doreen with her face wrapped up in Mammy's scarf, crying sore because she is heart scared of the dentist.

We had tea a bit early because I thought somebody might offer to take us to Cranee, and if they did we could hardly go without our tea. I told Mrs McFarland what we might be going to do, and she said she would look after George and Mervyn and wee James. She only had to mention that she knew of a good story about a rabbit and George could hardly wait to get down to her house. Mervyn is not fond of told stories, he would rather read them himself. Since he learned to read he has started on her bookcase and is reading all he can.

I have found out that a long time ago Mrs McFarland had a son. His name was Hamish and he was drowned at sea when he was nineteen years old. She never mentions him, it was Mammy who told me. It is said that Mrs McFarland keeps all his books and a picture he painted in Mrs Conlan's class at school and a piece of stone he fetched her when he was away at Cleggan Lodge with the Scouts. He was in the Merchant Navy and fell overboard and was never found. Mammy said that at the time it happened Mrs McFarland was living near the sea, where she could see a lighthouse three miles out, but after he drowned she could not bear it so came back here where she was born.

Maybe that is why she likes boys. If Mammy would let them, our three wee ones would be down there all day. She does not let them stay because Mrs McFarland would make them their tea.

112

Mrs McFarland only has her pension and it takes it all to pay her rent and coal and feed herself.

'I tell you what,' said Bertie after tea, 'we will borrow wheels off Maurice French, I know he has some, and see if we can't make a cart for the peats with that box John Gordon threw Daddy off the lorry last weekend. We could get some down in that anyway.'

'You could not make a bogie,' said Mria nastily.

'If you wait a while you will see,' said Bertie.

So he and Alec went back up to Maurice French's with the box. It was ten past five.

At six they came back from Maurice's with a cart on four wheels. I could not believe they had made it themselves. Bertie said that Maurice had only tightened the screws for them, that was all. The wheels had two axles attached to them but they could not fasten the axles to the box because they went round with the wheels. They were thinking of asking him for a wheen of three-inch nails when he gave them four of the things he has to hold the water-pipes to the pig-house walls. It took two screws to fasten each axle to the box and Bertie said his right wrist will not be the same again from trying to get the screws in. There was a brace and bit hanging on the wall that would have made the job easier but he did not like to ask. He thought Maurice was doing well enough to give him the use of the wheels, and showing him how to fasten them to the body.

We took our polythene raincoats, because the Moss is no place for a Christian and it raining, and I wrote a note for Mammy in case she thought we were mad. Then a row started because Alec wanted to come and I knew he would not be able for the long walk. It is over three miles and he is only eight years of age. We could not leave him in the house by himself and he would not go down to Mrs McFarland's with the rest, he said they were only wee boys and that he was a big boy.

It was the soldier who saved the situation. He was digging in their back garden and he came over and said to Bertie, 'Is there anybody here that can gather potatoes? I am in desperate need of help.'

You could see that he was not, but Bertie caught on and said

113

that our Alec was the best in the family at gathering potatoes, and that he would come himself, only Alec was better at it. Alec was mollyfied, and he went with the soldier at once. I would love to see the potatoes they dug in that garden. It was in marigolds since ever I mind!

The walk was longer than I remembered but at least there was no traffic. There would not need to be any for our cart had no steering and no brakes. We had our raincoats and a bottle of cold tea and a box of matches, and that was all.

I am sure it must have been half-seven before we arrived, but the peats were dry enough. We packed them very carefully into the cart so that we could bring the most possible. When it was loaded the cart was far heavier than I had thought it would be. I suggested we should sit down and rest for half an hour before we started for home. I could remember how tired we were the time we had gone to the other moss, and it would be easier for us to get home if we were not dying for a ride in the cart. So we lit a wee fire with twigs and bog fir and sat around it drinking cold tea. It was getting dusk by this time and the air was misty. I could see the lights come on in the town and then on the main road, the sky became very cold and blue and a star came out, the whitest white I ever saw. But I could not stay to admire it, it was time we were all away.

We gathered ourselves up and took hold of the cart and pushed. It bumped and shuddered over the bog lane until it was a wonder how it held together. When we reached the road it was a great relief, it is a long time since this road was fixed but of course it is tarmacadam, not just grass and roots like the bog lane.

It was completely dark before long. I was so tired I could have laid down on the road and cried, but that would not have helped. Mria was crying from about half-way home, her feet were so sore. If I had known before we left home that she had her old red plastic sandals on, I would have made her change to waders, but I did not notice until she complained. There was nothing to do but let her off pushing the cart and make her walk on the grass at the side of the road. It was so dark at the last that we could hardly see where we were going. By this time we were on the Pack Bridge Road. It has lamps but they are a long way apart, they cast our shadows before us for half a mile.

At last we came to the end of our road, and Mammy was standing there.

'Are you not foundered?' she asked us.

We were too hot to speak nearly, because getting the cart down the last big hill was a terrible job. We had to go in front of it and lean our backs against it every step of the way. Bertie cut two big sticks in the hedge and gave one to me. When we had to have a rest we used them for brakes by pushing them under the front of the cart and heaving the ends up, but we did not stop for long, I can tell you, in case the sticks broke. If the cart had got away from us it would have thundered down the hill and across the Black Road, and likely killed somebody.

'Where is Daddy?' I asked.

'He is never home yet,' she said. 'It is forecast rain and they will be getting in the bales by floodlights till twelve tonight, unless they finish sooner. How in under God did the four of you do it? The soldier said you had a nerve. Where did you get the cart?'

'It is Daddy's box on Maurice's wheels,' said Bertie. 'I wish I had put shafts on her, she will not steer. We can't take her in the lane, Mammy, we are clean beat.'

'We will think of something,' she said. 'Come on and leave it.'

She gathered Mria and Agnes into her coat, the way a hen gathers chicks under her wings, and we all went home. Bertie and I took the tarp and our kitchen clothes-line to cover the cart in case it rained or somebody stole the peat. Just as we got back to the cart a car stopped beside us. Three men got out of it. Paul and Kevin and an airman.

The airman saw us in the car headlights and asked, 'Aren't you two Ethel Skeffington's weans? What are you doing out so late?'

'Mammy knows,' I said. 'We have brought down peats from Cranee and can't get them home. The cart has no brakes.'

'Well, that's no problem,' said the man. 'Eh, boys?'

'Divil a bit,' said Paul.

The man was about as big as both of them rolled together and he had a bright brass badge, or maybe it was silver, on his sleeve. The three of them took a grip on the cart and pushed it down into

Arcady for us. I was that glad I nearly cried. Sure they could have gone by and not bothered.

Mammy heard the cart and came out at once to tell us we should not have done it, and then she called out, 'Tom Scott! I thought you were in England.'

'How are you, Ethel?' asked the airman. 'You are looking the best. I wish Charlotte looked as good as you.'

'Now, now,' she said, reprovingly, 'I could not guarantee to look like this if I was married to you! You are looking grand yourself. Any family?'

'Four,' said the man.

Said Mammy, 'You are just not trying.'

Paul and Kevin burst out laughing.

'You should talk,' said the man, laughing too. 'Sure you've only the two.'

'I have seven, and a half more, inside,' said Mammy, with great dignity.

They all laughed. Then they went down to McCann's and we went into our house. Agnes and Mria were just finishing bread and jam and cocoa. Of course all the rest had been in bed for hours. Mria's face was all covered with dust from the peat, and the tears had made clean rivers down it, but she had stopped crying. Mrs Conlan's bucket had been fixed long ago and Mria had her feet in it. It was full of warm water, and the two kettles were boiling.

I felt much better after I had eaten two rounds of loaf and jam and drunk a big mug of cocoa. Mammy bathed us all, and I fell asleep as soon as I was in bed.

We were all very tired the next day and did not get up until eleven, but it was worth it. Gilbert Taylor's harvest was all in, but the rain started on Sunday night and lasted untill Wednesday, so we did not go back to Cranee until the following Saturday. I do not know what Daddy was doing all week. He did not say. I only know he was fixing the lorry in the evenings.

Thursday it was dry, and cold and stormy. Old Joe Cooper's grey shirt was on the line, the pegs let go and it blew away. If our Mervyn had not met it, it would be going yet. On Friday the sun came out, but the storm still blew till around dinnertime. We were late coming from school and when we reached home there was a terrible to-do because our George had found out what happens to wee pigs when Maurice French sells them. He never knew before. If it was not for the stupid big lump of a lorry-driver he would not know now. He was sitting on the steps roaring and crying, and Mammy could not pacify him. She had tried everything short of a beating, not that that would not have done any good. He was not being bad, he just could not help it. Old Joe Cooper heard the noise and came up to see if he was murdered. So George tried to tell him what was wrong. He was clean by himself and could not, but Old Joe Cooper understood.

Joe sat down beside him on the steps and said, 'I wish you would come down and give me a hand. I was standing at the river when a paper-bag came by and stuck in the rushes. I picked it up to see what was inside, and it was a wee kitten. It is alive but it is not very good. It is too wee to lick so you have to feed it by hand. I have not the patience.'

'Has it its eyes open?' asked Mammy. 'Is it not illegal to drown them?'

'It has, it has,' he said, and stood up, leaning on his stick. 'Are you coming?' he asked George.

George did not even stop to blow his nose, and it could have done with it. Away he went after Joe. They were away ages, and at teatime Mammy sent me down to bring George up. He was sitting on a creepie at Old Joe Cooper's fire, with a wee grey kitten in his arms. I was afraid to speak in case it was dead, but then I heard it purring.

'It is purring in its sleep,' said George, all pleased.

'Just lay it down on the rug,' said Joe 'and away to your tea. Sure you can play with it tomorrow if you don't hurt it. It is only a wee soft thing so it is terrible easy to kill it.'

George did not want to leave it, but I told him it was tired after all its adventures and would need a good night's rest, so he came. He never mentioned the wee pigs that had grown up and gone to be killed, he had forgotten all about them.

'What should I call the kitten?' he asked Daddy, when he had told him about it.

'Call it Duff,' said Daddy. 'It is a duff job looking after it.'

When Joe Cooper heard that the kitten's name was Duff, he laughed for five minutes. I do not know why.

'We will get up early tomorrow,' Daddy told us, 'because we are going to Cranee for the day.'

We were glad to hear it.

Most of us went, from Mervyn to Daddy. Mammy stayed at home with George and wee James, and Doreen. At the last minute Mammy kept her at home because her mouth was still sore where she had her tooth out.

It was a lovely day but we had no time to look at the view. Daddy said he had a plan of campain. Agnes and I would pare the bank and he would dig peats, Mria and Alec would stand them to dry, Bertie and Mervyn would load the lorry with the ones we cut the last time.

When we heard the horn of the Belfast train coming down we stopped for a drop of tea. Mammy had put up a big stack of pilchard sandwiches with chopped raw onions in them, and soda scones with margarine, and a pound of tomatoes, so there was plenty for us all. After our tea Bertie came across to Daddy and said the lorry was full and there were more peats dried than would go into her, so Daddy said he would drive down home with them and come back. We needed more tea anyway. So away he went. He took Alec and Mervyn with him because they were tired, but they could stack peats at home in the garden with Mammy to keep an eye on them and show them how. Daddy was back before the Limited Stop bus came up the Belfast Road, and that was good going.

Bertie had the peat spade and was trying to cut peats, but he found it was not as easy as it looked. Agnes and I pared a good bit more of the bank, but it was no easier than it had been at the beginning because there was a lot of bog fir and we had no hatchet. Daddy told us to give up on that bank, and he found us an easier one. It pared like fun. He cut away at the old bank till he arrived at the fir, and then gave up and came to our one. We cut more peats that afternoon than we ever did in one afternoon before.

We made a fire for the tea and sat round it, eating and laughing and telling jokes until we were rested. For about an hour after that we worked on, but it began to get cold, so we threw the spades on the lorry and got in and drove home in style. Mammy and Alec and Mervyn had the peats stacked and were just going to put our tarp on them, but they had to wait till we had stacked what we had brought. Some of them were still a bit damp, but they would dry with the wind blowing through them in the stack. In spite of all we had eaten we were all mad hungry, and Mammy said she would sooner keep us for a week than a fortnight, but she made chips with tomato ketchup for us all.

Wee James was in his bed and Mervyn was going there, but George was down in Joe Cooper's so I went down to get him. I might have known he would be nursing the kitten again, but this time it was awake and chewing his finger. Its paws are white with pink soles and its nose is pink. I do not like cats much but I like this one, next to Harper's orange tom. I forgot to mention Harper's cat is called Shomberg, I do not know why. I wish people would not call their cats such crazy names, and I would love to know why they do.

Duff wanted to follow George, but Joe Cooper put it in his pocket. His coat is old-fashioned and his pockets have pleats down the middle of them, so there was enough room for Duff. He just lay down out of sight and I suppose he fell asleep.

'Duff is lovely,' said George to me as we went up to our house. He was so happy to have Duff that he did not attend to anything. He had a look on his face like the look on Mammy's when she is putting wee James to bed.

Later on I asked Mammy for the dictionary and looked up campain and found it is campaign. I thought as much.

OCTOBER

We have been up at Cranee Moss twice more, on Saturdays because Daddy is working at the castle. He is putting big stones along both sides of the front drive and painting them white. Before that he was slashing back the bushes at the edges of the drive, and as it is over half a mile long you can see he has not had an easy time. The garden has all gone to wilderness, so when he has finished the stones and weeded the paths he is to help Tom Lamont. The golden-rod is as high as me. And the delphiniums are as high as Tom Lamont, in fact they are higher, for he is a very wee man.

Daddy says this is because his mother was frightened by a leprechaun, but I don't believe that. There is no such thing as a leprechaun, it is just one of the silly things that the like of Miss Diamond would believe in, you would think with her father being the rector she would have a bit of sense.

The American woman has arrived with her wee girl and the wee girl's governess. I have not seen them yet, but Daddy has. He says the American woman was a film star long ago, and he can remember her riding in a donkey-race in a film. I would like to see her but he says we are not to set foot on the castle grounds or he might get the sack. As the pay is all right and it is a long job we do not want that to happen. It is a great relief to Mammy that he is settled.

Mammy is much better and is not sick any more, but her ankles are swollen up like baps. She goes to see Dr Emily regularly, for she has not got a job now. She is looking after our clothes for the winter, and keeping house. It is lovely to come home and find her there, and not out working like when she was in the Imperial Hotel. My blue coat is getting too short already, she says she will have to get me a new one and let Agnes have the blue one. I have my school garbardine this year so the winter will not be too bad. Mammy is making me a velvet dress with long sleeves out of Mrs Conlan's curtains. She is making it too big in case I grow again. Isn't she the great hand at sewing. Sure she has hands for anything.

Agnes and I do not come home from school as early as we used to, because now we have to walk for over half an hour instead of a quarter, but every Friday we scrub the kitchen floor for Mammy, and the bit of balcony outside our house. It is a lot cleaner than it used to be, because you could not have watched Hector. I am sorry he was drowned, but that is true. Even wee James never did the things Hector did. The worst that happens now is that the boys forget to wipe their feet. We had no boot scraper, but Daddy found a piece of rabbit-fencing wire netting, buried in Cranee Moss, and folded it in two, and stamped it flat, and if it is not a great scraper it is better than nothing. There was a whole lot of material left after Mammy made my dress so she dyed it red with stuff she got in Gorman's and made four sets of velvet curtains for our four windows. We never had curtains before. Daddy got four brass rods somewhere and put them up for us. It is a lot warmer now at night with the curtains shut.

On Friday night Daddy went out with Seumas McCann to play cards at another man's house, and Mammy waited up for him the way she always does.

I woke up when I heard him come in. I thought it must be three in the morning, for Arcady was silent except for the swish of the river and a dog barking in the distance. With that, the clock in the town church struck three, and I was glad I was right.

I heard him stop outside the door, maybe because Mammy had no light on.

He whispered, 'Ethel, are you asleep?'

'Not at all,' she said, 'I am saying my catechism. What is it?'

'Come out here a minute.'

I heard them on the balcony, and then she came in and told me to get dressed, in a whisper in my ear. I got up and went into the kitchen. I had put on my knickers and jersey and skirt. Mammy slipped down to the closet and fetched me her old short coat.

'Put that on and go with your Daddy,' she whispered to me.

I was mad to know why but I knew better than ask in case I woke the rest. I did as I was bid and away we went, Daddy and I, down the Water Walks and over the Iron Bridge and along the main road for a minute or two and across it and up a lane to the town dump. I had known it was there, of course, but I had never been in it, especially not at night.

'Are there rats here?' I asked.

'Stay you here,' said Daddy, and went on to the dump. He heaved and pulled at something and got it out. He wrestled it on to the grass by the lane.

It was twice as big as he was but he was so active I could hardly see what it was. The minute it flopped on the grass I recognised it for a roll of lino, inside out of course.

'I spotted it yesterday,' said Daddy, panting. 'There is a bed here too. I did not know till I tripped over it. My shins are peeled like bananas. Hold you this.' He reached into the dump and shoved something at me.

It was the head or foot of a wee iron bed. The paint was all chipped but that was all was wrong with it. He dragged out another bit and hit an oil drum, the noise rang out for miles.

'Go home and take that with you,' he said. 'And fetch Agnes and Bertie, quick. Don't speak or put a light on. There's stuff here could set us up for life if we could get it home. Can you manage that?'

'I can,' I said. I hung one of the ends of the wee bed on my shoulder and away I went. It was bright moonlight so I did not have to mind where I put my feet for I could see where I was going. Once, crossing the Iron Bridge, I scraped the bed against the girder at the side, but it did not make much noise.

The others, from Mria up, were up and dressed and waiting for me, and Mammy had whispered where we were and what we were doing. As soon as I had carried in the bed they followed me down the Water Walks at a trot. Daddy had the lino sorted when we reached the dump. He must have taken our clothes-line without Mammy seeing him, for he had tied the lino like a parcel, with loops between the circles where the clothes-line was round the lino roll.

'Line up,' he said.

We lined up.

'Now,' he said, 'this is the idea. It is too heavy for me or for any two of you. So I will carry the front end and you four can carry the back end, two each side, with a hand through the loop.' He arranged me and Mria on one side and Bertie and Agnes on the other, and gave us a loop each. Then he took a loop at his end and said, 'Lift!'

The lino came up as if it was a roll of feathers. He gave the order for quick march, and we did. It seemed to be only a few minutes till we were home. The door swung open silently. We all went in and Mammy shut the door after us. We thought that was all, but Daddy was away again like a rocket as soon as he had untied the clothes-line. Naturally we had to follow.

I was getting a bit tired but Agnes ran all the way and he gave her the other end of the bed to bring back. By the time we got to him he had found the middle part of the bed and Bertie and Mria were able to take it easily. Then Daddy and I searched about until we found an old pram.

'What are the wheels like?' I asked.

'Wheels nothing,' he said. 'This will do the way it is, we might need it yet. Here.' He put some heavy things in it.

I thought they were bricks. They clinked as I pushed it to the lane.

'Half a minute,' said Daddy. He gathered something off the dump and wedged it well down amongst the bricks to stop them clinking. Then he picked up something black, it was like a box with legs, and said, 'We'll leave the pram for one of the others.'

We set off for home with the black box between us. It was heavy.

Mammy had the fire on so we could see to some extent, but not much. She had lined up the wee bed against the wall, still in three pieces, and the lino was well back out of the way. It was like a moonlight flitting.

'Let Agnes help wheel the pram back,' said Daddy.

The next trip we got a long black thing which turned out to be a stove-pipe. Daddy put that in the pram, with a lot of lids from a

123

stove, an oven door, two shelves and two more bricks. By that time I could hardly move the pram, it was so heavy, but Agnes helped me to push it. Bertie and Mria carried an old bicycle because it would not push, and Daddy carried a big roll of stuff.

Once over the Iron Bridge, he sat down on the ground and said, 'Will you move as hard as you can, and come back and help me with this. I am not fit to carry it any farther.'

We could have done with the rest ourselves, and Mammy made us stop and catch our breath before we went out again.

Daddy had opened the big roll of stuff out longways. It turned out to be a narrow rug, and here, wasn't it about forty feet long. He arranged us about ten or maybe eight feet apart beside the rug. We all bent down at once and picked it up. It was not as easy as carrying the lino but it was not too difficult either. He waited till we all had a good grip, and then we set off. It was so like playing trains it was all I could do not to say 'Chuff!' as we went.

Mammy met us and gave us a lift up the steps with it, and asked Daddy, 'Did you know what that was you brought in?'

'It is an escalator carpet,' he said, 'absolutely endless.'

'I mean the wee stove,' said Mammy. 'What are we to do with that? We have an open fire.'

'This has a wee oven,' he said, sitting down and wiping his face on his sleeve.

'And no door to it,' said Mammy.

'The door is in the pram,' I said. 'We have all the lids but one.'

'The bike is no good,' said Bertie. 'It has no chain or pedals or saddle or handgrips and the back forks are rotten.'

'It has wheels, you gawm!' said Daddy, and that disposed of Bertie.

Mammy said, 'That carpet is soaking. How are we to dry it.'

'Cut out the bad bits, and burn them to dry the good bits,' said Daddy.

'You are a genius,' she said admiringly. 'Have you finished for the night?'

'I suppose we have,' he said. 'Enough is enough and more would be excessive. Exercise is a great mistake. It only makes a body hungry.'

124

So we all made toast and sat at the fire eating it until four in the morning.

Mammy said, 'I will skin you myself if one of you as much as breathes that we have got this stuff. Don't tell the rest, they are too wee to keep a secret. If you let on to anybody else they will ask you if everything else we have is off the dump too. Do you see what I mean?'

We saw. It would have been just too stupid to tell.

Doreen was mad when she woke up and saw what we had got.

'It arrived after you were in bed,' said Mammy to her. 'Do I need your permission to let it in?' And that disposed of her.

In spite of the late night we all got up early, except Mammy. She had stayed up to make the wee ones their breakfasts, and hadn't gone to bed at all. The minute Daddy had finished his breakfast, and Mammy had boiled the kettle for the dishes, he lifted the grate of our open fireplace clean out and began to build up the space with bricks from our fallen-down garden wall. As soon as it was nine he set off in the lorry for cement and sand. It was four and six for cement and three shillings for sand, I heard him telling Mammy. Before he went he sent Bertie with Mrs Conlan's bucket for cow manure from Maurice French's other farm. He also told him that if he had time later he should take the wheels off the old bike and throw the frame in the river.

Mammy got some cold water and a cloth and some soap and began to wash the old pram inside and out. The inside was just bogging dirty but she persevered, at the fourth scrubbing it came up white. Before she began you would not have known whether it was meant to be grey or yellow. It had been a nice pram and it was still pretty now that it was clean. Then she called me and Agnes and Mria and we began to open out the roll of carpet so that she could inspect it properly in daylight.

'Roll on,' she said. 'This bit is all right, except that it is a bit threadbare in the middle.'

She rolled up her end and we unrolled ours. We came to a bit about ten feet long that was not worn at all. Then there another worn bit, and a badly worn bit, and a longer very good bit, and that was all.

'Come on, girl,' said Mammy to me, 'you get the big knife.'

It was terrible work cutting the carpet, but I did it where she showed me. She held it, for she said if anybody had to get cut it had better be her. But nobody was cut. The carpet made two long rugs, one worn short rug, and one huge long good piece.

'Could I not hang them on the line?' I asked. 'It is very blowy and they would dry.'

'They would be far too heavy for our line,' said Mammy. 'Hang them on the balcony railing.'

We did that, and I kept Agnes and Mria running to the garden for bricks to peg down the ends in case the carpet fell into the yard. The big piece took fifteen bricks to keep it in place. It was so long it hung down past Old Joe Cooper's bedroom windows, but I knew he would not care because he was already up, he had the pan on and it was sizzling.

'Do you know, I believe we will have stair carpet,' said Mammy. 'If we cut this up the middle would it be wide enough?'

I took the brush and laid it across the stairs, then pushed my hand up the shaft till it was level with the banisters. We then laid the brush against the width of the carpet and decided it would be just wide enough when we cut it in half. Luckily there was no pattern on it, so no one would be any the wiser as to whether it was or was not stair carpet.

'Get me one of Mervyn's chalks,' said Mammy, and pushed the hair out of her eyes. She was awfully hot, for it was hard work dragging carpet about. She got up off the floor and took her purse out of the knife drawer, then called in Alec and Doreen. She sent them to Gorman's to pay her bill and get two boxes of brass-headed nails and one of big tacks, and a stone of potatoes and a pound of lard.

That was when Daddy came back. He had everything unpacked before Bertie came staggering back with the cow manure. Daddy took it from him and carried it to the steps.

'Get on with dismantling the old bike, Bertie,' he said.

So Bertie was out of what occurred next, because he was otherwise engaged.

Mammy looked out to see what was happening and when she saw the bucket she said, 'You are not bringing that in here.

And that is final.'

'Am I not?' asked Daddy, and carried it up the steps and set it down on the balcony outside our front window. He mixed dry sand and cement for a while and then added the cow manure and water. Mammy looked at it critically.

'That is not cement,' she said. 'I would call that a rare styaghy.'

And it was.

Daddy took down the bricks at the fireplace, then set up the wee stove and put its own firebricks inside it. On went the oven door and all the lids. He put the pipe carefully in position, slanting up a bit into the chimney, then he made me hold the pipe until he had built up the bricks and cement to the right height. I stood back while he carefully built round it with bits of brick and more cement, and finished it all off with a coat of cement so that you could not see the old bricks at all.

He stood back and put the trowel in a bucket of water to wash off the cement before it hardened, then he said, 'There, Ethel!'

Mammy said, 'Well, that was well done, but where are we to cook the dinner?'

'In the garden,' he said. 'It can't be helped. But it is early enough yet, surely?'

'With all you lot to feed?' said Mammy. 'Doreen, love, come on and peel potatoes till I tell you to leave off, about twenty-two or twenty-four.'

So there was Doreen on the balcony peeling potatoes, and Mammy and Alec and Mervyn in the garden putting bricks together to make a sort of fireplace, and wee James pulling out bits of peat from the stack to start the fire, and George trying to swing the pump to get more water, and Bertie with one wheel off the old bike but with the worst still to come, and Mria and Agnes and I getting the plates and preparing the table because we might cook in the garden but we would hardly eat there. I went out to see how things were getting on outside. Daddy had washed out the bucket and the tools, cleaned the loose cement off the balcony and repaired our door-step with it, and laid a board over it in case we forgot and stepped on it.

Mammy was frying chips over the open fire and made us stay

away from her in case the pan went on fire. She said she should get danger money. But the pan did not go on fire, in fact they were grand chips. We felt able for anything when we had eaten them. Naturally we could not wash the dishes, for we had no hot water.

'McCall's have a sale of wallpaper,' said Daddy. 'Some of it is only three and six a roll.'

I knew what he was thinking. We would never get off the marks Hector had made on the kitchen walls. Mammy had scrubbed but there were still stains.

'How much would we want?' asked Mammy. 'Would paint not be cheaper?'

'You would need a lot of coats of paint,' he said, 'and it is not a paint sale. The one coat of paper would do it. This is a rare occasion, Ethel, and we must rise to it.'

'Your feet are off the ground. I will come with you in case you float away altogether,' said Mammy.

She told us not to go in unless it rained, because she was afraid we might touch the stove and make the pipe and the bricks fall down and ruin everything. Than away they went, and I noticed that she was wearing the red shoes from Mrs Conlan's. Daddy had soled and heeled them for her.

It was three o'clock before the lorry came back. Mammy had a whitewash brush and whitening and a big parcel of paper rolls. Daddy had borrowed steps from McCall's, and he also had a big tin of paint and a four-inch brush. I could hardly wait till the paper was unwrapped to see what it was like, so Mammy unrolled a piece for us to see. It was white and quite thin but it had a pattern of red flowers and gold and black leaves.

Then Daddy called us round him in the yard and said, 'This is my plan of campaign.'

When he is going to do something big he lets us all in on it, but the rule is that you are to do what he says and *nothing else*. You are not to help or interfere with anyone else. If you did there would be hellish confusion. Daddy said that, I would not.

First we moved all the furniture out on to the balcony or into the low back bedroom. There are stairs at both ends of the balcony so nobody was put to any trouble getting past. Then Mammy took down the curtains, Daddy opened the steps and shinned up them and swept the ceiling with the floorbrush, Bertie and I mixed the ceiling whitening and buttermilk with a small squeeze of washing-blue. Then Mammy prised the lid off the paint and fetched Bertie's polythene coat and hood. The minute Bertie and I had the whitening ready she put him into his coat, gave him the paintbrush and showed him how to paint. It was like jelly, the paint, which was a good thing because there were no drips. Daddy had said that Bertie and Agnes and I would have to take turns at the painting, and that Bertie was to begin while he was whitening the ceiling. Agnes and I had to stay outside until he had finished. I will say he did not take long, then he came down the steps, opened the windows at top and bottom, told Alec to whitewash the inside of the closet and then clean out the bucket. After that he cleaned his hands, took the brush from Bertie, painted two doors like lightning, called me in to take my turn, and helped Mammy carry the table in from the balcony. Mammy told Bertie to go to the pump and wash the paint off his polythene coat, which he did. Mria had fetched water and Mammy sprinkled paste in to it, and stirred it furiously with a big wooden spoon. Agnes was down at the river swooshing the whitewash brush the instant Alec had finished with it, while Alec rinsed the bucket. Wee James and Mervyn and George were washing the kitchen chairs with soapy water and three old sponges. They did not do it very well, but sure it was just a made job to keep them occupied and not bothering us. Doreen was trying to boil the kettle on a wee fire of peats where we had cooked the dinner, and she was to call Mammy when it was ready. It was a lucky thing that Mammy had given all the kitchen paint a good scrubbing since she left work.

I had painted a good piece of skirting-board and the window-sill before Daddy called 'Time!' and Agnes came in to take her turn with the paint brush. The paint was sort of stiff, but you should have seen the change it made to everything. It was now white. Our paintwork had always been a sort of dark dirty yellow colour. While I had been painting Mammy and Daddy had cut and pasted four pieces of paper, and now Daddy opened the steps and went up and Mammy handed him the first piece. He just gave it a couple of shakes and it unfolded itself and stuck the top part to the wall, then he climbed down, smoothing the paper as he came, with both hands. By the time he had finished it and was up the ladder again, Mammy handed him another piece. He matched it carefully, and did the same with it as he had with the first piece of paper. It did not take sixty seconds to put on the other two pieces, then they began again to measure and match and cut and paste four more pieces.

'We will have to work awfully fast,' said Daddy, 'or else only paste three pieces at the time, Ethel. It is thin, but what would you expect.'

'Whatever you say,' said Mammy, slashing away with the paste and the brush.

But I noticed she pasted four pieces. If Mammy has made her mind up I doubt if the police could stop her.

In a minute or two it was again Bertie's turn for painting and he told Mammy that Doreen said the kettle would nearly do, so Mammy told me to hand Daddy the paper, and away she went hot-foot to set Doreen right. I think they did the dishes, but I never heard for certain. Daddy had stuck on the four pieces, and matched and cut four more, and was pasting them himself, when she came back. She lit a small fire of waste paper in the stove, and built a low fire on it, so that the stove and the pipe would heat very slowly and begin to dry the cement and the wet ceiling. Then it was my turn for painting, and Daddy said Bertie should keep an eye on the wee ones while he was having his rest. Mria came in and asked if it would be all right if she washed the splashes off the closet seat and floor. Mammy said, 'All right, but you will have to wash it about three times, because ceiling white is hard to remove. You do not need soap, but take two dusters and do your best.'

The skirting-board was painted on about three sides of the kitchen, and one of the window-sills, and two doors. I would have done the other door, but Daddy said not to, that he would. So I began the banisters. They were awful to do, because they had four sides each, the brush was too big and the paint was too thick so it went into the cracks and collected there.

'Stop,' said Daddy, 'till I help you. I should not have let you try that bit when you have never painted before.'

He cleaned up all the extra paint, with about six swipes of the brush, and finished the banisters. Then he sat down the tin and called Agnes for her turn, which was the rest of the skirting-board. He and Mammy slapped some more paper on the wall, and then he cut more while Mammy went out. In about five minutes, I thought, Alec stuck his head in and said 'Tea's up!' so we all went out and ate jam pieces and drank tea, standing about in the garden because the chairs were too wet and the steps too cold to sit on. The kitchen clock was sitting on its side as usual, but on the outside window-sill, and I was amazed to see that it was after six o'clock. I screwed my face round to match the clock's, and found it was twenty past six. Furthermore, it was dark. I could only see the clock at all by the lights of a car coming round the big bend on the Belfast Road.

We went in and hastily cleared up the mess, and Daddy finished the papering by himself. Mammy put some paraffin oil on a rag and cleaned Bertie's hands, and Agnes's and mine. They were not really very painty because of the nature of the paint. Agnes and I went out and dried the chairs that the wee ones had washed. Alec broke up another peat and put it carefully on the fire so that it smoked but did not blaze. I felt the rugs and found they were nearly dry. If it had not been a rather windy day they would not have dried till Christmas.

'This room will be very damp,' said Mammy from inside the house. 'The paper is damp, the ceiling is damp, the cement is wet and the paint is wet, forbye the smell would sicken you. Should we not put more of a fire in the stove?'

'The cement would crack,' said Daddy. 'What can't be cured must be endured. By this time tomorrow things will be different. If we leave the windows open all night, and we will have to or the paint will stick them shut, it will dry better before the morning.'

Mammy put the light on, and he began to paint the window-frame. I could see that they were both tired, but Mammy was white too. I rolled up the smaller rugs and fetched them in through to our room for the time being, and Agnes and Bertie and Mria helped me with the big ones. The biggest of the lot gave us a bad time and Bertie nearly fell over the balcony railing, only Agnes grabbed him by the leg just as his heels went up. We never told anybody. We would have got little thanks.

As we came past with the last of them, and I am sure it took an hour to haul them up and roll them and fetch them, Daddy said the painting was finished, and that there was not enough paint left in the tin to blind a field-mouse. He cleaned the brush and his hands and laid the brush on the high shelf. Mammy said she would bath wee James and George and Mervyn in our room. That she did, and then took them to their beds. Alec and Doreen were anxious to go too, they were hardly able to stand they were so tired.

With the wee ones out of the way Daddy said he would lay the lino. Mammy was dubious because she said it would tear if it was cold, but he said he would bet her five to three it would not. So we laid it.

Well, that was a trevallye, I can tell you.

Daddy unrolled a bit and slid the end against the wall under the window, and made Doreen and Alec stand on it to keep it there. When it was all unrolled, it was about three feet longer than the floor, so he cut that bit off with the breadknife. Mammy put a chair on a corner at that end and stood on the other corner herself. The only place the bare boards showed was at the front door.

Mammy said, 'I had better move the table in from the balcony.'

But Daddy said, 'Not yet, Ethel, I am thinking.'

'Think faster,' said Mammy. 'It is going to come on rain any minute.'

Daddy took the piece of lino he had cut off and fitted it onto the narrow place by the front door. It fitted exactly. There was a slight overlap, but two long tacks fixed that: he just slid the extra under the edge of the first piece, and nailed it down tidily. Mammy slipped another crumbly peat in the stove, and shut the damper almost fully. Daddy and Bertie would have fetched the stuff from the balcony, but instead Mammy gave Agnes and Mria and me wet soapy cloths and told us to wash the floor, which we did. The lino was so smooth it was nearly a pleasure, compared to scrubbing the splintery boards. (I mean compared with.) The lino had been marked quite a lot by high heels, but it was clean and nice.

'Will we put up the curtains?' I asked, as Daddy and Bertie carried in the chairs, and the old bench, and the big box the water-buckets sit on, and the wall cupboard, and the delf that stays in it.

'The wind would only blow them against the wet paint,' said Mammy. I do not know about you, but I am dead tired.'

'So am I,' said Alec and Doreen together.

'Well, go to bed,' said Mammy crossly, and sat down.

'Not yet!' cried Daddy as they moved. 'Not till I put a couple of tacks in the lino. There. Away you go.'

Doreen went into our room and Alec went upstairs, and that was the last we heard of them till the morning. I was so tired myself I could have lain down on the new lino. At this moment Mria gave a terrible screech that made us all jump like elastic. She had put her hand on the new stove to see if it was warm, and it was. She thought it was not because she could not see any flames. Mammy slapped a taste of margarine on her hand and told her she was not mortally wounded, then took her on her knee. Mria was crying, but she was too tired to do more than sniffle. Soon she went to bed, and so did Bertie. That left Mammy and Daddy and Agnes and me, and it was after eleven o'clock. The whole place was cold and bright and smelt of paint, but sure it was like a palace. It was nearly as nice as Mrs Conlan's. Mammy stuck a saucepan down on the stove and boiled water in no time at all, to make cocoa for the four of us. Then we locked the door and went to bed.

In the morning I heard Mammy up, and she was singing. She does not often sing so I listened to hear what it was, and here wasn't it a hymn. I got up and slipped into the kitchen with my clothes on my arm, to dress in front of the fire. The delf was still on the table, because when they fetched in the cupboard last night they were too tired to put the delf back in. Mammy woke George and Mervyn and by the time they came down I was dressed. The paint on the windows was dry and Mammy had shut them, but the curtains were not up yet. She had put down the best bit of carpet across the floor between the stove and the table. The wee stove had quite a good fire in it and the cement looked light-coloured, as if it might be nearly dry. The fireguard was up in case any of the rest of them did what Mria had done, one burned hand in the house was plenty for the time being.

Mammy came in and cleared the plates and delf off the table into the cupboard where they belonged. When the table was empty I put the cloth on it, and she gave me my breakfast. By this time the rest were up, and we could hear them moving about.

'What are we going to do today?' I asked.

'For once I am going to do some work,' said Mammy for a joke, because what else was she doing all day yesterday, and you could not daunt her. 'I know it is Sunday,' she said, 'but we want this place tidied as quickly as possible. Your Daddy will put the curtains up and I will lay the rugs upstairs, and perhaps the stair carpet too.'

As soon as the others were up they ate their breakfast and she sent them all out for a walk, except for us four older ones.

She said, 'If any of you are thinking of going up to the dump to look for more, please do it after dark. Where did all this stuff come from anyway, I mean whose was it?'

Daddy said, 'It is all from the castle, except maybe the pram. That is the stair carpet, there would have been about twenty yards of it. The American widow is going to buy more when she gets her head shired after the flit. That's not the half of the lino, it was in the kitchen and a lot of it was marked with black scorches, as if they had dropped hot stove-lids on it a time or two. There was a fellow in the kitchen, now I think of it, laying blue vinyl tiles all day Friday. The wee stove came out of the stables, it was in the way when they decided to turn the stable into a garage. The wee bed was out of a sort of a servant's room, over the stable, a quare hole yon was for a man to have to sleep in, with a big green damp patch on the wall behind the bed, and the cotton cover black with mildew.'

'How do you know all this?' she asked. 'I thought I was all

through the house and we had missed nothing.'

'They were in the wee room that was over the stable,' said Daddy, 'the boss wanted it for a playroom for the wee girl. There is a builder in it now, only it is Sunday, he was ripping the old plaster off the walls on Thursday when we went up to throw out the bed.'

'Why didn't you ask for them?' asked Mammy.

'The boss was on top of the conservatory,' he said, 'digging out old putty with a knife, and saying a long prayer over a joiner that never come. A blind man would know she was not in a giving mood. I thought better of it, and if it meant looking for the things over the length and breadth of the country, sure there is no harm done.'

'Maybe she is not a giver, but she feeds you well and she pays you on the nail. You will be getting fat next.'

'You can't fatten a thoroughbred,' said Daddy, and got up and flexed his arms. 'Now where is this stair carpet, Ethel?' he added.

We were not long in carpeting the stairs because Daddy had a plan of campaign as usual. He cut the long piece of carpet up the middle and turned the raw edge next the wall, and I handed tacks and the hammer, and Agnes and Bertie and Mria kept control of the rest of the carpet, and unrolled it when he said, and Mammy stayed out of the way in case she would get hurt. Once it was tacked in place, Daddy added two brass-headed tacks at each side of each step to hold it firm, and then another bit was unrolled and he did the next step. The stairs were completely covered from the wall to the foot of the banisters, and they looked just like anybody's stairs. It looked so rich. Mrs McCann has carpet on her stairs and so have the Ryans, but the Lyles and Pettigrews have lino. Up till now we never had anything but the bare wood. Daddy and Mammy put up the curtains next, and then laid a bit of rug in the low back room where Doreen and Mria and Agnes and I sleep. That was where the pram and the wee bed were, for the time being.

It is a funny shape of room, two feet wider than the bed is long, but as long as the kitchen is wide, that is, about twelve feet. It has one window and a fireplace but we have never yet had a fire in it.

The bed is a great big one and holds us all with a bit of an argument now and then. The wallpaper is pink but faded. There is a mirror with spots on it over the mantel-shelf, and it leans forward a good distance because we could not see ourselves in it at all if it was hung straight. No one has said yet who is to sleep in the wee bed, but as we have not got a mattress for it there is no need to decide just yet.

Agnes and I went to boil the potatoes for the dinner so we missed what happened next, we only saw the results later. The rest went staggering up the stairs with the remains of the carpet, because Mammy said worn or not it was far too good to throw out just yet, and she laid a piece in each of the two upper bed-rooms, between the beds. Bertie said it would be lovely to land out of bed on that when there was frost in the winter-time.

Mammy stood in the passage between the two rooms and looked at the wee top back room where Bertie and Alec and wee James sleep, in two beds, and at the front room where she and Daddy and Mervyn and George sleep in another two beds, and at the dressing-table and the rugs, and at my velvet dress hanging on the wall on a hanger till she gets time to boil it and put the hem up. The wind came in through the open window of the big room and moved the curtains.

She went across to straighten them and said, very low, 'Thank God for it all.'

I never heard her say that before. Maybe it was because we have not had very much until now.

Mria's hand was worse burned than we had thought, and I had to take her to the doctor after school on Monday. It was Dr John's day and he said she ought to have known better than touch a stove when the fire was on. I agreed with him and he asked me how I did. I said, 'Fine.'

'Does you arm never trouble you?' he asked me.

'No,' I replied.

'Never?' he asked, as if he did not believe me.

'I do not notice,' I said, 'I am always doing something. If I was to do something outrajus it would hurt and I might lose my grip.'

'Ethel will never be dead while you are alive,' he said. 'You have enough spunk for a dozen. Tell your mother to let the child's hand alone, to keep it covered, not to put it in water, and come back on Thursday till I see it. Give this to your mother. It is for burns. Tell her I want her to try it if any of you get burned, and let me know if it is any good. It is a sample.'

He gave me a flat blue tin of what he had just put on Mria's hand, and I knew rightly it was no sample, it was a present. I know because Mrs Despard the chemist has it in her shop, in the glass cupboard where you stand to wait for a prescription, and it is three and sixpence a box.

Dr John is kind. He just loves people, even when they are so stupid they nearly make him go mad.

I think maybe God is a little like Dr John, and a little like Albert Dunwoody too. There is no codding with Albert Dunwoody, he is a very honest man and he makes me want to be the same. And I know why Mammy gave him a pound, it was to cover the damages. She must have found out somehow that Daddy took the two pieces out of his truck, and felt she was bound to pay for them. How could you take a present off a man when you had stolen things from him already?

Another good thing has happened.

Daddy's boss has been about in her grounds at the castle and she says the back plantation is an abomination, and will Daddy clear it out and dig drains and put in stick bridges over them and cart away the dead branches and trees. There has not been a thing done to it since 1939, Daddy says, and it is just full of dead timber. He asked the boss did she mean to sell it for her, and she said he could play checkers with it for all she cared, so long as he took it away first. Daddy is delighted, because with the winter coming the people in the town will be mad for blocks for their parlour fires. He says he will need a bush saw but that is a detail.

So after work was finished on Saturday we went back with him after he had eaten his dinner, and we found that a lot of the fallen logs were so rotten that you only had to hit them against the ground or a stump, or jump on them, and they would break like fun. We broke until we had a big pile of them, then Daddy came with a great big roll of hens'-meal-bags he had borrowed off Albert Dunwoody, so we started to stuff the sticks into the bags.

'Put in as many as possible,' he said. 'We will give good value because we are getting the stuff for nothing.'

When the bags were full he and Bertie swung them up on the lorry and away he went to sell them. I am sure he was away over two hours, but when he returned he had a bush saw with him, and all the bags were lying in the lorry, empty. Bertie and I fetched him branches to saw, while as fast as he sawed them Agnes and Mria and Alec and Doreen collected them and put them into the bags. At the coming of dark we had cleared quite a big space of fallen branches, all that were left were small twigs too wet to burn, and they would give no heat if they did.

The next Saturday we did the same, and cleared a lot more ground because Daddy told us his plan of campaign. I wondered why he had not begun on the drains because I could see no sign of any digging, so I asked him.

'I began at the lough side,' he told me, 'and I have dug I am sure a half mile of them this past week.'

'Why did you begin at the lough?' I asked.

'To let the water out as I went,' he told me patiently. 'If I had started at the road for example I would have nothing but a long trench full of glar to work in until I cleared a way to the lough to let it out.'

'You are smart, Daddy,' I said.

'Don't tell anybody,' he whispered. 'There's only two of us know!'

We piled that day's sawn logs and blocks into the lorry and Daddy drove off while the rest of us were to make our own way home. I have been out in the dark many a time but I got a funny feeling that this plantation was not a nice place to be in after dark, so I said to Bertie, 'I'm scared.'

He took to his heels, with Agnes and Mria after him. The wee ones were not with us that day. We ran until we reached the back-drive gate. The back drive is a horrid place, with big overgrown evergreens and fir trees. They looked in the gloom as if

138

they might suddenly snatch at you going past. It was the worst way to go home that ever was invented. We came out on the main road near McKenna's Stores and had to walk a mile up the Cribben Road before we hit the other end of the Water Walks, at the Iron Bridge where they got me out of the river the day Hector was drowned. We had to go up the Water Walks in the dark, all the way to Arcady. It would have been far better if we had come out by the front drive of the castle because then we had only a short distance to go to the Back Road, and a mile to the end of the Arcady Lane.

I love Saturdays. There is always plenty to do, and with Daddy you never know what you will be doing next.

Alec and Mervyn were scrubbing out an empty pig-house for Maurice French at his other farm, so were away all day. Mrs French gave them champ for their dinner and Maurice gave them half a crown each. Alec loves sloshing with water and Mervyn is just as bad, so when they heard they could use the stirrup-pump there was no holding them.

Mammy boiled my velvet dress and it was a great success. The dye came out where it was a good green and went into where it was a bad faded green, and now you would never know that it was ever faded. Mammy had a search and found an Irish lace collar of her own, and tacked it on. It is easily the most beautiful dress I have ever had.

Our house is lovely to come home to these cold evenings, with the wee stove just glowing warm. Mammy says the next thing we need is a blanket or two, but the way everything has come to us this year it would be foolish to ask for them. We are to wait and see. At the beginning of this year Daddy was not working and we had nothing. I had not even a coat. Now Daddy has a steady job and Mammy is better herself because she has not to watch Hector all the time. That is not meant to be kind, it is meant to be true. She could never take a job while he was there because he was so bad and hard to look after that she could not ask anybody to do it. I am sorry he was drowned but God knows I could not help it, my hand would not hold the branch any more. Besides, he did not suffer very long. Mammy could not talk to me about it, but Mrs

Henessey told me that some time after it happened, when I thanked her for trying to save us. She said if I would think of it I would see that it was the best thing for Hector, because who would have looked after him if he grew up? She had something there. We could never let anybody into the house while he was there for fear of what he might do. One time the Welfare Nurse came to see wee James, and Hector threw one of wee James's dirty nappies at her. She told Mammy it did not matter but I am sure she had to go home and change before she made her next call for her apron was ruined. She knew Hector was backward and she did not say a cross word, but that does not mean she was not cross. I am sure she was. So was Mammy, but what was there she could do? He did not understand.

About the end of October we had four days' rain and that finished any chance of getting more sticks until they had dried. We had been up to Cranee several evenings through the week, and fetched down all the peats we had cut, so that our stack of peats in the garden was the biggest stack I had ever seen.

Mammy has found out how to heat the stove oven. You do it with four peats and the damper a third open and the stove door shut. You keep four peats sitting by ready to put in the stove the minute the fire goes down a little.

On Hallowe'en Mammy sent us across to Gorman's for margarine, flour, sugar, four pounds of cooking apples and a pie dish. We never had a pie dish before either, with an open fire it would have been no use at all.

It was Vera Gorman who served us. She passed the Qualifying and is at the Grammar School, but she does not like it and says the amount of homework would frighten you. And besides, her mammy says she will have to learn to serve in the shop for there is so much to do in connection with the Post Office she has that she has not got the time to mind the shop as well. Vera says it is the pensions and the allowances that make the work, and if her mammy made a mistake and paid somebody too much she would have to pay back the money herself. I do not know at all why they keep a shop and a post office anyhow, because Vera's daddy has a good job in Belfast, and her aunt who lives with them has a good job too for she is a sister at the hospital. You would think they would have plenty among their hands. But Vera's daddy has a car and her aunt Doris has a car, and my Daddy says what with road tax and insurance and the licence it costs five shillings a day even to have a car in the garage, and that if you take it out on the road the petrol and oil are extra, never mind the fine if you crossed a white line and a policeman saw you at it. A lorry can earn its living, but a car is just foolishness. That is what my Daddy says.

But it would make you laugh to think that the Gormans do not consider themselves well in. Mrs Gorman does a very big trade all over this district. When you have a certain amount of tick she has a talk with you and if you do not pay her something on account she would ask you for it in front of somebody. People say this is not a nice thing for her to do, but she can do it in a pleasant way, and I say she is right. Why should she feed people for nothing? Besides she is only asking for what is hers. But I am a wee bit afraid of her.

That apple pie Mammy made was the very best I ever tasted. It was as good as Mrs Conlan's any day. We all sat around eating pie until it was all gone, and Mammy said that after this we can have pie quite often, because she can make other sorts of pies, and maybe even roasts, only a roast for us all would be very expensive.

'More than five shillings?' I asked.

'More than fifteen,' said Mammy, 'if we are to have more than one bite each. However, I will think about it.'

She is looking fat and well and has a good colour, and her ankles do not swell any more, because she got tablets from Doctor Emily and that did the trick. Dr Emily says if Mammy feels even a wee bit sick she is to let her know at once, and she will come. I am glad Mammy is not so bad these days because I was frightened when her ankles swelled. I do not know very much about it, but I know that is very bad.

I would like to see Mrs Conlan again, for I have not seen her to talk to since the day of the bonfire. I would love to do something for her because I know we owe her a lot. The weather is colder now so Mammy wears Mrs Conlan's sister's things. The skirts and the coat are warm and smart for going in the bus or to Gorman's. Mammy mended the coat's torn pocket and sewed on buttons, so it is as good as new. Her hair is growing out dark because she has stopped putting on peroxide, she says she has decided to be a brunette for a change. This is only one of her jokes. Daddy says her hair is the colour of a six-weeks-old mouse.

'Where did you ever see a six-weeks-old mouse?' she asked him.

'Come on and I'll show you,' he said.

Mammy laughed and said, 'Once bitten twice shy.'

Daddy laughed too.

Mostly I understand what they are laughing at, but this time I did not. It is about something they both know that I don't.

I am learning to say a piece of poetry at the Intermediate School. They have more poems there than you ever heard of and some of them are just marvellous, even reading them makes me cry nearly. When I have this one learned I will go up to Mrs Conlan's, but not before, because she might ask me to say it for her and it would make both of us feel bad if I did not manage to do it perfectly. So I know better than to go up just yet.

NOVEMBER

The dark evenings are here again, Bertie and Agnes and I are just in after sitting on the ditch of Harper's Plantation and watching the moon rise. The sky is clear on top and misty around the edge, so when the moon first appeared it looked very large and mysterious and had a face on it. Bertie spoiled it all by saying a satellite was on its way there. This may well be true but I would rather not have heard it just then. All the birds had gone home to perch for the night, and the river was running very quietly though it was nearly up to the planks of the Stick Bridge. There has been a lot of rain in the past week, so the Ryans are worried in case the river comes over the bank and floods their house. It happened one time before, the water came into the kitchen and they were weeks getting it dry. Since that time Dermot made the doorstep higher and built a wee wall about two feet high so that the water would have to rise about five feet to get in the door.

We are on the first floor and it cannot happen to us. I know I would not like it if it did.

Nobody has taken the empty house between Lyle's & Pettigrew's. Mrs Lyle's house is empty still, because she is in hospital this long time and not expected to get better, but she gets her rent sent to the rent man for she thinks she will live and she wants to keep her home. The Pettigrews are still here but they have paid for a piece of land on the other side of the town near the factory, and the foundations of their bungalow have been dug. The men could go no farther with it because they found a spring and most of the site is in glar, Daddy says, but it is the contractor's job to turn the flow away from the house and go on with the building.

'They will have their own private river,' said Mammy. 'I do not blame them for trying to have style. A little style is what we are all lost for. There should be more of it about.' But she was only

143

joking to keep her heart up.

Vera Gorman says her mammy nearly took a weak turn the other day. Mrs Pettigrew jumped off the bus, came running into the shop and bought a pound of ham and half a dozen eggs. Mrs Gorman only had the best ham left and it was six shillings and sixpence a pound, but Mrs Pettigrew shelled out the money without a cough and the minute she got home she put the pan on.

Mammy says she knows rightly that the sight of us roaming about the place eating chips and pancakes and handfuls of pie (that was the boys, I had a plate) got on Mrs Pettigrew's nerves till she had to make herself a square meal or run mad. I think it is a pity of Mrs Pettigrew. Daddy said there is not less than thirty pounds a week going into their house, because they both have good jobs, but sure they have a miserable time of it, neither in them nor on them, till the bugalow is finished and they have got their furniture. My mammy says it will be a miracle if they both keep their health. I would not like to live like that, for I am fond of my grub.

George and Mervyn were over at Mrs Henessey's earlier this evening, helping her to put her hens in for the night. Every single night the hens roost in a great laurel bush as big as a tree growing between Henessey's house and the river, so she has to get them out and put them in the henhouse. The rats that live in holes on the riverbank would get them before morning if she did not. She just goes out at dusk and shakes the laurel and for five minutes it rains hens, then George and Mervyn sort of whoosh them to the henhouse. The hens are a breed I do not know, paler than Mrs French's Rhode Island Reds and browner than Albert Dunwoody's Light Sussex. They are exceptionally nervous. I used to think Leghorns were the worst, but now I am not sure. The only person the hens are not frightened of is our George, but Mrs Henessey scares the living daylights out of them because she flaps her apron at them when she is whooshing them. They run all roads and directions from her. But it is all to the good because when George puts them in for her Mrs Henessey generally gives him an egg, and Mammy scrambles it for him with a taste of margarine.

144

It's strange, the noise a river makes at night. During the day you cannot hear it for the traffic, or the wind, or people making a fuss as they work, but at night it makes a kind of soft roar, and you can hear it lipping against the old tree near the ruins of the Beetling-house or the legs of the Stick Bridge.

We went up to the dump again that same night but we did not get anything much. Bertie found an old shovel and Agnes found a plastic sort of basin, a good big one, but here wasn't it cracked. It was not the sort of plastic you could melt and fix either, so we left it. Daddy and I each got a filthy five-gallon oil-drum, he said he could make them into peat-hods for the house if he could get the tops off. I must say I have seen him do a lot of impossible things, but I do not fancy his chances. As we were leaving the dump I slipped and put my foot in a hole, when I pulled it out a big pot was stuck on it. 'Horray!' I said and took it with me. There are some extravagant people about. Imagine throwing out a good aluminyum saucepan. Likely that is not how you spell it, but it will do till I get at the dictionary.

Mammy was delighted with the saucepan and gave it a good scrub, while Bertie cut a thick stick from the hedge and whittled it to make a handle for the shovel. We already have a shovel, or the remains of one you might say. I did not see Daddy taking the tops off the oil drums or making wire handles for them, because he and Bertie were outside at the time, but Bertie told me he did it with half a hedge shears that he found on the dump, and the back of our timber-axe. Bertie came in smelling of the stuff that was in the drums, and said he had to clean them out with newspaper. It smelled like bubble-gum and something else, and he told me it was not oil, it was anti-freeze. If you asked me it smelled anti-social, but I did not say so because it would have been wasted on Bertie.

On the Saturday I went to Gorman's for Mammy, brushed the bedrooms, made the beds, washed the dishes, peeled the potatoes for the dinner, then I was finished for the day. I asked Mammy if I could go up to Mrs Conlan's and she said yes. I washed my face and hands and brushed my hair and changed into my green velvet dress.

145

Mrs Conlan was just back from the town so I helped her carry in her parcels and waited till she put the car away. She is getting better at reversing it into the garage this winter, I think she will be able to do it without having to come into Arcady first.

'It is a long time since I have seen you,' she said to me. 'Are you quite well? And how is your mother?'

'Mammy is much better,' I replied. 'And how are you yourself?'

The fire only needed a poke to set it going, and in no time Mrs Conlan had tea made and a plate of cake out. It was lovely to see her again. She told me how the rest were doing at their lessons, and how pleased she was with Mervyn because she could not hold fit to him in reading books. Bertie and Mria and Agnes are nothing special at reading or sums, if Mammy did not keep at them they would hardly bother to learn their lessons, but Doreen and Alec are a bit smarter and now it looks as if Mervyn will do well, so I am glad. It would be nice for Mammy and Daddy to have a clever one in the family. I would like to be clever myself, especially at sums, but I doubt it was not to be.

I would have liked to tell Mrs Conlan about the things we had got since I saw her, but I dared not, because I had promised Mammy I would not. So I told her instead that Mervyn was started to read Mrs McFarland's son's books, and she was amazed.

'I only wish he was as good at his handwork,' she said, and smiled. 'Would you like to tell me about yourself?'

It was meeting her made me think of it, but now I knew I did not like the Intermediate School half as much as I thought. I hardly knew what to say. I could hardly tell Mrs Conlan that my teacher has a car and goes home the same road as Agnes and I do, but catch her offering us a lift if it is raining, the way Mrs Conlan always did. Mrs Conlan would stand no old nonsense, but she was good to us. You knew where you were with her. But Mrs Carpenter only teaches us.

But I said I liked it all right, only there were thirty-six in our class, and sometimes I never was asked to read, and we marked each other's sums.

'Why is that?' asked Mrs Conlan.

'It is because the teacher has not the time,' I said. 'She has too many of us to go over. She is kept very busy.'

'No,' said Mrs Conlan, 'I meant, why don't you like marking each other's sums? You sometimes did it with me. You remember when you were learning practice sums?'

'Ah but, Mrs Conlan,' I said, 'you lifted the books and you knew if we had them all right. At the Intermediate if I am right in all of them the teacher does not even know.'

If you had all your sums right at the wee school, the master put your book up for the rest to see. Of course tidiness was not enough, and having all the sums right was not enough either. You had to have both at once. That was the part that stuck me. I am sure my book was not up six times, the whole time I was at the wee school. My composition was never up at all. I wrote such long ones I had not the time to be bothered with the writing.

'But if you know that your sums are right,' said Mrs Conlan, 'does it matter that nobody sees them?'

I could tell she was interested, but how to answer without making her think I was being cheeky, that was the mystery! 'Well,' I said, cautiously, 'it is like speaking and getting no reply.' I thought I had said enough.

Maybe so did Mrs Conlan, because she asked me if I had learned any new poetry. I got up and stood the way she had taught me, and recited 'The Forsaken Merman' and never missed a word, although I nearly cried about the little mermaiden, her story is so sad.

I was at the Feis last year but I started to recite before the bell rang and lost points. Miss Diamond was too mad to speak, but Mrs Conlan just shrugged her shoulders. She was not pleased either, but sure the damage was done.

'Good, that was very good,' said Mrs Conlan. 'But change your voice volume a little, the way you were taught, when you recite a long poem. It makes it less monotonous.'

I said I would, and I saw her just glance at my dress. I could tell she was delighted to see me wearing what had been her parlour curtains. But she never said 'what's that, where did you get it, did your mother make it?' or anything else. Only a stupid person

147

would have been offended, she was letting on she had never seen or heard of such a thing as green velvet, and I just loved her for not letting on she saw it, for all I know she did. Mrs Conlan is a real lady. I never knew the beat of her.

It rained from when I got home from Mrs Conlan's. About eight o'clock on Sunday night the river rose and crept round the end of the wee wall Dermot had built, and crept up to Ryan's door-step and carried away a tin bath Monica had for the Monday wash.

The Ryans were watching TV and they nearly went mad. Monica ran out but she could go no farther because she was only in slippers. She had a coat over her head, but what use was that? And the tin bath was away down the river, turning round and round now and then as if to make sure she was still watching it. We saw the whole set from the window of our low back bedroom.

'It will be in the Lough if I don't get it,' cried Monica. 'Away quick, Dermot, and see if you can't catch it.'

Dermot did not want to go but he did not want to argue either, so away he went. He came back in an hour to tell us the Town Meadows were under water and the people in the prefabs were flooded out.

'Oh, God!' said Monica. 'Never mind the bath, come down to Bernadette's and fetch up her and the children, she must be at her wit's end.'

She had no wellingtons, so while she ran to borrow a pair from the McCann's, Dermot got bricks from the old garden wall and threw them down to lengthen the wall. Then he tore big sods out of the ditch and slapped them down and tramped them in tight upon the bricks, until he had built another bit of wall, and Fidelma flew out and started to sweep the water away with a brush. It did not seem to be rising any farther, but Paul and Kevin came out and said they would look after that end if Dermot and Monica wanted to go for Bernadette.

They hurried up Albert Dunwoody's lane, which is a short cut to the Town Meadows. Of course it is not a public road. At any other time they would not dream of going that way, but this was an emergency. There are gaps in the ditch between the lane and the riverbank, to drain rain off the lane, but this time the river was backing up the drains. It was dark before they got back with Bernadette Docherty and her four children. She is a cousin of theirs and is very good-looking and has long black hair and can talk with a cigarette in her mouth. Fidelma had a big fire on, so they bathed the children, fed them and put them to bed up in Bridie's room. I heard Mrs Docherty start to cry.

She said, 'The first thing I knew, Finola's teddy bear came swimming into the living-room on a tide of black water!'

But Fidelma comforted her and said, 'Sure you are safe here, the lot of you,' and made her a good feed of sausages and tomatoes.

Mr Docherty is a sailor and he is never home when he is wanted. Dermot later in the week told Daddy he never remembered about the tin bath till late on Monday, then he went down the river to see if he could see it. By that time the flood had gone down a good bit, and he found the tin bath sitting in one of Archie Agnew's fields. Mrs Docherty and the children stayed till the Tuesday and then the Ryans went down with her to clear out her prefab and light fires. Her prefab was not damaged and it was only flooded about three inches deep. She had vinyl on the floors, so all she had to do was lift the vinyl and dry the floors. Some of her neighbours had their beds soaked and their carpets completely destroyed. It was a shame. It seems that what caused the flood was a haystack that stuck in one of the arches of the town bridge. Archie Agnew's haystack, he only had the one, was swept away, so likely it was his. The water could not get through the bridge properly so it spread over the town meadows.

Many a time I have thought I would like to live in a prefab, but not now. Arcady is rough and old-fashioned but the teddy bears have never had to swim for it yet.

Daddy is saving hard for a new lorry. The tyres on the one he has are very bad and so are the brakes. Usually he delivers peats up the Belfast Road but now he keeps to the back roads in case the police stop him. Mammy wants him to sell the lorry now and be done with it before the police see the state it is in. He says he will be all right as long as he keeps out of their sight, but it is not easy in a ten-ton lorry.

A cow died on Gilbert Taylor's place at Ballycromkeen so he got Daddy to drive her to Stormount to find out why she died. She had no excuse, he said. The cow did not know that, so she died anyway. When Daddy came back he said the boys in white coats were quare and pleased to see her.

'What boys in white coats?' asked George. He was under the table looking for a toy tin car wee James had.

'A welcome committee,' said Daddy, 'what else. It's not often they see a cow from Ballycromkeen. She was a novelty.'

He could not let on to George that the cow was dead. George would have cried, he cannot bear to think of an animal suffering. If anything happens to Duff Cooper I do not know what George will do.

About the middle of the month Daddy came home and told Mammy he had seen a lorry he thought would do. But it was fifty pounds.

'You may put that notion out of your head now,' said Mammy. 'The winter is coming and I need to make the boys new trousers and sweaters yet, and they have not a sound pair of boots among the whole of them.'

I don't know when I heard her so serious.

Daddy knew it was no use, so he did not try to make her agree with him. He just drove off in the old lorry to finish carting stuff for a man in the town. When he came back he gave Mammy two pounds ten, and sat down and heard Bertie and Alec their lessons.

I would like to agree with Daddy but I think Mammy is right. Another winter like the last one would finish us.

Of course the very next time Daddy had the lorry in Ballycromkeen the police stopped us. Fortunately he had not taken the lorry into Ballycromkeen very often, so they did not know his face.

They asked him for his licence and insurance and log book. The log book was properly written up, but he said the licence and insurance were at home, so they asked him his name and address.

'Con Rafferty, Red Row, Davidstown Lane, Gortnamoniagh,'

he said, just like that. 'This is my wee girl Dolores. I would not have the child in the lorry with me this way but she's bad with the toothache and I was taking her to the dentist.'

I was dumbfounded. I never heard anybody tell such lies.

After they let us drive on Daddy said, 'That was a near shave.'

I said nothing. I thought they would be looking for us again soon, and he was only wasting his time trying to fool them. The police are fly boys. Very likely they are just as smart as Daddy is.

When we got into Arcady the policeman who got me out of the river the day Hector was drowned was standing yarning with Seumas McCann. He called me over and said to me, 'Tell your Daddy to get rid of that lorry as quick as he can and not to let on who tipped him off.'

So I told Daddy.

'Ha! Ha!' he said, exactly like Napoleon the Fourteenth, and drove away again at once.

When he came back it was pitch dark and his feet were sore, but he never mentioned the lorry, and I had the feeling he had it hidden. If it was me, I would have hidden it in Cranee.

Mammy could not stand the suspense and asked him where it was.

'Lex Todd has wanted it this long time,' said Daddy. 'He has one like it a wee bit newer, so it's likely that he only bought it for the spares. He gave me a fiver for it. And he'll not let on how long he's had her, nor where he bought her.' He opened and shut his toes at the fire till the steam rose out of his socks.

I was sorry the lorry was gone, but I was glad too. I knew rightly Daddy never insured her, and there is something funny about his licence, so it is just as well she is gone. If he does get a van later on, Bertie says it will be easier on the petrol.

Mammy knitted Daddy an Aran sweater in brown wool, and she burned his old army battledress at last. The Aran sweater suits him. I can see now that that battledress did not.

He came in from work one night and said to Mammy that the boss had been going through the attics and had found trunks with the old colonel's clothes. She had asked the solisitors what to do with them because she thought she had no right to them. They wrote back to say that she had bought the house as it stood so whatever she found was hers to do as she liked with. She called in Daddy and Tom Lamont and said they could take a trunk each and divide the stuff between them, or it would be burned. He told Mammy the things were of the very best, but old-fashioned.

'Bring all you can get,' said Mammy. 'This is my prayers answered. What you can't use I can cut down for the boys. Little did I think the colonel's trousers would ever hang on the end of my bed. If I make you a pair of drainpipes would you for the love of God get your hair cut.'

'I will,' said Daddy. 'She says I can take the trunk itself. Bertie, where are the bicycle wheels?'

He meant the wheels of the old bicycle Bertie found on the dump that time. He had got a bit of iron rod for an axle, but I did not know just how they would get the trunk to stay on it.

When they returned they had this big black canvas trunk with them. They were both clean done with pushing it so we all helped to drag it in. It was just stuffed with suits and trousers and a good overcoat and some scarves. Daddy told Mammy that the trousers fitted him from the toes to the oxters, then he went up and changed into a pair and he was right. Mammy said she could alter them, and pinned up the legs then and there. His toes had been sticking out at the bottom like a fringe at the hems. I do not know why they were comical, but they were.

Mammy studied how she could take them in for him, then said she could do it, and I had not a doubt of it. Two pairs were what you call Bedford Cord, and another pair were brown tweed and another pair black and another pair striped. There were two suits, one navy with a white blurred stripe, and the other a rich brown colour in a rough wool material. There was also a grey overcoat of lovely warm stuff, like Doctor John's winter one, and a tan-coloured suede waistcoat with a broken zip. Mammy measured the zip at once, to get another for it.

I like touching suede, it is as soft as wee James' cheek.

'Now,' said Mammy, 'change back. I will open the seams tonight and start in tomorrow.'

She was studying the trunk, and she remarked, 'That would

152

make a fine seat. Are you sure she meant you to keep it?'

'Tom Lamont got one too,' replied Daddy. 'He picked a black tin uniform case.'

'Try the boy!' she said admiringly. 'I suppose he thought it would be the best thing to keep his blankets in when he is not needing them.'

'Likely,' said Daddy.

As we went upstairs Mammy looked at the trunk, the overcoat and the other things scattered about, then said, 'Thank God for it all,' very low, but I heard her.

The alterations proved to be a terrible job. Anybody else but Mammy would have given up and said they were impossible, but she never gives up once she starts. By Friday night she had a pair of the colonel's trousers made into drainpipes for Daddy, and you should have seen him. He looked just lovely, except he needed his hair cut.

He and Bertie went into the town early on Saturday afternoon and both of them went to the barber, it was four shillings for the two of them. After he came back he said people were looking at him twice all the way home to see if it was him or not.

'I have often told you,' said Mammy, 'that you look just grand if you take a wee bit of trouble. Why don't you?'

'I will have to, I can see that,' he said, 'or you will be losing notion of me, Ethel.'

'You'd get blood from a turnip sooner,' said Mammy. 'Let that do you.'

That was a happy afternoon. Mammy was sewing velvet dresses for Agnes and Mria and Doreen, and she had finished them, all but the collars and belts, just before teatime. Mine had not shrunk when she boiled it, so she knew she was safe to set the hems and then I could sew them. She said she would let me slip-stitch them and not herringbone them, because it is a lot quicker. The belts were sewn, but they were still inside out and she had not the time to turn them. She had to rise and fry the sausages.

We usually have sausages for tea on Saturday and breakfast on Sunday now. This week she also bought a big piece of meat and stewed it with some kidney, she told me she was going to make a

153

steak-and-kidney pie for the dinner on Sunday. She had flour and margarine laid by on the high shelf, and Doreen loves to rub it in. The only thing is that you have to inspect Doreen's hands first, for she thinks they are clean enough no matter what she has been doing, and they almost never are. Doreen does not like brushing and making beds and washing dishes or clothes, but just let her at the fire and she will do her best to cook. It is very good because she is only eight and a half years old. Mammy made her a wee white apron and she wears it when she is cooking. She could not fry anything when we had the open fire, because Mammy was always afraid of the pan catching light, but now we have the wee stove there is little chance of that, so it is usually Doreen who fries the soda bread. She cannot fry sausages yet because she lets the pan get too hot.

Agnes was standing in her velvet dress, which came down nearly to her ankles, while Mammy set the hem and the sausages were beginning to give small spits and sizzles, Mria was just taking off her dress with the hem set and I was turning Doreen's dress belt right side out with a long knitting-needle, Doreen was minding the pan and Mervyn was in such a hurry for the sausages that he was putting the cloth on the table all crooked. Mammy lifted her eyes from Agnes's dress and tweaked the tablecloth straight, and stuck another pin in the hem, and with that there was a loud knock at the door.

Mammy said to me, 'Go and see what that is.'

A strange lady was standing on the balcony.

Mammy looked round and stopped still, then said, 'Hello, Mother, will you not come in?'

'Maybe I had better,' said the strange lady. 'There is a pair of eyes upon me this minute.'

I knew she must mean Mrs Pettigrew. When anything happens in Arcady she is always out cleaning her windows.

The lady came in and I shut the door.

Mammy said, 'You can take that off now, Agnes, and hang it up carefully. Doreen, love, that bread's burning, take it off quick. Mria, would you set the table and put out an extra cup and plate. Will you stay and take your tea, Mother?'

'I will take a cup of tea in my hand,' said the lady. She looked at,me and said, 'I am your granny. Did you not know you had a granny?'

She was wee and thin and not like Mammy at all. She had on a good black coat with a fur collar and a hat like a grey velvet pot with a feather for a handle, and a big black bag and a parcel. She had far more style than Mrs McFarland.

'I did not know I had a granny,' I said. 'None of us did.'

'What is your name?' she asked me.

I told her all our names.

'Have you not a wheen more boys?' she asked Mammy.

'Bertie is with is daddy outside somewhere,' said Mammy. 'And Alec is away a message, and George and wee James are likely down in Old Joe Cooper's. Mria, away and tell them their tea's ready.'

Alec, George and wee James came back together. Alec gave Mammy the change at once. They were shy with our granny but not for long. She was a bit like old Mrs French and they like her, so they soon came round. Then Bertie came in and was introduced. Mammy got him to help her to drag the colonel's trunk round to make a seat and the three wee ones sat on it. They had not enough room for their elbows, but Mammy cuts up their sausages and fried bread anyway. Mervyn can cut his own and George is not too bad at it, but today she did not want them to affront her by letting pieces of food skid off their plates on to the clean tablecloth. Our granny was sitting at the fire drinking tea and eating a buttered soda scone and Mammy was just pouring our tea when Daddy walked in.

He nearly fell down dead. I could see that he just did not know what to say.

But Granny never mismade herself. 'I was just passing,' she said, 'and I thought I would come over. It is a long time since I had seen Ethel, so thinks I, one of us might be taken in the night. You are looking bravely yourself. I heard about the wee lad you lost. It was an awful pity but God's ways are the best. I hear you are working at the castle.'

Daddy was embarrassed at the first but she talked till he was fit to answer her.

'How many weans have you now?' asked Granny. 'Is it eight?'

'Count them,' said Mammy, 'they are all here. That one at the end is Frances. Agnes is the one with the bow in her hair. The biggest boy is Bertie. Mria is the one with the glasses in her hand, Mria, would you give Agnes her glasses and stop codding with them before they break. Alec and Doreen are twins, you heard about them, I am sure. This other one is Mervyn. That is George beside you, and the wee one is James. There will be ten, I would not be surprised at that.'

'You have this place lovely, and you have reared your family well,' said Granny. 'And about the rest I will say no more. What can't be helped can't be helped. If I was hard on you before, I thought it was for your own good, but I am sorry now for some of the things I said.'

'Every word came true,' said Daddy. 'But we got by. We managed. Whiles not any better than you said we would, but we didn't starve. Would you like another taste of tea?'

'Would you pour it for me?' asked Granny.

'I would that,' he said, and got red in the face as if he was very pleased to do it.

'Do you never hear from Martha?' asked Granny.

'She came up here one day in the summer time,' Mammy told her. 'But she didn't stay as long as she thought she would.'

'You never told me,' said Daddy to Mammy.

'You would only have been mad at her and maybe had another row with her about me,' said Mammy calmly. 'I sent her away with a flea in her ear. I see Judith's like you, Joe, she is a lovely girl, no more like Martha than day's like night. Her mammy was saying all the usual things to me and Judith was that embarrassed she didn't know where to put herself.'

'I was fond of Martha once,' said Daddy. 'And I would go to see Judith, only Martha would take it for the first move next a surrender. Ethel here is worth a dozen of her.' And he put his arm round Mammy as far as it would reach.

Mammy reached him the chalk she had been marking the dress hems with. 'Here,' she said, 'put a mark and start over again.'

Granny and Daddy both laughed.

'Still the same Ethel,' said Granny, and the severe look was off her face now. 'Bad and all as you are,' she said to Daddy, 'you have made Ethel happy, and I could like you for it. You are straighter than I gave you credit for.'

'I'm not straight at all,' he said, 'I only wish I was. I leave a trail of lies and destruction wherever I go.'

'You got off the drink,' said Granny. 'This is one good thing. And you have made a good home for Ethel and your children, that is another good thing.'

'You are making me blush,' he said in a funny voice.

Mammy gave a loud laugh. 'Anything that would make you blush would make a crowbar sweat!' she said.

'The compliments are flying,' said Daddy drily. 'Would two or three of you clear away the dishes and wash them, then bring in the peats and get water and put on the griddle.'

'And bring the sheets off the line,' said Mammy. 'And put on the flat-irons to heat. It is not every day my mother comes to see me. Just you show her the way you can do things!'

So we did.

I brushed up the crumbs, made up the fire, put on the griddle and sat down to sew. While Agnes fetched the water Bertie and Mria fetched in the sheets and stretched them and folded them. Then Doreen washed the dishes and Mria dried them, and I gave Doreen her white cooking apron while Agnes put on the flat-irons to heat. Mammy put out the bakeboard, the flour and the buttermilk, and let Doreen mix the dough for soda bread. Daddy captured wee James just as he made for out, and Granny asked how old he was.

'He is two and nine months,' said Mammy. 'He is a rogue.'

Mervyn asked to go down to Mrs McFarland's until wee James had had his bath, and Mammy said he would be sent for as soon as she wanted him. George had already gone back to Old Joe Cooper's to play with Duff. Old Joe had told Mammy that he just loves that kitten and would not hurt it for worlds, and it is great to see a wee fellow that does not want to torment dumb animals.

Mammy and Granny talked about old times while Daddy bathed wee James in our room, and put him to sleep. He does not do this very often for he is not often in at wee James's bedtime, but wee James loves it, and goes to bed like an angel. Bertie took the rest out for a walk but I stayed with the grown ups because I was sewing and I wanted to finish the dresses. We would all be dressed alike, we four girls, and I would like that.

'That is lovely stuff,' said Granny, feeling it between her finger and thumb. 'Where did you get it?'

'Out of the winter curtains,' said Mammy calmly, and she never let on whose.

'I say, here, you are well at yourself,' said Granny. 'And rugs on the floor, and all!'

'It was not easy getting them,' said Mammy, as calm as you like. 'There was a deal of trouble went into it all, mother.'

I finished the hem of Agnes's frock and took it into our room to hang it up. Out of the window I could see Bertie and Agnes and Mria and Doreen and Alec going over to Gorman's to spend their money. Bertie had helped Maurice French through the week so he had a shilling, Mria had done two messages for the master so she had a shilling, Alec and Doreen had each got a prize of sixpence in their class at school for counting farther than the rest and for being able to write down all the numbers the teacher called out. Mammy had asked them earlier what money they had, and she was satisfied. She does not like us going to get sweets in Gorman's too often, because Mrs Gorman cannot stand people who pay cash for sweets and then try to get their bread on tick. Sometimes on a Thursday Mammy has to get bread on tick but she always pays it the minute she gets Daddy's wages. She has paid up all she owed Mrs Gorman last winter, and she tries not to get a single thing we don't need. It is lucky we are all fond of pilchards because they are only one and six a tin. We like eggs too, and it is unfortunate for eggs are nearly always about five shillings a dozen, and a dozen only does us for one meal unless Mammy makes French toast with them. It is delicious but it is not very eggy. And bacon is out of all buying, it is six and six a pound or nearly that. Stewing meat is four and six but it takes at least two pounds for the Sunday dinner. I just do not know how Mammy manages, but she does. She knits our jerseys, and now she has the

158

machine she makes us our clothes. The rest do not notice this, but I do. The soldier's wife gets steak and sausages and liver, and eggs by the dozen, and cakes and biscuits and tins of Coke, and all that is only for two people and the soldier has his dinner at the camp. She gets tins of soup and peaches and pineapple and pears. On the Twelfth Day we had two tins of pineapple for our tea, with bread and butter, but I have not tasted it since. I would be greedy with it if I had the chance. We have had apple pies several times since Hallowe'en, but the kind of pie I like best is made with minced beef and onions.

I came to my senses and realised that Granny was asking me something. 'I am sorry,' I said, 'I was thinking. What did you say.'

'I said that you and the other one that goes to the Intermediate could have your dinners at my house and then your Mammy would not have to pay for the school meals,' said Granny. 'You would get whatever was going, so I hope you are not too choosy.'

'I would like that very much,' I said. 'Thank you for thinking of it. The school meals are not much good. Even before we got the stove Mammy could make better ones.'

Granny laughed and said, 'I will have to be careful, Ethel, there is one that knows what is what. Well, if that is settled, I will be going. What time is your lunch-hour?'

We told her.

She said, 'I will be at the school gate for you on Monday to show you the way to my house, and after that you will come by yourselves. Now I will have to clear or I will miss the bus. Don't rise from your seat, Ethel, you have done enough, Frances will convoy me over the Stick Bridge. It has been nice to see you again, and I hope all will go well if I do not see you again before.'

'Thank you, mother,' said Mammy. She pulled Granny down and kissed her cheek.

Then Granny hurried out. She walked so fast she was half-way to the Stick Bridge before I caught up with her. She asked me was Mammy keeping well and I said her ankles had been swollen, but that lately she was much better because we were all trying to help her in the house.

'What was she doing at the Imperial Hotel?' asked Granny grimly.

159

'Daddy was not working at the time,' I said. 'But he has got a steady job now, with a good wage.'

'For how long?' she asked. 'What do you suppose will be wrong with this one?'

'I do not know,' I said. 'What was wrong with the others?'

'I am not saying one word against your daddy,' she said, 'but he has had more jobs in more places than anybody else I ever knew, and made less at it. If he had his deservings he would have a bungalow on the Belfast Road with a birdbath in the garden and a lawn to be mowing on Saturday, and likely a wee car.'

'We had a lorry,' I said. 'He sold it.'

'See to it he never gets another,' said Granny. 'With all of yous to feed he could never manage the insurance, and if the police get him with one and it not taxed he would get jail. He has tried it before and was let off with a caution.'

My blood ran cold because I remembered that day in Ballycromkeen when he gave the police the wrong name and address because they wanted to see his licence and insurance. Of course he could not show them the insurance, because from what Granny said he had none, and by this time I knew rightly his licence had been endorsed, because I had heard Mammy asking him was there any use in keeping it in the tin box on the high self.

'I will,' I told Granny. 'But you know I could not make him do anything.'

'You will have to try,' she said bluntly. 'Ethel has her hands full, and you are the eldest. It is up to you to help her, even if you are young yet. With a bit of practice, you could wind your Daddy round your finger.'

I did not like the sound of that. Daddy does not wind very easily, I could have told her, but the bus came, so I helped her in and the conductor armed her to a seat. She must have known him, or else he was very polite. She waved at me through the glass as the bus drove off, and I waved back. Then she gave a wee bounce to settle herself in her seat. In a minute the bus was out of sight.

I went back to Mammy and found that she had nearly finished baking, and was leaving Doreen to finish harning the bread while she started the ironing. I helped Doreen clear away and wash up.

Then Mammy sent for George and Mervyn. I gave them their baths when they arrived back, then Mammy heard them their prayers and they went to bed. Doreen was allowed to stay up until Alec came back, then they were bathed and went to bed too. By this time the ironing was finished. It was late but I picked up Mria's dress and started the hem.

'You will not be long at that, my lady,' said Mammy. 'It is hardly worth your while starting.'

I said it would always be a move in the right direction.

With that Daddy and Bertie and Agnes and Mria came in, all red in the face with the cold wind that was blowing. They did not say where they had been, but you would not need to ask for Daddy slammed a hare down on the table.

Mammy screamed, 'Take it out this minute! It will be living with fleas!'

He grabbed it, all abashed, and raced out to the closet with it, then hung it very high up in the roof so that nothing could get at it.

When he came in Mammy said, 'I am sorry I yelled at you, Joe, but I think I would die if we had fleas in the house.'

'That is all right,' said Daddy. 'I should have thought of that. Holy Smoke! I think I have a few.'

'You can keep them,' she said, 'I would not ask you for a share. Where did you get that?'

'I fell over it going up a field,' he said, 'It knew it was meant for us, so it waited.'

'It is very welcome,' said Mammy. 'When it has been hung and jugged and smothered in onions, it will be a change.'

'Would you kick up a row if I bought a bike?' asked Daddy.

'Why would I?' she asked. 'It is your own money and you need something to get to work on. I was thinking it would be handy for the castle, sure you waste half a day getting to the back of the woods. And if ever that fell through, you would have to have one to work for the farmers. How else would you make it to Ballycromkeen? Go ahead and buy it. But how much is it?'

'It is a young fellow has it,' he said. 'He wants money badly. He will take a tenner.'

'Have you that much?' asked Mammy.

'I have,' said Daddy. 'I put a bit by for a pram and things, but then they came by themselves. But it is for you to say if it is a good idea.'

'Well, get the bike,' she said. 'But get a receipt, and make the deal before witnesses. Till my dying day I will never forget Bella Blazer and the pram she sold me for our first one. Never!'

'What did she do, Mammy?' I asked.

'She sold me the pram, and an oul' wreck it was till I cleaned it. And charged me four pounds for it too. When your wee brother died she came down a day or two after and took it back, and told everybody she had only lent it to me. I fixed her! I boned into her in Guinan's one night late, and said, "Either you give me my pram back, or the four pounds I paid for it!" And first she said I never paid the four pounds and then she said she would give me two for it. With that Harry Guinan came out from behind the bar and said to her, "Give Ethel her four pounds, Bella." But she gave a skreigh of a laugh and said, "I will not then!" And he said, very quiet and sad, "Then that finishes you and me, Bella. You'll never darken my door again."'

'And what happened?' I asked Mammy.

Mammy laughed a wee bit. 'Then she pulled up her skirt and took a roll of money out of her stocking, and she gave me my four pounds. Mrs Guinan said, "You're doing well, Bella, is all that yours?" and Bella said, "Aye." But she was mad.'

'I will get a receipt,' said Daddy, 'before I lay a hand on the bike, or he lays hand on my money. Seumas will go with me.'

'Will you go in tonight?' asked Mammy.

'I will,' he replied, 'I had better make sure of her. I will just have time.'

Mammy screwed her face round and looked at the clock, which was lying on its side as usual. 'You will have to shift yourself,' she told him, 'it is a quarter past nine.'

Out he went, and Mammy told us to take our baths. Agnes and Mria and I had our baths in our bedroom, and we had to hurry because it was cold, and keep as quiet as we could because Doreen was lying asleep. But we managed. We went into the kitchen afterwards to get warm and to drink hot cocoa. It felt lovely, sitting at the fire in our pyjamas, with our toes gripping the rug where the fire had warmed it all day.

Mammy said, 'You could call that a good day, now, couldn't you?'

She was right. In one day we had got a granny, and Daddy had caught a hare, and bought a bicycle which he needed very badly. Agnes's dress was finished too. We all waited impatiently until half past ten, when Daddy would be back from Guinan's, to see if he had really got the bike. It sounded too good to be true.

And it was.

He came in all wet with rain and said, 'Well, Ethel, you were right. Seumas knew the wee bastard, and he knew rightly it wasn't his bike at all. He had lifted it off one of the neighbours over in the housing estate on the Dublin Road, past Katie Ganzie's. Seumas says it is a hand-built racer that cost maybe sixty pounds, so he went straight down and told the police on him. He said that the fellow that had it was saving three years for it, and he'd shop the dirty wee thief if it was the last thing he did. He was afraid if he told him to leave it back and only threatened him with the police he might throw it in the river and ruin it, and the boy that owned it would be no better off. So Constable McGarry went down, and lifted him and the bike on suspicion, so nobody gets the bike till they settle who it belongs to. I should have known! I should have known!'

There was a smell of drink off him but he was not drunk, only cross. Also he was disappointed. He could not help it.

We all went to bed. When I was saying my prayers I asked God to get my Daddy a bicycle, because he needed one pretty badly.

Also you do not need a licence to ride a plain bike, and it is just as well because if he had one likely that would be endorsed too.

DECEMBER

An awful thing happened in school today.

Mrs Carpenter has double-pneumonia so we had a new teacher who does not know our names. He is a nice man and his name is John Sanderson. He was asking us who we were so that he would get the roll marked.

When it was my turn Dennis Barkley shouted out, 'She is Frances Skeffington and her Daddy and Mammy are not married and there are ten of them.'

I said, 'My name is Frances Jane Brody.'

'Thank you, Frances,' said Mr Sanderson.

When he got to Dennis Barkley and Dennis had answered, Mr Sanderson said, 'Now, you have not replied fully. Just say, "My name is Dennis Barkley and I have a long tongue and no manners and I am a disgrace to my mother and father."'

Dennis had to say it whether he would or not. Mr Sanderson did not offer to hit him, or send him to the headmaster, or anything. He just looked at him as if here was a wee insect he had found. I must say he shut Dennis up, but the deed was done, because all the class heard him. At break-time I heard them talking about me and it was not easy to let on I had not heard them.

After dinner-time I went and got Agnes and we mitched. We had never done it before and it felt very wicked. Also, we were afraid Granny would see us and stop us.

Agnes did not know what was said till I told her, and by the time we were home she was crying and I nearly was. Mammy was lying down for a rest while wee James had his nap, and she was amazed to see us and not one bit pleased. But when she heard why we had come she was absolutely raging. She rolled off the bed and sat up. I put her shoes on for her because she was groping for them with her feet.

'Take a hold of wee James,' she said, 'till I get my coat. I am going to the telephone.' She got her purse and set off across the Iron Bridge.

I wondered who she was telephoning and what she was saying to them. It took her half an hour, though the telephone-box was only at the other end of the Iron Bridge.

When she came back she was out of breath and red in the face. I made her a cup of tea as soon as I saw her coming. Wee James never stirred. I had left him upstairs with the blanket over him.

Mammy asked Agnes, 'How old are you?'

'I am eleven and a half,' replied Agnes.

'That is old enough,' said Mammy. She stood on the chair, took down the tin box and opened it. She lifted out a lot of papers, then gave one to me and said, 'Read that out loud.'

I read it. It was involved, but I made out that it was a divorce paper, for Joseph Brody v. Martha Brody, nee McKibbin, and Argue Williams (undefended), and a lot more.

'What is this?' I asked. It was too difficult for me to read, let alone understand.

'It is your Daddy's divorce from Martha,' said Mammy, impatiently. 'Read that,' she said, and snapped the divorce paper from me and gave me another one.

It was much simpler. It said that Joseph Brody married Ethel Skeffington on the 21st January 1952. I was very glad. Never mind if it made Dennis Barkley a liar. I had been worried myself since Martha had come down on us, in case maybe what she had said was true. I had no way of knowing until now.

'Mammy,' I asked, 'may we look at the rest of these papers?'

She was going to say No, but then she relented. 'I will just finish my rest,' she said, and started to go upstairs. 'Be careful not to damage them, won't you.'

So we opened them all out and really studied them.

That was the first time I saw my own birth certificate. I was amazed. Because my full name was Frances Jane Van Alstyne Brody. Agnes was Agnes Elizabeth Brody, Mria was Mariana, Bertie was Robert Roy, Doreen was Doreen Alexandra, Alec was Alexander David, Mervyn was Mervyn Skeffington Brody, but

George and wee James were just themselves. And Hector's birth and death certificates were there. It was perfectly thrilling, to see all of us written down and accounted for, as if we were part of history. If I could get a piece of paper wide enough I would try to draw our family tree.

When Mammy came down from her rest we were quite calm again. We all made some tea and ate a soda scone each. Wee James wanted to go out to play so at the last Agnes took him for a walk to John Finlay's.

John Finlay has promised to get Mammy some cheap remnants from the mill so that she can make patchwork quilts. She was to send and fetch them and he would tell her how much they cost. Mammy says that if she makes and sells quilts first she should be able to buy us a blanket or two for the winter. The cold is always worse after Christmas so she is in a hurry to get started. There is a shop in the town that will pay her thirty shillings for each one, and they will provide the backing. I do not know if this is good or not, but Mammy says it will do for a start.

'Are you satisfied?' asked Mammy, gathering up the papers and tidying them away into the tin box, which she put back on the high shelf.

'I am, thank you,' I said. 'But Mammy, it was so shameful.'

'I have shut Master Barkley's mouth for him,' said Mammy. 'Never ask me how. I have rung the school and they will say nothing to you for mitching. You were not right to come home the way you did, but it will not happen again. If you are faced with something that is too much for you to handle yourself, come and tell me or your Daddy about it.'

'Here are the wee ones coming from the school,' I said.

'Oh, good,' she said. She took the buttermilk can and sixpence, and handed them to Alec.

He knew what to do and where to go without being told. He hit his knee when he fell on the steps two or three days ago and it is still bandaged. Mammy thought at the time he had put out his kneecap, but he was never unable to walk, so it cannot have been that. Anyhow, we did not think it odd that he was not back for some time. It was about half-three when he went, and on account of his knee we did not expect he would be back much before four-fifteen, but five came and he was never back. I could not stand the look on Mammy's face so I said I would go and get him. I knew she was afraid that something might have happened to him.

I would have given five shillings just then to see my Daddy coming in, but of course he was at work. I ran all the way to French's but I did not see Alec on the path. When I found him standing in Mrs French's kitchen I was so mad at him I could have killed him for frightening Mammy and all of us.

But before I could light on him for it old Mrs French said, 'Do not scold the child, it is just that I was so busy I could not get him the buttermilk.'

I whirled around to see where she was, and she was in the wee room off the kitchen where there is a sink and another stove, and she was killing hens as fast as she was able. She took their feet in one hand and their necks in the other, and pulled in a certain way until their necks clicked. They kicked for a couple of seconds but she said that they were already dead but were slow to catch on. She is only a wee woman so it was a long stretch for her arms, but she was very good at it.

She turned around to me and said, 'Catch this one's feet for me will you. I declare he is a yard when he is stretched.'

The rooster was a Jersey Black Giant and he was very nearly as big as she was.

When she and I had pulled its neck she said to me, 'If your Mammy would like a sitting job there are thirty-eight hens to be plucked and dressed for tomorrow morning. With the milking to do I can't do them in the morning so I have to do them now and I am clean beat.'

'Where is Maurice?' asked Alec accusingly. He should not have asked but he is too wee to know better.

'He is away up at the other farm,' said Mrs French. 'A cow got cut on barbed wire and made an awful mess of herself. I keep telling him to marry some big strong lump of a girl that has been through Loughry and knows her stuff, I am persecuted with work and getting past it.'

With that Daddy came in and told us to clear off home. The last

I saw of him he was reaching for a hen and ripping a handful of feathers out of it, a dead one of course.

I carried the can and Alec carried Daddy's torch. When we reached home I told Mammy about the plucking. She mixed the pancake batter and left me to put them on the griddle, then went up to French's. This time the pancakes were all right, only not very round, in fact they were all shapes, but they tasted all right. Agnes sprinkled sugar on them and I put them on the plates and Mria suggested that we should eat them with knives and forks because it would be tidier.

Well, that was a mercy, because who should come to the door but the clergyman who had come the time Hector was drowned. I knew his voice at once although I had not seen him. He looked just the way I thought he would, tall and thin and with a red face and glasses and a nice smile. I would not say he was young or handsome, he was too bony, but you could like him. If Mria had not had that idea about the knives and forks we would have been creesh and sugar to the eyebrows and elbows. Instead there we all were, sitting up with our knives and forks, like the quality.

It was I who went to the door, and I just stood looking at him. I was dumbfounded.

'Good evening,' he said to me. 'Is your father in?'

'Good evening, sir,' I said, because I was not sure what to call him. 'Won't you please come in and take a chair? Daddy and Mammy are out but they should be back quite soon.'

'Do they often leave you alone in the house?' he asked.

'Never,' I said. 'One or the other is always about, and sometimes Mrs McFarland looks after the wee ones. But tonight they had to go and help Mrs French pluck hens. Would you like a cup of tea or a pancake? The pancakes are all right, it was Mammy who mixed them before she left.'

'I would be very grateful for a cup of tea,' he said.

I made one for him, thank God the cup matched the saucer.

'Thank you,' he said, and took a drink of it and looked relieved.

Likely he thought it would be bad tea, but it was not, for Mammy says I make good tea.

He looked around at us and smiled and said, 'Would you not

tell me your names?'

I told him our names and then remembered that wee James was in bed, Mammy had bathed him and put him up while I was fetching Alec. He told us that his name was Hamilton, and that it was a funny thing but his name was George too. Our George was sitting on his knee by this time. I was mortified at George, but what could I do when the minister put him there and George liked it?

I was also afraid that some of the wee ones would not know any better than to call the minister George to his face, so I said, 'Mr Hamilton, isn't your church the grey one at the corner?'

'It is,' he said, 'and I would like to see you all there one of these days.'

'We could not come just yet,' I said. 'It is only lately that we have some clothes fit to come to church in. But the boys have no suits and we have no hats yet. Mammy will manage it somehow, she always does.'

'Would you like to come to Sunday School and learn about God?' asked Mr Hamilton.

'We know about God,' I said, 'Mammy teaches us every Sunday.'

'What does she teach you?' asked Mr Hamilton quickly.

He did not sound very pleased. I could not understand why. He should have been.

I did not know what to say, but George was already telling him.

'Not to be bad to wee cats and rabbits and mouses,' he said. 'They are only pets.'

'Not to tell lies,' said Mria, 'or you will be found out. And even if nobody says anything to you, you will look a fool.'

'Not to take things from other folks,' said Bertie. 'It would do you no good, because it would be took off you again somehow, some time.'

'That is very true,' said Mr Hamilton.

He was wrong there. A thing is either true or not true. It can't be half true or very true. Mrs Carpenter pointed that out to me and I understand it.

Bertie said, 'If you see a man needing help with a job, you

should help. You might need help yourself sometime.'

'What do you do on Sundays?' asked Mr Hamilton.

'In the mornings we learn scripture and Mammy asks us questions,' replied Agnes.

'What is meant by blessed are the meek, for they shall inherit the earth?' asked Mr Hamilton.

'In the end all the countries with atom bombs will kill each other, and the people who were not fighting will be left,' I said.

'But if the atom bombs poison the world for those who are left?' asked Mr Hamilton. He said it very quietly.

I thought before I spoke. Then I said, 'Even if there is nothing left but a grain of dust, it will be enough for God to start over again and make more people.'

Mr Hamilton said nothing at all and looked at me a bit surprised. I was surprised too. I never thought of it before.

Then he asked us if we could say any psalms, and he was listening to Mervyn saying psalm one when I thought I heard feet on the balcony.

I darted to the door, opened it and said, 'Daddy, Mr Hamilton is here.'

Mammy whipped off her old apron, dropped it on the balcony and kicked it away up past Lyle's door. Then they both came in and shook hands.

'I was just going to see you one of these days,' said Mammy. 'I made you a promise and I am sticking to it, but things are not too easy.'

'You have some very remarkable children,' said Mr Hamilton. 'Do you know they are not even worried about the end of the world?'

'Why would they be?' asked Mammy, laughing a wee bit, and sitting down. 'I am not very good at putting it into words for them, for I have not much education, but it is all written.'

'It is,' said Mr Hamilton. 'I came here prepared to argue, but I know when I have met my match. You make me quite ashamed that I doubted what upbringing they were getting. I believe the difficulty is hats?'

Mammy turned a look at me that made me nearly get under the

table. I felt about two inches high. She would not warm my ear in front of anybody but I was sure she would warm it the minute she got me to herself.

But Mr Hamilton glanced around, then smiled and said, 'What a lot of nice little girls. Do you know I have six nieces in the County Fermanagh, about the same ages as you.'

'Have you not any wee girls of your own?' asked Doreen.

'I have not,' he said.

'That is sad,' said Doreen, all sympathy.

'Well, I will have to wait my turn,' said Mr Hamilton.

Doreen nodded as wise as a wee old woman.

Mammy was standing by, ready to be affronted at her, but you could see that Mr Hamilton did not mind Doreen's questions.

However, Mammy looked at the clock and said, 'It is very late, away to your beds, the lot of you.'

So we went.

Our door when it is shut has a crack at the edge through which you can hear all that is going on in the kitchen even if you cannot see it, so I lay and listened until I fell asleep. Mr Hamilton seemed to get on the very best with Mammy and Daddy and I was very pleased.

On the next Saturday a big light parcel came for Mammy, and when she opened it there were four hats in it. They were all felt ones and different colours. Agnes and I had our school coats and we got the red hat and the blue one. Mria was to have my old light-blue coat and the mustard hat, and Doreen had a new coat, a pink one, and her hat nearly matched it.

So we four went to Sunday School and I liked it. Bertie and the boys could not go that Sunday, but before the next Sunday Mammy made a push and got them suits, it was no easy matter, but she did it. So that Sunday we all went to morning Sunday School and evening church, and that night after evening church there was such a spread at our house as never was because Mr Hamilton came and babtized us, from wee James to me, and gave us our proper names. Mrs McFarland and Joe Cooper and Mrs French came, and Maurice and Granny and Albert Dunwoody, because he is a church elder. Granny does not belong to our church but she came anyway. They all drank cups of tea but did not eat much, although Mammy had made sandwiches and a cake. I did not eat much myself, I was too excited.

I never knew till lately that I was Frances Jane Van Alstyne Brody.

Well, going to church has made a difference already, because this week Mrs Carpenter asked us to write about our church, and what would I have done if I had never been in it? One of the girls had to write that she had no church, her daddy is a Belfast man and he is an agnostic. I do not know what that is but it sounds bad to me. He will not let her or her mother go to church.

She said to me coming out of the school gate, 'What were you writing? I could not think of anything.'

'About our church,' I said, by-the-way I was amazed.

'But you do not go to church either,' she said, all surprised.

'I beg your pardon,' said Agnes, 'but we go to Cribben Church. So there.'

The girl's feelings were hurt and she would not even walk up the road with us, it was a pity because I was getting to like her.

Agnes has improved a lot this year and she is nicer to me and not so curious, but she can still cut an inch before the point, and that was one of the times.

The Christmas holidays began the Thursday before Christmas, and this year we will have something to remember, because Mrs French is sending us a hen, free.

'Is it because of you and Daddy helping with the plucking?' I asked.

'Aye,' said Mammy. 'She was in a quare pickle that night, the poor wee woman. But the cow is all right again and she would not have lived if Maurice had not stayed with her and done all he could till the vet came.'

I have often seen Christmas puddings in Gorman's and wondered what they tasted like. This Christmas we will all know for Mammy has bought two. She has bread ordered in Gorman's to tide us over the holiday, and four swede turnips laid by in our bedroom in a basket. She bought a hundredweight of potatoes from Albert Dunwoody, they are great big ones and your mouth would water thinking about what they will be like baked in the oven with a dab of margarine in them when they split. We are all to get an apple and an orange on Christmas morning, and Daddy has got two pounds of toffees on the high shelf, where we can't get at them until the big day.

Agnes and Bertie and Mria and I wanted to buy something for Mammy and Daddy. Last Christmas was awful, none of us had a ha'penny because we had to give every last one to Mammy to feed us, for Daddy was out of work, he had been out of work for two months. But this Christmas is going to be different.

We had a discussion on Burnt Island about what to buy for Mammy and Daddy. It was a good place for one because nobody could hear us. Bertie said he had saved the money he got from Gorman's for delivering things in the cart he made with the bicycle wheels, he put shafts on it quite some time ago and it is safe enough to steer now. I had saved all I got for doing messages for the soldier's wife. She is expecting again and nothing would tempt her to go over the Stick Bridge in case she falls, but the rest do not know yet, they think it is because she can't be bothered. Every time I go she gives me sixpence. Agnes had about six shillings she has saved from the money she gets for fetching water for Mrs McFarland and Old Joe Cooper, and Mria had half a crown. Now that Agnes and I are at the Intermediate, the master and Mrs Conlan get her to do things like cleaning the blackboard for a week, that is sixpence, or clearing out a cupboard, that is a shilling, or going across to Mrs Henry's to pay for the master's dinners, that only happens once a month but it is always another sixpence.

'We must get Mammy a hat,' said Mria, 'so that she can come to church along with us.'

Bertie and I just glanced at each other. We know rightly that Mammy will not be in church until after the baby is born, but Mria is not old enough to figure that out for herself.

'A nice warm scarf for each of them,' said Agnes. 'Daddy does be out in the cold all the time, and Mammy should take care of her chest.'

173

'What does a scarf cost?' asked Bertie.

'We could get one in Woolworth's for not very much,' I said, 'but we would be paying four bus fares to go and get them. It would waste five shillings and more. It is impossible for us all to go. I think Bertie should be the one, he has the most money.'

'I could not pick the things,' said Bertie.

'Well, we will have to do something quick,' I said. 'There is not much time left. We only have tomorrow, and then it is Christmas.'

We went home very soberly and thought about everything we could think of, but could not come to any conclusion. Daddy was out. When he came in the first things I saw were his boots, they were good enough once, but he had had them a long time and when he took them off his socks were soaking. I looked at Agnes and Bertie to see if they were thinking what I was thinking, and they seemed to be. Bertie waited till Daddy went up the stairs, and then followed him up. I heard him asking Daddy what he thought Mammy would like for Christmas. I dashed over and picked up Daddy's boot and looked at the size, it was eight. Then I started to stuff it with newspaper, that is the only way to dry a wet boot from the inside.

Bertie came down the stairs and said, 'Daddy says never mind what she would like, buy her two pairs of tights.'

Agnes and I both yelled '*What?*' but he said it was true. Daddy told him that Mammy had pains in her knees with the cold, and she would just love warm stretch tights. And he said to remember and get the biggest size of stretch ones. It was the last thing I would ever have thought of, because Mammy never wears stockings, winter or summer, but I was glad Bertie had thought to ask.

'What are we going to get Daddy?' asked Mria.

'A good pair of rubber or vinyl boots,' I said. 'Look at this, did you ever see worse?'

They saw what I meant.

'When can we go?' I added, to Bertie.

'Daddy says you are to go,' he said. 'And I am not sorry. I could not go into a shop for weemin's tights.'

'I do not care,' I said. 'How much money have we?'

We counted it out on the kitchen table, and there was three

174

pounds four shillings and twopence of Bertie's, and six and six of mine, and six shillings of Agnes's, and Mria's half-crown. It was four pounds, all but tenpence.

'What will I do if I have any over?' I asked.

'Get what you think for the rest of us,' said Bertie.

I was waiting opposite Gorman's for the bus into the town when a car stopped and a policeman offered me a lift. I would not take a lift with a strange man but a policeman is all right.

But here wasn't it the same policeman as stopped us in Ballycromkeen, the day Daddy said his name was Rafferty. I did not know where I was sitting, but I never let on. That day I was like a tramp because we had only been working, but today I had on my school coat and shoes, good grey knee-socks, a red tammie on my head and navy blue gloves my granny knitted for me. I decided I knew nothing about that other time, because how could I if that wasn't me?

'Has your daddy still got that truck?' asked the policeman.

'Not at all,' I said. 'He has not had a truck in ages.'

'Are you ever in Ballycromkeen?' he asked next.

'We have a moss in Cranee,' I replied. 'It takes me all my time getting as far as that, never mind Ballycromkeen, why it is miles.'

'Come off it, Dolores,' he said, 'I know who you are.'

'My name is not Dolores,' I said. 'It is Frances Jane Van Alstyne Brody.'

'Do you tell me that?' he said. 'I was sure it was Dolores. It was Dolores the last time we met.'

'I do not think I have ever met you,' I said, looking at him seriously. 'Are you not mixing me up with somebody else? There is Dolores Lennon at our school, she is older than me.'

'Dolores Rafferty,' he said.

I let on to be thinking, but I was scared. 'You should ask my sister,' I said. 'There is no Dolores but the one I know, but maybe she knows another one, she is in a different class.'

He looked at me with his piercing eyes. 'Are you sure you are Frances Brody?'

'Of course I am sure,' I asked. 'Ask Mr Hamilton, he babtized me.'

175

'Did he indeed?' he asked, baffled.

I did not know what he was thinking, but that was usual. The police do not mean you to know.

He stopped the car at Woolworth's. I got out and went up the street to Carson's. I bought a pair of wellingtons for Daddy, they were thirty-five shillings, wouldn't the price of things just kill you. I walked around the town for a while till I saw the kind of tights that are warm as well as stretchy, so I went in and asked to see the largest size. They would have fitted a hippopotamus, the girl stretched them to show me. I was well pleased when I heard they were only fifteen and eleven a pair, so I got two pairs of dark green ones. I did not think Mammy would want red or royal blue, and if I took black she would say they were for doing Irish dancing, or getting the old age pension, or something like that. I counted my change carefully, and set aside ninepence for a half-single on the bus home, that left thirteen and three. As I wandered about a bit more I found that the boots made a very heavy parcel. I reached a wee shop that was selling children's clothes very cheap. I could not buy anything else but gloves, so I bought four pairs at three and six each, even so that was my bus fare away. I would just have to walk home.

Well, I had walked it before so I could walk it again. There was a good footpath and the lights were lit already because it was midwinter and getting dark in the middle of the afternoon. I set off up the hill and made short work of the first mile. The boots were not very well tied and I was afraid they would come out of the parcel for they kept slipping. The tights and the gloves were in smaller parcels, and my purse was stone empty so it was no problem. The traffic was particularly heavy and I was wondering how I would cross the road without being hit, the drivers would not be able to see me in my navy coat. I thought it out as I came to Gorman's. Vera Gorman knocked on the inside of the shop window at me so I went in to see what she wanted.

She said her mammy was asleep because she had been sorting mail till four in the morning, and then stayed up to get the breakfast. It is not all fun being a postmistress, I can tell you. But sure there is a catch in everything. Vera had just finished her tea, her daddy was in the post-office part of the shop so she was in charge on the grocery side. Parcels and boxes of mixed groceries sat about all over the place, Bertie would have to deliver them tomorrow, and it Christmas Eve. I could see they were far too many and too heavy for him to take more than a few at a time, even with the cart.

I had an idea. So I asked, 'Would it be all right if Agnes and Mria helped Bertie tomorrow? There seems to be a quare lot still to go and I do not know that he could manage it.'

Vera said she did not know, she would have to ask her mammy, but her daddy had heard her and shouted in that of course it would be all right, the more the better. So that was fixed.

'The traffic is very bad out there,' said Mr Gorman. 'Will you be all right crossing the road?'

'If I had a big bit of newspaper,' I said, 'they would see me and not just drive over me, Mr Gorman.'

'Give her a bit, Vera. Don't let her get killed, there aren't too many like her.'

He is a very solemn man, but he was grinning and I grinned back. Vera gave me a bit of white bread-paper. It had been on the floor and was only for throwing out.

I went out and showed the bit of paper on my arm. Two cars slowed down and let me across half the road. I changed the paper to my other arm and waited. A bus slowed down and let me across the other half of the road, and just with that a car came by like a rocket from behind the bus, if I had still been on the road I would have been minced.

But I wasn't.

I folded up the paper, crept cautiously across the Stick Bridge and quietly into the house. I heard talking upstairs, so I put the parcels under our bed, took off my coat and tammie and gloves, then stood at the fire warming my toes.

Daddy shouted down, 'Is that you, Bertie?'

'No,' I called, 'it is me. Where are the wee ones?'

'They are in Joe Cooper's,' said Daddy, at the top of the stairs. 'Will you to to Mrs Conlan's as quick as you can and ask her to phone for Dr John?'

'Is it for Mammy?' I asked.

'Yes,' he said.

'I am all right,' shouted Mammy to me. 'Do not be frightened. But hurry.'

'Take my torch,' roared Daddy. 'It is in my pocket behind the door.'

Dr John was there in twenty minutes and drove Mammy to the hospital in his own car, he said there might not be any time to waste. Daddy went with them and came back later by himself. The rest had been fetched in and put to bed, Bertie and Agnes and I did that, but we could not go to bed ourselves till Daddy came back because he had gone out and forgotten the door key. He was very quiet and I did not like that. I was anxious already and it made me worse.

About seven in the morning I was lying awake, listening to the wind going eee around the house when there was a knock on the door. I ran to open it. It was Mrs Conlan to say she had just rung the hospital and Mammy was all right and the baby was another boy. We were all very glad. Then she asked us if we could manage the breakfast, so Agnes and I ran in and got dressed and showed her a thing or two. The fire was lighted, the stove brushed and the kettle boiling in about fifteen minutes. I broke up a soft dry peat and set the stove damper the way Mammy does to give it a good start. Agnes spread the plastic cloth, set the table, put out sugar and milk and margarine and a big plate of sliced bread, and I put the pan on while Bertie fetched two buckets of water.

'Well, that's wonderful,' said Mrs Conlan. 'I can see you don't need me at all!' She was all pleased, and the minute Daddy came down she handed him a big parcel. 'That's a few trifles for wee Brody,' she said. She went away quickly and would not wait to explain.

Daddy stood with the parcel in his arms until we made him open it so we would see what was in it. It was full of baby clothes. Likely they had belonged to Mrs Conlan's wee son that died when he was nine months old, I had heard about that but it was before I was born. I knew Mammy had not near enough baby clothes, especially nappies, but there were fourteen in that parcel.

Daddy said, 'I would need to go to the hospital this afternoon, so will yous look after yourselves, and don't catch cold or set the place on fire.'

We said we would.

Agnes remarked, 'If Mammy was here now she would be working at something.'

'It is Christmas Eve,' said Bertie. 'What would she be working at?'

'What is for today's dinner?' asked Mervyn.

'Ha, that's the mystery!' asked Agnes.

'Potatoes and margarine,' I said. 'I have it all planned. We just scrub the potatoes and cut off a thin piece of skin all round each of them, and leave them in the oven until they are ready.'

'That would take hours,' said Agnes, 'and a great baking fire. It would be less bother to boil them.'

I had to agree that she was right. The only thing was, serving them might turn out to be dangerous, because when there are enough potatoes in the pot it is even heavier than you would expect. In fact I am not fond of trying to lift it, because I am afraid my arm might give way and the water scald me or some of the rest of them. But I admitted that roasting the dinner would be very hard on the peats. It is true we have a big peat stack in the garden now, but with Cranee so far away and us not having the lorry any more I could not see how or when we could get more.

'Will we do any cleaning?' asked Mria. 'We might as well. It would pass the time for us.'

'We will make the beds and brush the bedrooms and wash the dishes,' I said, 'and give the lino a lick. After that we will see. There is ironing to do but I am not sure Mammy would like us to try it, you can only destroy something once.'

Doreen was drawing on the windows. 'Our windows are shocking,' she said. 'The soldier's wife cleans hers with spray stuff out of a blue bottle and they shine.'

'Mammy cleans ours with a bit of wet newspaper,' I said. 'and a cloth with the ghost of paraffin oil on it. If I find them for you, would you like to try?'

179

There would be no use in telling Doreen she *had* to clean the windows, she would not do it. So I tried offering to *let* her. And it worked. She got a chair and I damped a bit of paper. She polished away like mad, and finished them off with the rag Mammy kept for them under the wash stand. Of course they were no better cleaned than you would expect, because Doreen is not very big and this was the first time she had ever tried to clean them, but she was happily occupied.

Bertie was all set to go over to Gorman's when I told him that Mr Gorman said to bring the other two as well, and the cart. So away they went, in their polythene coats in case it rained, and their wellingtons. I told them to mind themselves crossing the road because if they were hurt or killed the shock would likely kill Mammy. They said they would be back about one, and that was them away.

Alec's knee still hurt him, but he said we would need peats. He took Mervyn and George and both the Girling buckets and was out for ages. They fetched in enough to last all day.

It takes two of us to make a bed, so Alec and Doreen helped me, and I did the brushing. Mervyn and George and wee James went down to Mrs McFarland's. They wanted to go to Old Cooper's but I would not let them, because it is the day he lifts his pension and he would be wanting to go to the town to do his shopping for the weekend. I saw him go, in his good raincoat, check cap and good brown boots he did not look any older than the master. He is just wonderful.

Everything worked out very well.

I did not have to risk pouring the water off the potatoes because the fire was hotter than I thought and they boiled dry. Mercifully the pot was none the worse, they only stuck to it the least little bit. I never let on to the rest, what they do not know does no harm.

Bertie and Agnes and Mria came in ravenous, although Mr Gorman had given them chewing-gum to help them to concentrate. The four wee ones came up from Mrs McFarland's and said she was going to the town too, and would I go down now and arm her across the Stick Bridge because she wanted to catch the half-one bus? And of course I did. Seumas McCann rides his bike over the Stick Bridge, so it is not as dangerous as you might imagine, but since Mrs McFarland had that toss she is frightened she might get another. I stayed with her till the bus came in sight and then made back home. Bertie and Agnes and Mria were just leaving, then Mria made us all laugh by saying she was on the two to ten shift.

'It is not as bad as that,' said Bertie. 'Mr Gorman will not let us go on after dark. He says that whatever is left then he will take round in his car. So that only gives us about three hours more.'

I was relieved when I heard that. I would not like them out after dark either, particularly with Daddy not her to stop them.

I was just clearing up after the dinner, and putting a fire on, when I heard a timid knock at the door. Wee James went and opened it. There stood Mrs McCann.

'Are you able to manage?' she asked me.

I said I was, but that I would appreciate a bit of advice tomorrow for a hen was coming and I did not know what to do with it. We never had a hen before. Mrs McCann said she would come up and show me when the time came, and I was satisfied. She is nearly as quiet as her husband, but when she says she will do a thing you can rely on her. I was glad she came, because all I know about hens is that you take out their insides and throw some away and keep the rest, but which is which I have no notion. It will need to go on very early in the day in case there is an accident or the fire goes out, with Mammy away anything could happen. I said a short prayer that I would have wit enough to get the better of the emergency. Then I felt better. I began to remember what Mammy had said. We were to have boiled fowl, roasted and boiled potatoes, stuffing and boiled swedes. I knew how to roast potatoes, and I had seen Mammy boiling swedes in the same pot with peeled potatoes, so that was all right. It was the stuffing that had me beaten. Then it occurred to me that the directions were likely on the packet, so I stood on a chair and looked in the cupboard for the packet of stuffing, and there it was. In fact it would be easy. Then I remembered we had only the one pie dish, and the roast potatoes would be in it. I examined all our pots and pans to see if I could get anything that would stand being in the hot oven, and sure I had forgotten a brown dish about eight inches across that was the remains of a wee enamel frying-pan. I remembered us using it at the cottage, only the handle came off later, and Mammy had been keeping washing-soda in it for a long time.

I got a porridge oats carton and emptied the washing-soda into that, then took the dish and a cloth and the tin of scouring-powder to the pump. When I came back in it was clean I can tell you! And that was how that problem was settled.

I was as worried as could be on Christmas Day itself, but everything seemed to happen without any trouble. The hen arrived without its feathers and with the insides you keep in a bowl, all washed and ready. Mrs French came with it herself. She was all surprised when she heard we had a new brother, and sent Mammy her best wishes. I think she got an eye-opener at how comfortable we were. The last time she was up was while Hector was still alive. Today the floor was washed, I had had another go at the windows, there was a good fire on and plenty of peats in. Agnes and Mria had stayed in to help me, but Daddy had heard what we were going to do and made sure I knew how, then he took the rest for a walk so that we would have peace to get on with it. Mrs French could not stop, but no sooner was she away than Mrs McCann came up, and together we put the hen in our big black pot with water and salt and chopped leeks from her garden. Mrs McCann said a taste of barley would improve matters if I knew where Mammy kept it. I had it out of the cupboard in a second and she put in twice what would lie on her hand. It did not look very much.

She said, 'If you put in more you would be having a sort of porridge instead of soup, Frances. Too much barley is worse than not enough. Now,' she went on, 'do not let him be lepping in the pot or he will be boiled to rags. Just keep a medium fire, or else push the pot a wee bit to the side. You are a great girl to be helping with the dinner like this. Your Mammy has you well reared, and that is a fact. And don't you work too hard, love. If you get stuck with anything, run down and ask me, I am not busy and it will be no trouble. Where are the potatoes?'

'They are in the oven,' I replied, 'I am roasting them. The turnips and potatoes are in this pot and we will put them on at a quarter to twelve, I think. This dish is for the stuffing.'

'Oh but you are wise!' she said.

I was surprised. Agnes and Mria looked interested.

'Why?' I asked.

'Why did you not put it in the bird?' asked Mrs McCann.

'I could not do it,' I replied, 'I do not know how. And it said on the packet that you could make stuffing in the oven fifteen minutes before the meal was to be served.'

'Tell your Mammy you are as wise as a wee old woman,' she said. 'the whole three of you!'

'Oh, Mrs McCann,' cried Agnes as she turned to to, 'what do you do with a pudding? We have two wrapped in paper and stone cold. How do you heat them?'

'I will lend you my steamer,' she said, and hurried away.

I thought she was crying. I wondered what she could be crying about. After a short time she came up with a thing like two saucepans, I had seen one of these in school but nobody had said what it was for.

'You put water in the bottom and have it boiling,' she told me. 'Then put the pudding in the top. Just give them a small slice each, it is very rich and more would only give them sore stomachs for the rest of the day. You had better pour milk on it, you have your hands full without making custard.'

I went out to the balcony with her and asked, 'Is anything, wrong, Mrs McCann?'

She looked at me and said, 'It is Christmas again and Nuala has not even sent me a card. Never you treat your mother like that, no matter what she does on you. It is not fair. You be good to your Mammy, Frances. Let nothing and nobody come between you.'

'I will not,' I said. 'Thank you very much for the steamer, Mrs McCann. I would love to do something for you, so if there is anything you want done, would you let me know?'

That is what Mammy says if she is obliged to somebody.

After that, all I had to do was keep the fire up and wait.

183

The dinner was grand, Daddy said so. We all got enough, and there was even some left. George wanted to take something to the kitten, so I gave him a little bit of hen skin, and he said the kitten thought it was a mouse and killed it twice before it would eat it. He did not stay down for long because we had him well warned to come back so we could give Daddy his new boots. Daddy did not even know we had a present for him.

Mervyn looked to see if George was coming. The snow had started. Everybody looked out of the window for a moment. While they were doing that I crept into our room to bring out the boots and the other parcels. When Daddy turned round from watching the snow fall there was this parcel on his chair.

'Where did that come from?' he asked.

'Santa brought it,' replied Bertie.

'Is it for wee James?' asked Daddy.

'No,' we said.

Wee James got four presents, a plastic car from Daddy, a book from Mrs Conlan, a wee spade from Mrs McFarland, and a trumpet from Old Joe Cooper.

'Is it for George?' asked Daddy.

'No,' we said.

George got a monkey on strings from Daddy, a box of puzzles from Mrs Conlan, and a velvet toy kitten from Old Joe Cooper.

'Is it for Mervyn?' asked Daddy.

'No,' we said.

For Mervyn got *five* books, three from Mrs McFarland and two from Mrs Conlan, all in good big print, and a pair of knitted gloves from Mrs French, I do not know why.

'Is it for the twins?' asked Daddy.

'No,' we said. We were sort of laughing and trying not to laugh, and squeaking with joy. Us four older ones, that is, the wee ones were not in on the secret.

The twins had got new coats for church, that had to be their present, and thank God they never seem to want much. They were well pleased with their coats, they wore them last Sunday. I never knew for years that twins are supposed to be like one another, ours aren't, but they are great friends.

184

'Well, is it for Mria?' asked Daddy.

'No,' we said.

Mria began to laugh. She explained afterwards that she was thinking what she would look like walking into school in size eight wellingtons.

'Is it for Bertie?' asked Daddy.

I could see he was getting puzzled and a wee bit anxious.

'No,' we said.

'Is it for Agnes?' he asked.

'No,' we said.

'Is it for you?' he asked me.

'No,' I replied, 'it is not.'

'Is it for your Mammy?' he asked, uneasily.

I could see he was afraid we had done some bad thing. I thought it was time to end the joke, so I gave him the parcel with the tights and said, 'This is for Mammy, but the parcel on the chair is for you, Daddy.'

He looked at Bertie. Bertie got red in the face and had nothing to say.

He opened the big parcel, and at first he could not speak. Then he looked at us very sharply and asked, 'Is this paid for?'

'Everything is,' I said. 'Are they the right size?'

'Size eight?' he asked, dreamily, looking at the boots.

'Yes,' I said.

'And what did you get for your Mammy?' he asked. He slid his old boots off and pulled the new ones on, tucking the legs of his drainpipes down into them.

'We got her two pairs of dark green stretch tights,' I told him. 'And there was money over, so we got gloves for the wee ones. Last winter they only had old socks on their hands.'

'What makes you think the tights would fit your Mammy?' he asked. 'She is a lot of woman you know.'

'They would fit a hippopotamus,' I said. 'I made the girl in the shop stretch them sideways before I could decide.'

Daddy looked at us as if he did not believe his eyes. 'Tell me this,' he said, 'where did you get that much money?'

'We earned it,' said Bertie. 'Gorman's gave me fifteen shillings

185

a week and I worked five weeks and a bit. The rest did messages and saved up.'

Daddy just gathered a bunch of us into his arms and said nothing. The ones he could not catch sort of burrowed into the heap until they were next to him. He did not say a word, but it felt just lovely.

It was time to visit the hospital. He took the parcel with the tights, and Mrs Conlan's parcel, and me. He told the rest that Agnes was in charge, and not to spoil the day by being bad, and off we went. The snow as only about an inch deep and we both had wellingtons.

'Daddy,' I said, when we were away from the house, 'when I was waiting for the bus yesterday a policeman gave me a lift. I think he was the one that stopped us in Ballycromkeen in the lorry and you said your name was Rafferty. He asked was I Dolores Rafferty and I said no. But he was suspicious.'

'If we come across him again,' said Daddy, 'don't you speak. Leave the talking to me.'

I was ready and willing to let him do the talking. The police are the boys to have the truth out of you if you don't watch yourself.

It was just as well I had remembered to warn Daddy, because a police car drew up nearly immediately, and a voice said, 'Well if it isn't Mr Rafferty.!'

'Where?' asked Daddy, glancing back at the Stick Bridge, then looking in the car.

'Is your name not Rafferty?' asked the policeman, all surprised.

'It is not,' said Daddy. 'My name is Brody. What is yours?'

'Do you know a Con Rafferty?' asked the policeman.

'I do not,' said Daddy at once.

I knew he was telling lies but he was so good at it you had to admire him.

'Are you going to the town?' asked the policeman. 'Would you take a lift?'

'We are,' said Daddy. 'My wife is in hospital and we are just taking her a few things. Thank you kindly for the lift.'

'About Rafferty,' said the policeman as we drove off, 'would he be a man resembling yourself now?'

186

'How would I know?' asked Daddy.

There was a thoughtful pause. Then the policeman asked, 'Have you a lorry?'

'You're joking,' said Daddy. 'I have not the time, even if I had the price of one.'

'You're working then?' asked the policeman.

'Aye, hard and sore, with ten of them at home,' said Daddy, 'there is no rest for the wicked. Were you wanting Rafferty?'

'No, no,' said the policeman, very off-handed, 'I was just asking.'

We walked the rest of the way to the hospital. It wanted some minutes to visiting-time, but the sister let us in. Mammy was lying propped on a pillow with her red cardigan on and a red ribbon in her hair. She looked just lovely. I could not help it, I went and hugged her, and she hugged me so hard she squeezed all my breath out and I said 'Uh!' Both of them laughed at me. We gave her the parcels and she said she would have the tightest tights in Ireland until she got her figure back and lost a bit of weight.

'What are you going to call the baby?' I asked.

'Noel,' she replied. 'Because he was a Christmas present. And I would like to name him for the black doctor, he is just great, he stayed with me all night.'

'I will prosecute him,' said Daddy, pretending to be angry.

Mammy gave a loud laugh and said, 'I will go farther than that, Joe, last night I would rather have had him than you! You are able for a lot of things but last night you would have been licked.'

'I know,' he said. 'God, but I am glad you are all right, Ethel. The world would not be the same place without you. What is the doctor's name, Sambo?'

'Don't be so bloody ignorant!' she said before she could stop herself. 'Oh, Joe, you are making me mad at you already, and he is a real gentleman. He could have gone to his bed and left me with the sister, but he did not because he could see I was frightened.'

And with that in came the black doctor. I had seen him before, because he was the one who wrote on the plaster DO NOT TOUCH the time I broke my arm. He did not look very happy. He is very dark but not black, and has brown eyes and is taller than Daddy.

187

'Hello,' said Daddy to him. 'Are you the doctor that looked after my wife here?'

He said he was.

'We would like to thank you for the trouble you took looking after her when things were not going too well. And if you would not mind we would like to call the baby after you, if you would write your name down so that we would know how to spell it,' said Daddy.

I knew all the time the doctor would like that, and I was right.

He printed his name on a prescription paper, and that was how I knew it was Douzenkamp. It was an odd name but I liked it.

'It gets no easier,' said Mammy suddenly. 'And you lost your night's sleep. I am sure you were disgusted with me.'

'Not at all,' said the doctor politely. 'Babies do not recognise the eight-hour day.' He gave a sort of little smiling nod and went away.

I think he had forgotten what he came for.

'We can't stay long,' said Daddy. 'The wee ones are at home. This one and the next two cooked as good a dinner as ever I tasted, with a bit of help from Mrs McCann. I never thought she would come up, for you know she is that shy.'

And I told them what she had told me about Nuala.

Mammy said to me, 'Go out of that door and down the hall. There you will find a phone on a shelf and a directory hanging by it. Look up Garvey, 18 Castlemain Avenue, and write down the number. Then come back here and I will tell you what to do next.'

'Mind, now, Ethel,' said Daddy uneasily.

'I do not care,' said Mammy. 'Both of them think it is the other that is holding out.'

When I came back from looking up the number, Mammy had a sixpence in her hand. She told me how to dial, and what to say.

I went down the hall and set the sixpence in the groove while I spread out the paper so that I would not dial the wrong number. It was an old-fashioned phone, you dialled first and pushed button A when the other person answered. In my reciting voice I said, 'Is that Mrs Nuala Garvey, please?' When she said 'Yes', I went on, 'Will you please go to your mother at once. Please go to your mother at once. She is at her own home.' Then I hung up.

'You did that to perfection,' said Mammy. 'Bette Davis had better watch herself. Do not ever let on it was you who rang or me who thought of it. Mrs McCann would not like it.'

'We will have to go,' said Daddy. 'We have been here far too long as it is. You will be tired out and I will get my head on my hand from the sister.'

'Well, goodbye for now,' she said. 'And mind that wee James does not get the cold.'

'I will,' I said.

We caught the bus back home, and arrived just in time to save the fire from going out. We had a simple tea, because we had had such a good dinner that none of us wanted much. Daddy and Doreen washed the dishes and we all sat round the fire with the light out, telling stories. Daddy can tell stories that would make you laugh if you were dying. You should hear him telling The Three Bears like this.

Once upon a time there were three bears. Two of them should have had either more sense, or more wee bears. They used to go for a walk in the woods every day and the wee bear was bored stiff, he was aye wheenging to be carried, or getting left behind, or tripping on things. One day when they were out a wee girl called Goldilocks called at their house. Her bin was always full of empty peroxide bottles. She was as curious as a cat so she went into their house to see what they had for their breakfast. She tried it and said, 'EUGH!' She tried the next plate and said, 'EUGH!' She tried the third plate and if she had any sense she would have said, 'EUGH!' again, but she could not decide if it was for pasting wallpaper or cleaning the knives, so she ate it to find out. Then she went up to see if they had fitted carpet in the bedrooms and they had, so she tried the beds to see if they were Dunlopillo or inner-sprung and they were all as hard as washboards, so they cannot have had mattresses at all. Not a bit put about she lay down and fell asleep. And that was where the bears found her when they came home. Forget all that cod about who's been eating my dinner and who's been sleeping in my bed. The biggest bear raced to the cupboard and got a stick and stood guard over her while the second bear phoned for the police, and she got eighteen months' jail for breaking and entering, trespass and petty larceny.

He did not always tell it exactly like that, sometimes he finished with Goldilocks and the bears dancing the tango. He would get up and act them and you would have done yourself an injury laughing at him.

When we had done laughing Daddy said we could sing carols and he would get the tea for once. The curtains still were not drawn and the sky outside was a deep rich blue with white falling snow coming down. We were singing 'See amid the winter's snow' at the time. I felt the way I did that night in Cranee when I saw a star come out. I was so happy I nearly cried. Altogether it was a lovely Christmas.

We managed as best we could without Mammy, but it was hard enough work, and Daddy appreciated it, because on the Saturday before the New Year he took us for a walk to Cranee and back. Mria did not want to come and Alec and Doreen thought it would be too far. Besides they had a mysterious date with Mrs Henessey. So in the end the wee ones went down to Mrs French and Old Joe Cooper, and it was only Bertie and Agnes and me who went to Cranee.

The snow did not lie for even a full day and it had rained all the rest of the week, so when we reached the bog at Cranee we found that the bank we had worked on first had fallen down and filled in the pool under it. The pool could not have been bottomless at all or one bank slipping would not have filled it. The fallen loam was filled with bits of bog fir and some big dark thing like the trunk of a tree. It was about six feet long. I was turning away when I saw the edge of it, it was hard like leather and there was something hanging out of it. I could not speak. I reached out and caught Daddy's sleeve, and hung on. Because I was afraid.

'What is it?' he asked.

'Look at it,' I said. 'It has a hand. Oh, Daddy, I am frightened of it.'

'Stay you and I will see what it is,' he said.

We stayed. I do not know about the others but I would not have gone one step forward for a pension of ten pounds a minute. Daddy went to the thing, it was green with the wet and nearly as long as his leg, got down on his knees and pushed back the wrapping. Because it was all wet it came away easily. A bit of rush-coloured cloth like what meal bags are made of broke off and fell on the edge of the water. It was quiet, quiet, there was nothing but bog and sky and us for miles.

After a while Daddy laid the cover back, then came to us and said, 'It is nothing to be afraid of. It is somebody who was buried in the bog a long time ago. He had a sword.'

'As old as that?' asked Bertie. His voice sounded very wee.

'As old as that,' said Daddy, and turned to me. 'You saw him first. What do you want to do about it? Will we tell the police, or Mr Hamilton, or nobody? Will we take his sword and his brooch, or will we not?'

'Could you not just hap him in the earth again and then let him alone?' I asked. 'He did not think when he was buried there that we would dig him up and be ignorant with his remains. I would not like to take anything from him. Oh, Daddy, supposing it was you, if you had been killed in the desert.'

'How long was the sword?' asked Bertie. 'Was it iron or bronze?'

'I suppose it was bronze,' said Daddy, climbing to the top of the bank and kicking down big sods or turf till the parcel was covered.

'He was a Norseman,' said Bertie. 'I knew they came up the Bann, about a thousand years ago, but I never thought they would have come this far. The master told us about them. I would have liked a Norseman's sword, but I would not have it in the house for any money.'

'Good,' said Daddy.

Everything was buried again, but I will not forget that bony black hand until the day I die.

Daddy stepped back and put his left hand on my shoulder, then stood facing the fallen bank and saluted. He said nothing more, and neither did we.

About half-way home, he said to us, 'Tell nobody. They would not understand. They would come up from all about and spoil our moss and dig him up and take his brooch and his sword. Even if you only told the master he would have the boys down from the university, and before you knew where you were they would have him whipped away and stuck in a museum. If he was here, and old enough to fight, he might have been married to a local girl, and left a family behind him when he died. For all you know some of his blood might be in us for we have been here time out of mind. Would you have Old Joe Cooper stuffed and put in a show when he dies? Well, then! Where's the difference?'

Bertie and Agnes said nothing, and I was thinking too hard to speak. All that Daddy had said was true. But a dead Norseman is not a very tidy thing to find in your own moss. I thought of the night we went up by ourselves to bring down peats, and thought that he must have been there all the time. . . and it was pitch dark when we left.

Oh, if that hand had caught me by the ankle I would have died without a squeak! It was too much like King Log and King Stork, I never liked that story because I did not understand it. But oh gosh I understood it now!

We were away down the road before anybody spoke again.

Then Bertie asked, 'Should we not put some mark?'

'On his grave?' asked Daddy. 'What need is there for that?'

'So we would know to stay away,' said Bertie, 'and give him peace.'

'So,' said Daddy, 'I will see about it the next time I am in Cranee. I see what you mean, son. And I mean what I say about telling nobody. Not Mria, nor Alec, nor your Mammy. *Nobody.* D'you get that?'

We said we did, but he never said one word about not writing it down. I like writing things down and I have my books in a tin box Mammy gave me. Forbye you could not read them if you did find them. I just put the last letter of a word on to the front of the next word, and write x for y. It looks terribly strange but I am used to it and I can read it myself and the rest can not. Now and again they ask me what I am writing but I just say, 'Whole lots of things.' And that has to do them.